THE LITIGATION GUY

By VINCE AIELLO

Published by SarEth Publishing House
SarEth Publishing House
Carlsbad, California

First Edition: October 2013

Printed in the United States of America

ISBN 978-0-9883413-3-3

SPHN 13-0506080810

SarEth Publishing House

Also by Vince Aiello

LEGAL DETRIMENT

*For my mother, **Dora**, who taught me to appreciate moving pictures.*

*For my father, **Paul**, who taught me how to be a raconteur.*

When you look in the mirror, if you don't see my face – a mean, cold-hearted, merciless prick – you (will) never be successful as a lawyer.

-Roger Legion
Legal Detriment

PROLOGUE

SAN DIEGO
1980

The weather at night in San Diego is the same as it is during the day: perfect. San Diego has always possessed the tranquil innocence of a beautiful child. A child that is gazed upon by some in admiration and by others in deviance. If only the waters of the Pacific Ocean could protect this beautiful cherub from those predators who come to prey upon its virtue. Like a glass of pure water, the only way it can become polluted is from outside sources.

On this Thursday night, at 1:45 a.m., a cool breeze blew down Broadway, San Diego's main downtown street, from the ocean. Nothing more than a windbreaker was required. The streets and sidewalks were empty, except for a few homeless people, who hovered slowly with zombie focus. The street lights changed with mechanical precision, without vehicles or pedestrians to control.

The streets south of Broadway were an area littered with liquor stores, tattoo parlors and porno theaters. Many people avoided it in the daylight and at night, it took on a menacing persona.

As a taxi cab headed east on Broadway, a well-dressed man sprinted in the same direction and saw the approaching lights. He frantically waived his arms to hail the cab and it stopped at the corner of Fourth and Broadway. The white cab had the words 'Magic Carpet' written on the door.

The man quickly slid into the back seat and looked over his shoulder, first to glance at the sidewalk and then to look down Broadway. The driver looked at his passenger and saw his tailored Brooks Brothers suit, silk, yellow tie, and starched white shirt. He gave off the sense of hurried affluence.

"Where to?" the driver inquired.

"Hotel Del," the passenger responded.

The driver scribbled the location on a clipboard, while the passenger regained his breath and continued to nervously look over his shoulder.

"Hotel del Coronado it is," the driver said as he shifted the car into drive and commenced the meter that would eventually determine the cost of the trip.

The driver was of Middle Eastern descent, approximately 30 years old, with black hair. He wore a big smile and, in person, he was a far cry from his posted 'mug shot' driver's license photo that indicated his name was Habib Abbaspour.

"You in town for a convention?" Habib queried without a tinge of accent.

"No," the passenger acknowledged in a much more tranquil tone.

"Well, I hope you're not spending your vacation in this parta town. I won't even pick up a fare south of Broadway. All lowlifes and degenerates."

"I heard they wanna put a mall over here," the passenger said with impending optimism.

7

"Whatta they gonna do with these homeless people? Put'em out to sea?"

"Only if somebody can make money off it." The man's voice echoed in a tone of surrender.

The comment brought a smile to Habib's face and he adjusted the rear-view mirror for a better glimpse of his passenger. The taxi was now proceeding onto the Coronado Bay Bridge, which connected San Diego with the City of Coronado, home of the oldest wooden structure hotel on the West Coast of the United States, the Hotel del Coronado. The bridge was slightly more than two miles long and curved to achieve a height that allowed ships to easily traverse under it. It was the third most popular place in the United States to commit suicide just after the Golden Gate Bridge in San Francisco and the Aurora Bridge in Seattle.

The passenger peered out the window with a fastidious gaze and only occasionally looked over his shoulder. As Habib scanned him in the mirror, a look of recognition came over his face.

"You look familiar," Habib's speech was meted as he thought. "I've seen you someplace before. Let me think."

There was a quick pause and suddenly Habib snapped his fingers and pointed his index finger forward.

"I know. You're that lawyer who advertises on TV," and after a quick moment, "Dexter Frye – the Litigation Guy. You don't ration the passion."

The identification brought a smile to Dexter's face. "You must watch alotta TV."

"Not really. But I do like your jingle. The only show that I like is _Hawaii 5-0_. And I just heard today they're gonna cancel it," Habib's tone was resentful. He changed the subject. "You like bein' a lawyer?"

Dexter contemplated the question. "I thought I did." He then glanced at Habib's driver's license to learn his name. "Do you like driving a cab, Habib?"

"If you do it right, you can make a livin'. My wife, Paniz, and I got a kid and between me and her, it seems like we're working 24 hours a day."

"Do you think it's dangerous work?" Dexter wondered.

"What? Driving a cab? Nah, you just gotta be careful."

"Remember that Zodiac killer," Dexter quizzed, "up in San Francisco - back in the late '60s, early '70s? The last guy he killed was a cab driver."

"Really? I wonder why he killed a cabbie?"

"Maybe he didn't like the ride."

At this point in the taxi ride, the cab was coming onto the apex of the bridge where it curves and sweeps down into Coronado. The night air on the bridge was suddenly filled with red and blue lights from the beacons of at least eight San Diego police cars in pursuit of Habib's taxi. Habib checked his speed and slowed down even though he had never exceeded the speed limit.

"Holy cow! You should see all the cops behind me. If I get a ticket, you're gonna help me out, right?" Habib nervously inquired.

Dexter looked over his shoulder and back to Habib.

"If I can, I will. Stop the car," Dexter told him.

"I'm in the middle of the bridge. I can't stop," replied Habib.

Dexter pulled out a .45 caliber semi-automatic Colt 1911 pistol from his waistband behind his back. He pointed it behind Habib's right ear.

"Habib," Dexter's voice was calm and measured. "I want you to go home to your wife and kid tonight. Stop the car, but don't turn it off."

Habib saw the gun and halted the taxi. The police cars all slowed down when they saw Habib's red tail lights and began to slowly creep up toward it. A voice was then heard over a loudspeaker.

"Cab driver. Proceed across the bridge."

Dexter quickly spoke up. "Don't listen to'em. You know the cops can lie to ya? I never thought that was right. If the search is for the truth, where do lies fit in?"

"Listen, friend, I don't want any trouble," Habib retorted with a matter-of-fact plea.

"You know, I'm glad you called me 'friend.'" Dexter reached into his pocket and pulled out a $100 bill. "Take this," he said as he handed the bill to Habib. "When I tell you, I want you to lay on the horn and put it in reverse. Don't move the car or they'll open fire on ya. You understand?"

"Yeah. What do they want?"

"They want me to shut-up. And that's a tough thing for a lawyer to do." Dexter looked over his shoulder and gazed at the lanes filled with police cars and officers. They now stood outside of their cars utilizing the doors as shields, while aiming guns at the cab.

"Habib," Dexter requested his attention one more time and Habib stared at Dexter from the front seat. "I've enjoyed the ride."

The loudspeaker voice once again came to life. "Driver, let me see your hands and slowly step out of the vehicle."

Habib looked at them in the side-view mirror. He again looked back at Dexter.

"NOW!" Dexter exclaimed as Habib laid on the horn, but instead of putting the car in reverse, Habib put it in drive. There was a split second of confusion and the police believed that the cab was about to take off with Dexter. The police started to re-enter their vehicles when Dexter bailed out of the cab and vaulted up onto and over the 34-inch high railing of the bridge, all while carrying his semi-automatic pistol.

"GUN!" was screamed out by an anonymous policeman's voice.

As soon as the word was uttered, the police fusillade commenced on Dexter and one of the bullets struck him on the right side of his neck. Like a squib in a movie, it looked like blood had exploded out of him. While in mid-air, vaulting off the bridge, Dexter brought his right shoulder up to acknowledge the pain, and with a slight twist of his body, extended out his right arm back toward the policemen and squeezed off one shot. The bullet found a target and hit one of the officers in the center of the forehead, killing him instantly. Dexter's body fell straight down 200 feet to the water below. A policeman closest to the point where Dexter jumped reached the side of the bridge just in time to see the splash of Dexter's body hitting the water like a cannonball and waves of water could be seen bursting up.

The policemen who saw Dexter's body hit the water returned to the confusion of the officers surrounding the dead cop. Several of them knelt around the slain patrolman in a futile attempt to provide first aid. One officer moved with robotic precision attempting to keep him resuscitated, all while the life force had clearly left his body. His tears acknowledged the futility of his efforts.

"Where the hell is that ambulance?" one of the kneeling officers spoke out in vociferous frustration. He then turned to another officer, "John, call dispatch and find out where it is. Then, call the Harbor Patrol and tell'em to find this son-of-a bitch."

As moonlight and a robust breeze enveloped the bridge, an ambulance could be seen in the distance, racing to the scene of the crime.

Part 1

CHAPTER 1

33 YEARS LATER

Roger Legion sat at his mahogany desk this Monday morning studying a flat screen monitor as he reviewed attorney billings from the week before. His tailor-made, black, pinstripe suit, starched, white shirt and yellow, silk tie were sterling; his gold cufflinks gave off the essence of affluence, while his Italian, leather shoes completed a uniform that, in Roger Legion's mind, was ready for courtroom battle.

He was the eponymous leader of Legion and Associates, an insurance defense law firm considered to be one of the best law firms in the city of San Diego. Roger exuded confidence and a vice grip on all aspects of his firm's operation. In the 37 years that he has been a member of the State Bar of California, he never lost a case that he took to trial and he viewed the courtroom as an arena to play out a bloodlust sport. He did not 'practice' law because that was an activity engaged in by a novice. He engineered the law and manipulated it to his client's advantage. His opponents were adversaries that were to be crushed and regret the day they ever challenged Roger Legion or one of his lawyers.

Roger completed a trial the week before and today would be the second full day of jury deliberations. He represented an ambulance company, whose employees allowed a developmentally disabled man to slip from a gurney and sustain brain injuries. The plaintiff attorney was seeking $6.7 million and Roger had offered $375,000 from the insurance company that retained him.

Roger was in excellent physical condition for a man in his mid-60s; he looked 20 years younger than his age and was always impeccably dressed. In the office, he never removed his suit coat because he felt it was necessary to set an example for the other attorneys to always be ready for anything they may encounter.

Outside the windows of his corner office, located on the 24th floor of the America's Finest City Building, the sun blazed down on the San Diego landscape. As usual, the high temperature this day would be in the low 70s. The view from Roger Legion's floor-to-ceiling windows encompassed the Pacific Ocean and a portion of the San Diego Bay, where ocean liners and naval ships came and went with methodical regularity.

There were 15 attorneys in the firm and their primary job was to account for their time. Every phone call, letter, or thought was a 'billing event' that could be charged to a file. These events were to be captured and monetized. Roger reviewed the entries for logic, diction, and the amount of time that was charged. He wanted no surprises after the bills were sent to the insurance companies. He also knew that when attorneys became lazy, they might start padding the time amounts or simply fictionalizing them.

His desk was uncluttered with the exception of a flat screen computer monitor, small, manila folder, the office phone and his cell phone. The rest of the office included leather chairs and sofa, mahogany wood on the non-windowed walls, and various awards for his legal work throughout the years.

As Roger continued to read a billing entry for the third time, in an effort to comprehend it, his cell phone came to life. The Caller ID indicated 'County of San Diego' with a number that he did not recognize.

"Hello," he answered in a serious tone.

"Roger, this is Mark Jurecki, out at Los Colinas. How are ya?"

Mark Jurecki was a sergeant with the San Diego County Sheriff's Department. He spent 20 years with the San Diego Police Department then retired and was striving to obtain a second pension before, as Mark would often say, his "clock runs out." Years earlier, Roger Legion helped Mark's wife, Beth, with a successful Worker's Compensation Board appeal against the Post Office.

Mark was in charge of inmate intake at the Los Colinas Detention Center in Santee, California. This was the facility where accused female criminals were brought after their arrest.

"I'm good, Mark. How are you?" Legion inquired.

"Good. Listen, one a the city patrol units stopped a car in the Tierrasanta area a couple of hours ago for having a taillight out. A simple equipment violation. A young lady was drivin' and when the patrol officer asks for her license, he sees, right out on the console, a bindle. It was an ounce of pure coke. He asked her where she got it and at first, she says she got it from a lawyer. He read her her rights and she clammed up. But she also said that *you* were her lawyer."

"What's her name?" Legion asked with a sharp focus on every word uttered by Mark.

"Jill Burdick."

Roger thought for a second before responding.

"I know her," replied Legion.

Jill Burdick was a claims representative at Acitu Mutual, a major client of Legion and Associates.

"I thought you might want to get involved before this gets outta hand."

"I'll come over there right now."

"All right," Mark told him. "When you get to the counter over here, ask for me, don't mention her."

"I'll do it. Thanks, Mark. I'll be there in about 30 minutes."

"Okay, I'll see ya then," Mark answered and both men ended the call.

Legion turned to his computer monitor and, with several key strokes, determined the dollar amount of billings sent to Jill Burdick from Legion and Associates in the first half of this year. The total was nearly $275,000. He slowly removed his reading glasses from his face down to the desk. Roger clasped his hands and stared at the wall opposite his desk without focus. He was troubled by Mark's comment that Jill originally said that the cocaine was given to her by a lawyer.

Legion arose from the desk and quickly exited his office. He walked down the hallway that ran the length of the floor to a bank of elevators located on the south side of the building. This was the reception area for Legion and Associates. The only non-attorney on this floor was the receptionist, named Nina. She was in her mid-40s, petite, with shoulder length hair and a China doll complexion that accented her congenial personality.

As he waited for the elevator, Legion called out to Nina.

"Nina, I'll be back shortly. We have a new attorney starting today. His name is Luke Cordel. If I'm not back when he shows up, call Louise and tell her to get him started on whatever paperwork she needs." After a moment, he added, "If the court calls for me, put them through to Louise."

"I will, Mr. Legion." As Nina uttered those words, one set of elevator doors opened. Roger entered the elevator and Nina watched his stern visage with a smile as the doors closed in front of him.

CHAPTER 2

Diane Abrams was jarred awake by the clamorous sounds of a vacuum cleaner being used right next to her bed. For a moment, she was unsure of where she was. Diane was dreaming about figure skating, where she was on an ice rink performing a flawless routine with pirouettes, three turns, mohawks, and crossovers. The crowd erupted in applause when her REM-induced sojourn abruptly ceased.

She was in her early 30s, with radiant blue eyes, perfectly flushed cheeks, mauve lips, and brown hair that projected natural beauty. She was like a beacon in a lighthouse; all eyes were drawn to her. She gave up hope of an acting career to become a medical assistant and placed all of her energy in supporting her husband and his dreams.

Diane's husband, Lester, was operating a vacuum cleaner wearing underwear and socks after knocking a plant off of his dresser. He was 5 feet, 6 inches tall, three inches shorter than Diane, and had a rather scrawny physique. He was good-looking in a suit and could turn on the charm machine when he needed it. His voice boomed over the turbulence of the vacuum and when he saw she was awake, he turned it off.

"Tell our maid, what's-her-name, Consuelo?" his terse tone evidenced his annoyance.

"Juani," Diane replied.

"Tell Juani, she's fired!"

"Why?"

"Stupid bitch put the goddamn plant on top-a the dresser right where I put all the stuff from my pockets."

"Lester, Juani put the plant by the window; you moved it over to the dresser."

"Bullshit. You either fire her or you find a way to pay for her." Lester's pejorative demand drew Diane's ire.

"What's wrong with you?" Diane asked sitting up in the bed.

"Ever try paying the bills around here?" he said gritting his teeth. "And all you do is sit around here all day doin' nothing! And we got another mouth on the way."

Diane was four months pregnant and this bundle of joy was not planned. Diane was excited about the baby because she knew Lester was so selfish that he would never plan to have a child.

"Lester, I lost my leg. Or don't you remember? My car was hit by a tractor trailer, remember? I was in the hospital for 12 weeks, does that sound familiar? I know you were busy sitting in your office acting like you're digging a ditch while you're making lunch plans and telling everybody how much you're gonna get from _my_ accident."

"I," Lester started to speak and Diane cut him off.

"One more word and I'm outta here. And if I leave, I'm not coming back. Then, you can start putting a value on your law license because I'm entitled to half of it. Remember, I paid for it. So, 50% of your value as a lawyer plus child support. I don't want to argue with you, but I am not going to put up with your shit, 'Mr. Legion lawyer'."

Lester had been a lawyer at Legion and Associates for the past 10 years and he was developing a reputation for being extremely proficient in the courtroom. Earlier in the year, he obtained a defense verdict against a high profile plaintiff attorney in a products liability case. He considered everything that Roger Legion said to be "gospel" and he would never vary from Legion's script. Although he fancied the message, he did not share a similar fondness for the messenger. Lester felt that Roger was part of a bygone era. His goal was to show Roger Legion that his student was now the master.

Lester gazed at Diane as if he was positioned for a Mexican standoff. In that moment, his singular thought was how easy it would be to snap her neck. Then a smile came over his face.

"I'm sorry," he said with just a slightly repentant tone. The tension in the room began to mitigate as Lester's cell phone rang. It was on the nightstand next to Diane and she picked it up and saw the caller identification read 'R. Legion.' She handed the phone to Lester.

"Yes," he said. "Where?" A short moment passed. "What time? I'll be there." Lester ended the call.

"Will you please help me to the bathroom?" Diane asked as she swung her one leg off the bed and reached to the floor to pick up her crutch. "My sister can't take me to physical therapy tomorrow, so can you take me?"

"Yeah, just remind me." Lester assisted in raising Diane off the bed and she commenced a labored hop to the bathroom. His voice was calm, but his anger was well shrouded.

CHAPTER 3

Alton Burchesky entered his home office carrying a 4-pack of medium-sized boxes that were covered in cellophane and also had a thick, plastic strap that held the flattened boxes together. The room appeared to be a tribute to the 1960s in both motif and dust. The walls were cluttered with family photos in cheap frames and portraits of fishermen purchased at S.S. Kresge's, the predecessor to K-Mart. He positioned the boxes on the floor next to the desk and walked over to a set of shelves on the left hand side of the room. From an open box of latex gloves on one of the shelves, he yanked out 2 gloves like tissues and put them on.

On a higher shelf was an all-in-one stereo system that resembled a large boom box. It was obviously an older model because it did not play compact discs, but it did play cassette tapes. Alton swiped a cassette tape off the shelf next to the stereo and loaded it in. He looked around on the shelves and then went to the desk, where he found a started roll of Office Depot strapping tape. Alton then took a 4-inch Buck knife out of his pocket and with one swing motion, locked the blade in an open position. He then slashed the plastic strap and the cellophane off the boxes.

Suddenly, he recalled the tape that he placed into the cassette player. He walked over and pushed 'PLAY.' He pulled one of the flattened boxes out from the center of the 4-pack, commenced folding it into a box shape, and taped it into place. On the cassette tape was a jingle from a radio ad, which he listened to without emotion:

If you get in trouble, my oh my,
And all you really wanna, do is cry.
Well, there's one thing that you oughta try,
Tell 'em your lawyer is Dexter Frye.

Dexter will get you a settlement,
So you don't have to worry, about the rent.
You can afford him, wait and see,
'Cause Dexter works on contingency.

Dexter Frye, Dexter Frye, Dexter Frye,
The Litigation Guy.

Alton then approached the closet in the office and on the shelf there was a small pile of <u>San Diego Union-Tribune</u> newspapers. Based on their condition, they appeared not to be read. Alton clutched the top 3 copies and they were all for the same day, a Sunday, approximately 8 years earlier. He took one paper and placed the other 2 copies back on the shelf. He then proceeded to the cassette player and flipped the tape over. He again pushed the 'PLAY' button and heard another version of the jingle:

If you're the victim of a slip and fall,
There's really only one, guy to call.

Hearing his name will make them sigh,
Tell 'em your lawyer is Dexter Frye.

Insurance companies go round and round.
Dexter will knock them to the ground.
So, if you need a lawyer, don't be shy.
We both know that Dexter's your guy.

Dexter Frye, Dexter Frye, Dexter Frye,
The Litigation Guy.

While the jingle played, Alton removed the first section of the paper and placed it on the desk, so the entire page could be perused. A headline at the bottom of the page read, "25 YEARS LATER: WHAT REALLY HAPPENED TO *THE LITIGATION GUY*?" He opened the paper and found the article, which comprised 2 full pages. At the bottom of the pages were 11 photographs of individuals that were, according to the newspaper, involved with the events when Dexter Frye jumped off the Coronado Bay Bridge. In addition to the name that accompanied each photograph, it also indicated whether or not the person was deceased.

Alton reached into the center drawer of the desk and retrieved a black Sharpie. He placed an 'X' through each photograph of a deceased person. In addition to Dexter Frye, who was not listed as deceased, 5 photographs remained. Of those photos, the one in the far right corner was Roger Legion.

He capped the Sharpie and put it back in the drawer.

Alton was 34 years old, approximately 6 feet tall, 180 pounds, with a muscular build. He had a flat top military haircut and a 3-inch scar on his right cheek. He also wore a uniform that contained a shoulder patch. The image on the shoulder patch represented character, integrity, knowledge, honor, loyalty, and courtesy. The words on the patch were 'CALIFORNIA HIGHWAY PATROL.'

CHAPTER 4

The Los Colinas Detention Facility looked more like a high school than a jail. Located in Santee, California, approximately a 20-minute ride from downtown San Diego, it contained 11 housing buildings on 15 acres of land. It was originally built in 1967 as a juvenile detention facility and subsequently, converted to an adult women's detention facility in 1979.

While the outside of the buildings appeared to be rather mundane, the inside reflected a dark, dank, unappealing environment that was literally dark. The interior was lit by fluorescent bulbs that did not appear to be very bright. The walls and floor were painted an industrial gray and green, and the smell of a bleach-type cleaning agent effused the interior.

Roger Legion removed his watch, pocket change, and cell phone before passing through a metal detector and into the lobby. There were no less than 20 people in 3 lines to inquire, in various languages, about their desire to visit an inmate. There was also an attorney line with no waiting. Roger Legion proceeded to the attorney line and received immediate service.

"Can I help you?" a rather large, African-American woman asked.

"I'm here to see Mark Jurecki."

"Can I get your name?"

"Roger Legion," he said and the woman pushed several buttons on her phone. She looked at Legion with a big smile as she waited. Then, a voice answered her phone.

"Roger Legion is here to see you." She then waited for a quick response and looked up at Legion. "He'll be right out."

Roger stepped away from the counter and heard his name called out. Mark Jurecki approached at a fast gait. Mark was approximately 6 feet tall, 175 pounds, with black hair, graying around the temples. He approached Legion like a family member finding a long, lost relative.

"How are ya?" Mark asked as he extended his hand to shake Roger's hand. "Com'on back to my office."

Roger followed Mark down a darkened hallway, but did not enter any of the offices. Mark stopped as did Roger. He then stepped closer to Roger to speak in a hushed voice.

"I'll bring her to one of the attorney conference rooms. We haven't processed her yet. Wait right here. It'll only take a sec."

Mark left the hallway and returned in less than 60 seconds. He motioned to Roger to follow him.

Jill Burdick was plopped down on a chair in an attorney conference room that was rather well lit compared to the hallways and lobby area. The room had 4 walls that were half glass with a rectangular stainless steel table and 2 stainless steel swivel chairs bolted to the floor on opposite sides of the table. Jill wore a handcuff on her left wrist that had a longer chain than regular handcuffs and the other handcuff was fastened to a steel ring that was welded to the table.

Jill was in her mid-30s, curvaceous but not heavyset, with strawberry, blond hair. She possessed innate beauty, which was often expressed by a smile. Her cherubic cheeks could illuminate a room.

Jill wore black slacks, a white, button blouse, and a teal blazer. Her tears had caused the makeup around her eyes to cascade down her cheeks. Her uncomfortableness was trumped by fear. Mark Jurecki would not answer any of her questions and she was well over 2 hours late for work.

From the darkness of the hallway, Roger Legion emerged. For a moment, she wondered how he appeared there, because she did not see him approach the room.

"Roger, I'm sorry." Tears welled up in her eyes. "I didn't know what to do. I didn't know who to call." The sentences came out between sobs. Legion stood there and raised his left hand in front of her. A serene feeling came over her and she realized that he wanted her to cease talking.

"I believe I can help you. But I have to make sure you wanna be helped."

She stopped crying and gently nodded her head.

"Where did you get those drugs?" Roger asked in a calm, serious tone.

"I don't want to get the guy in trouble."

"Well, you're in quite a bit of trouble right now. You're facing at least a felony charge. What do you think Acitu Mutual is gonna do when they find out you've been arrested for drug possession?" Her silence telegraphed the answer to the question. "Do you think anyone else is ever gonna hire you?" Her silence was renewed. "Let's try it again: Where did you get those drugs?"

"I got 'em from Lester Abrams."

Roger's face did not change expression.

"Did he give them to you or did you pay for them?" Legion asked.

"I paid, but he said it was a great deal. He said they would help me lose weight." Her voice started to crack and her eyes began to well up with tears.

"Does anyone else know that you bought drugs?"

"No."

"Don't lie to me." Legion had an astute ability for detecting mendacious deception.

"No! I swear to God."

Legion turned, reached for the door handle, and returned to the darkness of the hallway. Jill lowered her face into her hands and began to sob uncontrollably.

Mark Jurecki waited for Legion at the end of the hallway. Roger walked up to him and Mark moved in close to him to again speak in a hushed tone.

"Do you want it to disappear?" Mark asked.

"Yeah," Legion responded.

"Okay, we're still gonna give her the fix-it ticket, so we don't have a gap in the log."

"What's the cost of the impound?" Legion asked.

"Nothing. I'll say we brought it in on some bad outta state warrant information. It's rare, but it does happen. It's over at the lot on 9th Avenue. You remember a guy named Sheets? He used to be a mechanic down at the old headquarters building. Cut his hand real good. Went for permanent disability and they only gave him partial. So, now he babysits that lot. I'll call over there and tell him you're on your way."

The two men looked at each other for a moment.

"We good?" Mark asked.

"We're good," replied Legion.

"You parked out in front?" Mark had one more inquiry.

"Yeah."

"On the side of this building," Mark said pointing, "there's a delivery entrance. That's the door she'll come out. You can drive right up to it. You still got a Caddie?"

Legion nodded affirmatively.

"Tell your friend to get that taillight fixed today."

"Thanks, Mark." Legion extended his hand for a final handshake with Mark.

"Anything for you, my friend."

Roger left the building and Mark escorted Jill out of it.

Inside Roger's late model Cadillac CTS-V, Jill looked out the window for most of the ride and was silent. When they approached the 9th Avenue impound lot, Roger pulled into a parking spot on the street to give Jill a final admonition.

"You're gonna forget this ever happened, right?" It was actually more of a statement than a question.

She turned to him and simply said, "Yes."

"You're not gonna tell your mother, your best friend, your priest, anybody, right?"

"Right," she answered in a more affirmative tone.

"If someone does find out, you and I are gonna have a problem. And I don't think you want that."

"No."

"I want you to go home, clean up, and get the taillight on your car fixed. You know how to take care of a fix-it ticket?"

"Yeah. I had one once before."

"All right. I'll call Lisa Leffort at Acitu and tell her we were at court together. You didn't feel well and I sent you home." Lisa Leffort was the claims manager at the San Diego office of Acitu Mutual Insurance Company. "Tomorrow, you go to work as if nothing happened." Jill nodded her head in affirmation. "Next time you get involved with something like this, I won't be able to help you. You understand?"

"Yes," Jill replied with her voice sounding like she just stepped off a bloodcurdling roller-coaster.

"Let's go get your car," Roger said as he pulled the latch on his door to open it.

"Wait," Jill said as she reached over and pulled his bicep, so he would stay in the car. "Acitu is talking about pulling the files from your law firm."

Roger needed to comprehend that statement for a quick moment. "Where did you hear that?" His tone was deadly serious.

"There was a conference call, last Thursday, with Lisa Leffort. She was told not to say anything to you. She said that if they pulled the files from you, she would quit."

"Did they say why or who they would send them to?"

"No. That information is supposed to be coming."

"You're gonna tell me as soon as you know, right?" His voice echoed more of a demand than an inquiry.

"Absolutely. As soon as I know."

They both exited the car and walked toward the impound lot.

CHAPTER 5

Lester Abrams arrived at the Bistro West restaurant in Carlsbad, California slightly after twelve o'clock for a noon lunch meeting. Lester was always rather dilatory with his appointments. When he advised the maître d' of his arrival, he was informed that the rest of his party had already arrived.

The Bistro West restaurant was an upscale eatery famous for putting their own 'spin' on sandwiches, comfort food, fish, or a nice steak. They grew all the vegetables used in preparation of their dishes and the atmosphere was perfect for a discreet business lunch.

"Gentlemen," Lester said as he arrived at a table, "sorry, I'm late."

At the table were two partners and one associate attorney from the San Diego office of the law firm of Bantree, Tasker & Matast, usually referred to as just 'Bantree.'

The associate, Tim Hurn, was in his early 30s, with a slight build, receding hairline and glasses. He was happy to see Lester and spoke up immediately.

"You're not late. We just ordered our first round," Tim said. He then turned his attention to introductions. "Les, this is Walter

Stoller and this Earl Oepkes." Lester responded to each introduction with a handshake.

"Nice to meet you, Les," Walter Stoller replied.

"Same here," said Earl.

"We gotta get this guy a drink," Walter said. He raised his hand, snapped his fingers, and their waiter, named Wyatt, appeared at the table. It was clear that Walter was the alpha of the group. He had well-coifed white hair, but was in his mid-40s. His clothing boasted European designers and he had diamonds in his cufflinks. His hands were clasped and his chair was slightly away from the table allowing him to cross one leg atop the other.

"Can I get you something to drink?" the waiter, dressed in black, inquired of Lester.

Lester looked around the table and saw that all 3 of the men had an alcoholic beverage.

"Cutty and Seven on the rocks," Lester responded. The waiter acknowledged his request and moved away from the table.

"Do you always get the same drink?" Walter asked.

"If they have it." Lester spoke with a smile.

For some reason, the comment made Earl Oepkes laugh. Earl looked harried like a man who had been up all night playing poker or slept in his clothes the night before. His clothing was much less expensive than Walter's. Earl was heavyset and his clothes were one size too small on him. His jowls hung over his shirt collar and his tie appeared to be more of a noose than a clothing accessory.

"I think it's good for a man to have a signature drink," Walter said. "It shows decisiveness and character."

"I wanna thank you guys for having this lunch up here," Lester told them. "If we did it down in the city," he paused for a moment, "you know, people talk."

"We understand," Earl said. "But it's no inconvenience for us, we have an office here in Carlsbad."

"So, how do you know Tim?" Walter asked.

"I told ya, we went to law school together." Tim said and Walter shot him a quick, daggered glance. Tim understood that Walter wanted Lester to answer the questions. Tim retreated and smiled. He understood the law firm pecking order.

"So, how's Roger Legion?" Walter's tone moved from casual to insidious.

"He's all right." As Lester answered, the waiter set his drink in front of him.

"Is he still the same miserable prick he was born?"

"Most days. Some days worse."

"Now, why would someone want to stay at a place like that?" Walter's serious tone endured.

"The pay's good, the reputation's good, and you can say what you want about the guy, but he will back you up. Every law firm has a resident prick. He's just up front about it."

Walter looked at Lester without emotion.

"What do you do at Legion's office?"

"I bill time."

Walter pointed at Lester and looked at Earl, then Tim. "Now, that's a lawyer's answer." Walter uncrossed his legs, moved his chair closer to the table and leaned forward to add a further degree of seriousness to the conversation.

"We're in the process of making serious inroads for business with some insurance companies that have long, established relationships with certain firms. We've made a decision not to add new associates because we have neither the time nor the patience to deal with the learning curve. We would like to see if we could recruit some talent from established firms."

"So why am I the lucky recipient of your potential largesse?" Lester asked.

"Frankly, we've seen you in action and we like what we see. We're impressed," Earl said.

"Well, thank you." Lester graciously accepted the compliment. An awkward silence followed. "So, these things usually come down to dollars."

"I don't think that'll be a problem," Walter said. "The offer, if made, would be a full partnership, with perks. A half million dollar minimum. But before we get to that, the question I have for you is: What is it you bring to the table?"

Lester appreciated the tenor of the conversation and decided the time for self-promotion had arrived.

"I've developed a relationship with every insurance claims person that I deal with. And I can tell you, with all sincerity, that they don't just like me, they love me. The Acitu account is definitely in play for movement. I have a relationship with all the local people, the regional office in Sacramento, and the home office. Upper management still has some resentment against Legion over the death of Pauline Murray."

"Why's that?" Walter asked.

"Her killer was a Legion lawyer. One that had a grudge against Roger."

Eighteen months earlier a former Legion lawyer was blamed for the murder of an Acitu claims manager. That same lawyer was also held responsible for the death of another Legion attorney and died in a gun battle with various criminals in the main conference room at Legion & Associates.

"You mean Paul Clifford, right?"

"Yeah. So 'but for' Roger Legion, Pauline Murray would be alive today."

"You really think you could swing that account?" Walter sounded as if he was doubtful of Lester's claims.

"As long as you put up the necessary financial backing," Lester told him with certainty. "I can't do it over the phone. It takes time and face-to-face interaction. Boots on the ground. That way I can assess the situation and get a vibe on these people. I can make it happen.

"Legion's track record is sterling," Earl chimed in. "He can deliver the goods."

"He's a good lawyer, but he's not down in the trenches," Lester told them. "He doesn't have his finger on the pulse. He depends on his lawyers for that."

Walter looked at Earl and then back to Lester.

"I think we can do business. See what you can do to make the transition as smooth as possible. Take your time. If Legion gets a whiff of this, all hell will break loose. And I don't have time to fight a battle with him. We'll make Tim, here, our point man. You deal with him. Earl will take care of all the negotiation details. After today, don't contact me. For the record, I will deny any knowledge of this conversation."

Walter extended his hand to Lester and they shook hands over the table.

"Can I ask you guys a question?" Lester asked after acquiring new found confidence from the conversation. "I heard a story once that one of the perks you guys have over there is that you bring in comfort girls every once in a while to relieve stress. Is that true?"

Walter raised his hand and snapped his fingers to call their waiter, Wyatt, over to the table. Walter then focused on Lester.

"We don't want to give up all of our secrets." As the waiter arrived at the table, Walter told him, "We need another round."

Lester admired Walter's bravado and could easily envision himself fitting into the culture of this law firm.

CHAPTER 6

Inside the Deus X Machine Shop, located just off Sampson Street in the Logan Heights area of San Diego, the 20,000 square foot warehouse was filled with a cacophony of pneumatic tools, welders, cutting torches, drill presses, and generators that allowed for fabrication of various pieces of metal. The building was 2 stories high, which allowed for the use of scissor lifts and small winches. It was windowless, but fans and an exhaust system circulated fresh air through the building.

There were 2 overhead doors on one side of the building to allow trucks to enter for loading, unloading, or if a truck needed body work. Each side of the building also contained a man door for entrance and exit purposes. The overhead doors were 20 feet high to allow even a tractor trailer to enter. At the south end of the building was a paint bay to allow anything, including something as large as a truck, to be painted. There was also a segregated area, approximately 20 feet by 20 feet that had walls of heavy, clear plastic. This was a clean room that was utilized for precision electronic work. Its purpose was to eliminate or minimize any excess dust while performing delicate work.

At the north end of the building, away from the fabrication, loud noise, and flying sparks was the company office. It was located on the 2nd floor and there was a metal walkway that ran the entire length of the north width of the building and halfway down the east and west side of the structure. A full wall separated the production area from the administration area, approximately one-third of the length of the building from the north end. At one end of that wall was enough room to drive a tractor trailer inside the entire length of the building.

From the 2nd floor walkway, you could observe all the operations within the building. There was one metal staircase from the west side of the walkway down to the first floor. Also on the 2nd floor were barrack-style rooms, to allow one shift of men to sleep, while another shift worked.

From the office emerged Remy Kalm. He was 36 years old, 6 feet tall, with black hair, combed back, and an athletic build. He wore jeans, a blue t-shirt, and a leather vest. Remy was a French national from Nice, who served 3 years in the military and was on his way to becoming a soccer superstar before being sidelined by a knee injury.

"My Brock man," Remy yelled out in a French accent above the noise of the interior. He sauntered along the western walkway to the stairs and began to descend them.

The person Remy called out to was Bob Brockman. He was a computer-loving geek, who wanted to be a California beach boy/gangster. He wore glasses and his head was totally shaved. In the back of his head was a tattoo that simply read, "I.T.C.O.B." which stood for "I took care of business." Brockman was of the belief that motorcycle gangs would obtain that tattoo after killing someone. He believed that it made him look tough. He wore a

Hurley t-shirt, shorts, and flip-flops. He met Remy when he was a student at Ohio State studying electrical engineering.

Brockman had a computer desk in the middle of the floor at the north end of the building. He would only leave his chair to sleep, eat, or go to the bathroom. On top of his desk were 3 computer keyboards, six 24-inch monitors, 3 abreast, 2 high, to allow for maximum multi-tasking, and a box of Cap'n Crunch cereal.

"Yo, yo, yo, my frog friend! What up, dawg? The man of Brock is in the house."

"How's it coming?" Remy asked as he reached the first floor.

"Like taxes in April, baby!"

"You keeping to the timeline?"

"I own the timeline, my Champagne-swilling amigo. You worry too much. Eat some cheese." Brockman's eyes returned to the computer monitors, moving from one to the other.

Remy looked at him in amazement. Brockman was eccentric, but Remy had faith in the work product he could produce.

"Remy," a voice yelled out from the southern end of the building where all the machine work was being performed. The voice belonged to Remy's brother, Emile. If he had an accent, it was not noticeable. He was muscular with a white t-shirt, dirtied by work and sweat. His face wore a 5-day beard growth. "Come and see the latest delivery."

Remy moved at a fast gait down to the southern end of the building to a supply room that consisted of a counter and shelving around the perimeter of the room. The shelves were filled with metal parts, welding accessories, and various nautical and painting products. On the counter was a wooden box with transit instructions taped to the exterior. Emile took a crow bar and pried the top of the box. Inside, lined up next to each other were 5 Heckler & Koch

MP5K submachine guns. Remy pulled one from the box to examine it.

"*Trés bien*," Remy said as he appreciated the weapon. "This is exactly what I asked for." Remy returned the gun to the box, which also contained a magazine for each gun with 30 nine millimeter bullets within each magazine. The final item in the box was a Glock C18 machine pistol. It looked like a regular handgun, but could fire 9 millimeter bullets like a machine gun at a rate of 1,100 per minute.

Remy's ringtone of *La Marseillaise*, the French national anthem, began to play. He looked at the Caller ID that said "Brian Sweeney." He answered it.

"'Ello," he said attempting to minimize his accent.

"Remy, it's Sweeney." Brian Sweeney ran a bar in San Clemente, north of San Diego County in Orange County, called the Swing & A Miss. Remy and Brian were cellmates for two years at the Clinton Correctional Facility in Dannemorra, New York. Remy was in for credit card fraud and Brian was serving time for car theft.

"Sweeney, how are you?" Remy's accent had returned.

"Good. Listen, I got a regular, comes in here all the time, and he needs a little help with somethin' and I think it's right up your alley."

"I 'ave this project going on and I don't 'ave time."

"Well, I thought you might wanna make time for this guy. He's a cop."

Sweeney's comment piqued Remy's curiosity.

"What kind of cop?" Remy asked.

"California Highway Patrol."

Remy thought for a moment and nodded his head affirmatively.

"Okay, I'll call you tomorrow and we'll set up a time."

Remy ended the phone call and looked forward to his tête-á-tête with Sweeney's friend.

CHAPTER 7

Roger Legion emerged from the elevator on to the 24th floor and gave a quick scan of the lobby before calling over to the receptionist, Nina.

"Did Mr. Cordel come in?" he asked.

"He's in the conference room," Nina replied.

"Is Mr. Abrams here?" Roger asked.

"He hasn't come in yet," Nina immediately responded.

Roger moved to the closest conference room door. The conference room was separated from the lobby by a sculpted alabaster glass wall and 2 entrances, one at each end of the glass wall. Roger entered and saw Luke Cordel looking out at the ocean and the cruise ships parked along the ocean front.

"Luke," Roger said upon entering. "Welcome to Legion and Associates." Legion smiled and walked over to him extending his hand.

"Nice to see you, sir," Luke replied and his hand met Roger's with a vice-like grip.

Luke was 6 feet, 2 inches tall, 195 pounds, and appeared to be carved from a piece of granite. Even with a suit on, his physical fitness was evident. His hair was black, soft eyebrows, no facial hair, and a bright complexion that was nicely tanned. A slight smile was a natural condition for his face. He wore a blue, pinstripe suit, white shirt, and a striped, red and blue tie.

"You been waitin' long?" Roger asked.

"Not really. I met Louise and she gave me some forms to fill out."

"All right. Grab 'em," Legion said referring to the forms, "and we'll go back to my office."

Legion walked over to the other door to the conference room and as he exited, he turned to Luke.

"Did you park in the building?"

"Yes, sir, I did."

"Nina will validate your parking," Legion said pointing to her. "We should have a space for ya tomorrow."

Legion led Luke to Legion's corner office. When they entered, he closed the door.

"Sit," Roger told Luke. Luke sat in one of the chairs in front of the desk and Roger sat in his chair behind the desk.

"Are you ready to get to work?" Roger inquired with a serious, smirky smile.

"Yes, sir," Luke's alacrity was refreshing.

"The way we operate around here is somewhat of a pod system. Each attorney, including myself, has files assigned to them. We work in groups of three. Two of the attorneys have a normal work load and the 3rd attorney has a lighter load. We call that attorney the 'lead' lawyer. That attorney is responsible for reviewing and having knowledge of everything going on for all 3 attorneys. So, if you're not here and I need to know something about one of your files, I should be able to contact that 3rd attorney to get the answer. Understand?"

"Yes, sir."

"You're gonna hear alotta things about me here and I presume most of them are true. I'm the guy responsible for this mule train, so I demand a certain level of performance."

"I understand."

"You wanna be a litigator?" Legion asked.

"I believe I would be good at that, sir."

"You'll get the opportunity here. I will show you how to do the dance. You pay attention to what I teach you and then, when you walk into a courtroom, you will be feared." Legion's icy gaze locked on to Luke. "Lesson number one: Lawyers like to put the word 'esquire' after their name. You know where that word comes from?"

"No, sir."

"In medieval times, it referred to the shield bearer for a knight. The guy in training to become a knight. I don't want any of the attorneys here to be esquires. I want them all to be knights. Knights that only know the sweet taste of victory and don't even know what defeat is." Legion leaned back in his chair. "I use a lot of military analogies here. I like to say we weaponize the facts and we bludgeon our adversaries with them. I have never lost in trial because I have never trusted an adversary. 'All war is based on deception', you know who said that?"

"Sun Tzu, *The Art of War*."

"Very good. You were at Pendleton, right?"

Legion was referring to Camp Pendleton located in northern San Diego County.

"Yes, sir. Fox Company, 2nd Battalion, 5th Marine Regiment, an infantry battalion."

"I'm a fellow leatherneck and I'm grateful for your service. Your work with the marines will serve you well here. You seem like a nice guy. Some lawyers confuse niceness for weakness and try to capitalize on it. We work in a profession where courtesies are requested. I am not against extending a courtesy, but it's a two-way street. Somebody wants something, they better be ready to give something. That's how we do it here. Understand?"

"Yes, sir."

"I'm also gonna teach you how to read people. When I read a deposition transcript, it's only words on a page. I need you to bring it to life. How they look, how they act, and how they react. I wanna know if they have any visible tattoos and any piercings. Most juries believe that branding and self-mutilation are mental disorders. That's the key: picking a jury. Your client's fate is in the hands of 12 people who are too stupid to figure out how to get out of jury duty. That's why most cases are settled. If there was any science to it, I would take every case to verdict." Legion was done with his proselytizing. "All right?"

"Yes, sir." Luke responded.

"How many suits do you own?" Legion asked.

"Two." He answered unsure of the purpose of the question.

"You're gonna need 3 more. Go and see my tailor, Gianni. He's on Fourth Avenue below Broadway." Legion reached into his top, left-hand drawer and took out a business card. He put the business card on the desk and slid it over to Luke.

"Sir, I don't believe I can afford suits like you wear."

"Yes, you can. The firm will pick up the tab and you pay it back either fifty dollars or a hundred dollars every paycheck. It's a no interest loan. If you need shoes, socks, shirts, or ties, he's got that stuff, too. I don't wanna see you wear the same stuff two days in a row. If I notice it, others will also. You can go during the day, because he's not open at night."

"Thank you, sir."

"Initially, you shadow me for a few days then we'll get you connected with a couple of the other guys. I try to always keep my door open. If you have a question, ask – don't proceed blindly. No one stands alone at this firm. Now, com'on, let me give ya a tour." Both men arose from their chairs.

"One final thing:," Legion said, "you don't have to call me 'sir', but I do like it."

"Roger that," Luke acknowledged his comment followed by a broad smile.

CHAPTER 8

On the 8th floor of the W Hotel on West B Street in downtown San Diego, Clare Luconi was on top of Lester Abrams engaging in one of their accustomed 'afternoon delight' sessions. Clare was a court reporter and, approximately a year earlier, a plaintiff and his attorney failed to appear at a scheduled deposition. Clare and Lester decided to have a drink with a carnal passion chaser. Since then they met weekly, sometimes twice a week at various hotels throughout downtown, always attempting to avoid prying eyes.

Clare was 34 years old, 5 feet, 2 inches tall, approximately 100 pounds, on a petite frame. If you analogized her body to a luxury vehicle, the adjective to describe her would be 'tight.' Little body fat, narrow hips, and breasts that were enhanced perfectly by saline and a plastic surgeon's artistry.

Clare arched her naked body back, not in satisfaction, but rather in frustration.

"You pulled the trigger kinda quick, don't you think?" her snarky attitude regarding Lester's performance demanded a reply.

"What are ya, in a hurry?" Lester retorted.

"You apparently are." Her tone was matter-of-fact.

"I've been under alotta stress. God damn work! And I gotta deal with that stupid, sow, crippled wife of mine. To boot, she's gonna shit out a kid, so she can stay on the couch, bon-bon, gravy train for 18 years. I shoulda forced her to go to doctor wire hanger." Lester's pejorative rant recalled his bitterness that his wife, Diane, refused to have an abortion.

"Just get a divorce," Clare said as she slid off of him and lied down on her side next to him.

"Not until I settle her car accident. I'm gonna get the entire policy. $5,000,000. It should be all mine. She wouldn't get shit off 'em without me. Stupid bitch. The thought of cutting that bovine an alimony or child support check makes me sick to my stomach."

"So, what happened when I called your phone?"

"She saw the 'R. Legion' on the Caller ID and shit her pants. Probably too frigging stupid to know how to answer it." Lester then warned her, "If you ever hear a woman's voice, hang up."

"Once anyone sees Roger Legion's name, they start to shake in their boots," Clare casually mentioned. The comment immediately set Lester off.

"I don't need his bullshit name to settle a case. You think an insurance company is gonna cut a check, just because a guy's name is on a pleading? That's not how it works. They gotta know that you're willing to stay in the fight until the verdict is read. You can't be bullied, because you are the bully. And you have to know how to make it as expensive as possible for them."

Lester's didactic efforts were not impressing Clare. She did not want to agitate him any further.

"When are we gonna go away?" Clare asked as she ran her fingers through his minimal chest hairs.

"I'm working on something that should allow me to walk away from Legion with a big payday. But it's gonna take a little time. When I have Legion in my rear-view, we'll go anywhere you want: Europe, Japan, Australia."

"I'd like to go to the Bahamas," Clare was quick to interject.

"We're there. Just tell me again that you don't want kids."

"You kidding? I can't take care of myself."

"Okay, baby. We're gonna own it."

Clare lit up with a devilish smile.

"Are you ready for round two?" she asked.

"Find out. Use your mouth for somethin' other than talkin'."

Clare proceeded to the task at hand, while Lester leaned his head back on the pillow, closed his eyes, and guided her head up and down.

CHAPTER 9

When Roger Legion and Luke Cordel entered the law firm kitchen on the 24th floor of the America's Finest City Building, the lights came on automatically.

"Nothing too fancy, here," Roger told him. "There are coffee mugs or paper cups, and we have one of these coffee makers that allows you to make all different kinds of coffee. My secretary, Louise, brings in bagels or doughnuts every morning. If you want something special, just tell her." He then pointed to a large soft drink dispensing machine. "The sodas and water are 25 cents. If you don't have a quarter or a dollar, it makes change, ask Nina up front, she's got some petty cash. Or ask one of the other guys. If they don't have a quarter to give ya, I don't want'em working here."

Luke concurred with every fact shared by Legion.

"The next area down is the library. These days, it's easier to research online, but some guys like the book in their hands, so they can go in there and get it. You can also just sit down in there and read. Some people like the solitude away from the phone. The books don't leave the room. If you try to do that, an alarm will sound. If you want to take one of the books out, one of the ladies downstairs is our designated librarian. She will check it out for you. These books are too expensive to go missing."

Roger and Luke began their door-to-door trek searching for any attorneys in their offices for a royal introduction to Luke. Luke met more than half of the attorneys as he and Roger walked the perimeter of the floor. Roger assured him that he would meet the rest of the attorneys over the next several days or at the Friday attorney meeting.

As they passed Lester Abrams' office, Roger stopped and gazed at it. His casual countenance took on a hardened gaze.

"We're gonna go down to the 23rd floor. After this visit, you should never have to go there again. Your pod will have a secretary assigned to it. There is a pool of typists, paralegals, and law clerks. They all have a unique proficiency, so either my secretary or one of the other experienced secretaries will match you up with what you need. You want anything done, you either pick up the phone or send an e-mail. They pick the person, you don't. We also have runners. They pick stuff up, they drop stuff off. If you need something, they get it up here now. They don't do any technical work on the files. Is this making sense?"

"Yes, sir," Luke acknowledged.

"No one from the 23rd floor is allowed to be here unless they have a reason. If they don't, they will be severely reprimanded and depending on my mood, they may be fired. I also require all the support staff to address an attorney as 'Mister' and their last name. No variation on that rule is allowed. Understand?"

Luke nodded his head in agreement.

"We have an I-T guy, you know, information technology guy, named Roy."

"I'm scheduled to meet with him tomorrow," Luke interjected.

"Good. Any problems with your computer, printer, or phone, call him. They'll give you a new phone tomorrow. As for the phone, feel free to turn off your current cell phone service and you can transfer your number to the law firm phone. You can make personal calls, I don't care. But just remember that the purpose of the phone is that you will answer it when I call."

"Sounds fair," Luke told him.

"I don't know if you'll be sayin' that when I call you at three o'clock in the morning." Luke wasn't sure if Roger was serious or joking. Legion looked at him with a mischievous smile.

"As long as you get your work done, you and I will never have a problem. Let's go."

Roger and Luke walked over to the elevator banks and a set of elevator doors opened as soon as Roger pressed the call button. Upon entering the elevator, Roger pushed the '23' button and the doors began to slowly close.

"Are you married?" Roger asked.

"No," Luke reply was nonchalant.

"You got a girlfriend?"

"No."

"Everything happens in time. Speaking of which, Louise will be giving you a lesson in our billing system. It's important to pay attention for that one."

Luke nodded in agreement as Roger was struck with an idea.

"I wanna take a little detour and introduce you to someone on the 1st floor."

Roger stepped forward to push the lobby button just as the elevator doors opened. A young lady stood in front of the doors with an armful of papers engaged in conversation with someone in the distance. She was 28 years old, 5 feet, 7 inches tall, blue eyes, with a slender frame. Her hair was shoulder length, wavy, parted on the side, with combined highlights and natural lowlights. Her makeup was minimal, because she didn't need it. Her natural beauty provided her radiance. She exuded the elegance of a living piece of art. Her refinement radiated from her eyeglasses to her heels. She was the type of woman who would put on a dress from Target and make it look like it came from Neiman Marcus. Both Roger and Luke held the doors open.

"Get the one with the initial edits," a voice called to her.

"The first draft or the second draft?" the young lady in front of the elevator called out.

"The first draft will have the redline edits."

"Okay," she said and hurried into the elevator after realizing she was holding it up. As she entered, she said to Luke, "Twenty-four, please."

"We're going down to the lobby," Luke advised after the elevator doors closed.

"Oh, I must've got on the wrong one." As she finished her sentence, she became cognizant that Roger Legion was one of the passengers. Roger and Luke were each in a rear corner of the elevator and the young lady stood between them and in front of them. She nervously looked at the floor as the elevator descended.

"What's your name, young lady?" Roger posed his inquiry in a serious tone. She looked up to respond to him.

"Karla," she uttered and hesitated for a moment, "Karla Mulry." Her mind raced and she wondered if she would get in trouble for getting on the wrong elevator.

"Are you having a good day today, Karla?" Legion asked.

"Yes, Mr. Legion," she said trying to force a smile. She returned to her position staring at the floor while facing the elevator doors.

Luke wanted to say something to her. Like a harried driver in search of a parking space, he decided to pounce on the opportunity.

"Hi, my name is Loo. . ."

He was immediately cut off by Legion. "Mr. Cordel."

Karla turned to Luke and seemed to swallow.

"Pleased to meet you, Mr. Cordel."

A smile came over Roger Legion and the elevator reached the lobby. Luke thought the ride was instantaneous and Karla felt like she was underwater with no access to air for the entire ride.

The elevator doors opened and both men stepped off. The bouquet of her essence stayed with Luke. As the doors began to close, Luke looked back and said, "Nice to meet you, Karla."

CHAPTER 10

A.F.C. News or America's Finest City News was an unpretentious convenience store located on the eastern side of the lobby of the America's Finest City Building. It sold newspapers, magazines, paperbacks, candy, gum, chips and soda. It served the needs of those in a hurry or those within the 30 floors of the building that did not wish to travel very far.

Roger led the way in, closely followed by Luke. At the cash register sat an older, African-American man, heavyset, with short, gray, curly hair and several days of beard growth. He wore a grandfather's sweater and his glasses had thick, black frames with obsidian lenses. He had an infectious smile, which did not change until Roger's voice broke the silence.

"Roux," Roger declared as he stood before him.

"Is that Mista Legion?" His southern accent was distinct and his sanguine smile amplified. Luke then realized that Roux was blind. "I shoulda know'd it was you from your aftershave."

"It's soap and water." Roger informed him.

"That's why I like it. How are ya, sir?" Roux's ebullience filled the room.

"I'm good. How you doing?"

"Same ole, same ole. Still waitin' for my numbers to come in on the lottery."

"Keep up the good work. I got a new guy started today. I want you to meet him."

"Where is this boy?" Roux asked as he stood from his chair and made a tactile trek along the counter until he reached the end of it.

"Luke Cordel," Roger said to him, "this is Roux. R-O-U-X."

"Nice to meet ya, Luke." Roux held out his hand aimlessly until Luke placed his hand in it to shake.

"Nice to meet you, Roux."

"If you ever need anything from this place, you can sign for it and Roux will send us a bill," Roger told Luke.

"Then, if you don't pay, I send LeRoy up to collect. He's one-a the brothers."

"We don't have to worry cause he's blind too, so, he can't find the place." Roger's jocular comment caused Roger and Roux to chuckle. Luke smiled.

"Hey Luke, how 'bout you and I do a little skirt-chasing? Ladies can't resist a man with a white cane. I'll tell'em you're my seein' eye guy."

"Just tell me when and where," Luke told him.

"I'll tell ya when, you tell me where. I'm as blind as a white man in the projects."

Luke and Roger looked at each other and again had to chuckle. A young woman walked up to the counter to purchase a bottle of water.

"We're not in line," Luke told the woman.

Roux spoke up, "Customer, huh?"

"Yeah," Roger told him.

"Where is that boy? MATHIAS!" Roux screamed out to the back room. "Where are ya, boy? We got customers, don't be triflin'."

"I'm here, Roux," Mathias said as he emerged from a storage room. He was an 18-year-old, clean cut, high school student. He proceeded to the counter to attend to the customer.

"How's he workin' out?" Roger asked.

"He's a good kid," Roux told him. "Jehovah Witness. Those people don't steal."

"Any problems, you let me know," Roger told him.

"I will Mr. Legion," Roux put his hand out in the direction of Roger's voice and Roger clasped it with both hands to shake it.

"It's always a pleasure, my friend," Roger's sincerity was evident.

"As is mine. Now Luke," the tempo of his voice changed. It now possessed a smart-ass tinge, "don't forget, you and I got an appointment to go get some coochi-cooch."

"We'll do it," Luke assured him.

"Take it easy, gentlemen," Roux told them as he commenced his journey along the counter back to his perch.

Roger and Luke returned to the elevators to conclude their tour with a visit to the 23rd floor.

CHAPTER 11

The elevator system in the America's Finest City Building had a unique feature: a prospective passenger would select their floor from a computer screen located adjacent to the bank of elevators. The passenger was then advised which elevator to board for a direct, non-stop trip to their destination. This system was only available in the lobby and parking garage of the building.

Roger requested the 23rd floor and the elevator system screen advised him to board the 'C' elevator. As Luke and Roger awaited the elevator, Roger's cell phone rang. He removed the phone from the inside breast pocket of his suit coat and examined it. The Caller ID read 'County of San Diego' as it had earlier that day when he received the call regarding Jill Burdick. The number was different and there was a possibility that the jury from his trial may have reached a verdict. Roger answered it.

"Hello."

"Roger, it's Vic," the voice responded.

Vic Nagpal was a court bailiff and the union representative for the courthouse bailiffs in the downtown courthouse. He was not the bailiff for Roger's trial, but he kept close tabs on all the major cases occurring in the courthouse. Years earlier, Roger represented his wife and daughter when they were the victims of an auto accident.

"Vic, how are ya?" Roger asked.

"Good. I just wanted to let you know," Vic paused for a moment and the volume of his voice lowered, "they're talking seven figures and they're almost ready to put a fork in it."

"All right," Roger's voice was ponderous but his mind moved at warp speed to calculate his next move for this situation.

"Listen, your Semitic friend, he just called in. He's at Dobson's right now." Vic was referring to the plaintiff attorney from Roger's trial, Hillel Geisser, who was known as Hilly. Dobson's Bar & Restaurant was an attorney favorite for a 'power lunch.' It was a place where the 'high powered suits' closed deals while consuming excellent food and drink.

"Thanks, Vic," Roger told him.

"Work your magic," Vic told him and ended the call.

As Roger pushed a button on his phone to end the call, the doors to the 'C' elevator opened.

"Change in plans," Roger said to Luke. "Let's go to lunch."

"Lead the way," Luke declared and they exited the building.

CHAPTER 12

Dobson's Bar & Restaurant has been a San Diego landmark for decades. Located in the heart of downtown, it was a venue to be seen and to see the powerful from the legal, government, and private industry worlds. The highly polished wooden interior reminded the patron of a high-end depression-era speakeasy. It was complete with a mezzanine area that allowed customers to watch the human soap opera of business play out.

Due to its popularity, reservations were always a good idea. When Roger Legion entered, he never had a reservation, but was always treated like royalty, from the management to the bus boys. And he was always seated immediately.

When he arrived this early Monday afternoon, he whispered something to the maître d' and was rapidly escorted to the inner sanctum of the restaurant. He scanned the crowd until he locked on to the focus of his search.

Hillel Geisser, or 'Hilly' as he liked to be called, was in his mid-50s, heavyset, bald, with a French cuff white shirt, at least 3 rings on his fingers, and cuff links that boasted a noticeable 'G'. He was nearly finished with his Prime Flat Iron steak, which he appeared to be intently enjoying.

The maître d', followed by Roger and Luke, moved closer to him.

"Hilly, what are ya slummin'?" Roger inquired to command his attention.

"If you eat here, then the answer's yes," he told him and finished his answer with a smile. "How are ya, Roger?" Hilly inquired as he extended his hand to shake hands with Roger.

"Good. How 'bout you?" Roger asked.

"Well, I'm still eatin', so that's a good sign."

"Did you try the mussel bisque? Outta this world. Hey, I want to introduce you to a new guy that started with me today," Roger told him. "This is Luke Cordel. Luke, this is Hilly Geisser."

Luke and Hilly shook hands and both said, almost simultaneously, "Nice to meet you."

"I wish I had somebody I could send down here to take a verdict," Hilly lamented in a flustered tone.

"Where's your office?" Luke asked.

"La Jolla and Beverly Hills," Hilly responded. He turned his attention to Roger. "Is today gonna be the day?"

"Your guess is as good as mine," Roger replied.

"What's your experience, who does time favor?" Hilly was interested in Roger's opinion.

"I've had short ones and I've had long ones, but they've always been defense ones," Roger's voice was matter-of-fact.

"Is he always this modest?" Hilly asked Luke. He then backtracked. "Oh right, you started today."

"They probably decided liability and they're gettin' hung up on numbers," Roger told him.

"If you weren't such a cheap son-of-a-bitch, we coulda settled this thing."

"Not when you want millions a dollars. At that level, the decisions are easy to make."

"Your client still wanna shut it down?"

"It's an insurance company. The only thing they want is certainty."

Luke toggled back and forth between both men as they spoke. Something about their interaction was mesmerizing.

"You were at 375," Hilly said referring to Roger's $375,000 offer to settle. "Get me 750 and we'll call it a day."

Roger needed no time to think. "Still too rich for my blood. I was thinking 400."

"400! You're a pisser, you know that. 500. That's it," Hilly responded.

"Split it with me. 450," as Roger spoke, he extended his hand to shake and confirm the deal.

Hilly looked at his hand and then his eyes traveled north to meet Roger's eyes.

"You gotta call anybody?" Hilly asked Roger.

"Nope. You gotta call anybody?"

"No," Hilly put out his hand and shook with Roger. "450 it is."

"There's only one condition," Roger said before clasping his hand. "We go right now and put it on the record."

"No problem," Hilly told him as they shook hands.

Roger turned to Luke. "Let's go."

Hilly called his waiter over to request his bill. They waited for Hilly to pay his bill and the 3 men proceeded to the courthouse.

Roger showed no emotion. The mission was accomplished. It was business as usual at Legion and Associates.

CHAPTER 13

As the afternoon expired at the Deus X Machine Shop, Bob Brockman continued his relentless creation of electronic schematics on one screen, while working on several mathematical calculations that resembled hieroglyphics to the uninformed on another screen. He would occasionally let out a chuckle caused by an episode of _All in the Family_ that he listened to on his iPod.

Suddenly, an alarm within the building began to blare. It was accompanied by a computer voice repeating the words 'PERIMETER COMPROMISED.'

Remy raced out of his office on the 2nd floor and Brockman switched all 6 of his computer screens to the exterior video cameras on the north side of the building where the parking lot was located and the breach was detected.

A 1991 Toyota Camry had pulled into the parking lot and its lone occupant, a young woman in her late-30s, emerged from the vehicle and walked toward the buildings. She was tall, buxom, with blond hair, blue eyes, and a very distinctive bone structure. She wore jeans, boots, a red-hooded sweatshirt, and carried a purse with a strap on her shoulder. She was ready for work, but appeared alluring, while not attempting to look sexy at all.

Brockman typed in a number sequence and the alarm and voice were silenced.

"It's Uschi," Brockman yelled up to Remy.

"Let her in," Remy told him as he stood on the walkway against the railing on the 2nd floor looking down.

When she reached the door located at the office end of the building, she pushed a button and a buzzer rang inside. Once again, Brockman made a series of keystrokes and Uschi Horton heard a click that allowed her to enter the building.

Uschi looked over to Brockman, but he did not raise his head to acknowledge her. He had returned to his schematics, mathematics, and Archie Bunker.

"Uschi," Remy called out as he walked along the 2nd floor walkway to the metal staircase. She looked up at him and smiled. "How did it go?" he asked as he descended the stairs.

"I did exactly as you said," she advised with her slight German accent.

"I want to know what was said," Remy commanded.

"I met with an FBI special agent."

"What was his name?"

"Oliver Love."

"Are you serious?" Remy thought it was an odd name for an FBI agent.

"I have his card," Uschi responded like a loyal Aryan following orders.

"What did he say?" Remy asked.

"I told him I worked at a bar in San Clemente, Swing & A Miss, and I heard these guys speaking German. They were talking about radioactive material coming into the Port of Los Angeles. One guy said that he knew the shipment details and they had big plans for it."

The Swing & A Miss was the bar owned by Remy's friend, Sweeney.

"So, what did Special Agent Oliver Love say?"

"He asked if I heard any information about time periods and I told him I heard something about the end of the month."

"Did he ask you about names?"

"I told him, just like you said, one guy's name was Erhardt and the other was Stryker. He recognized the name, Erhardt, and he showed me the same picture you showed me. He was very interested."

Uschi's last sentence brought a smile to his face. Uschi's nervousness was becoming more noticeable.

"What else did he say?" Remy's voice was forced and impatient.

"He said he would come to the bar to observe. If the men came in again, he wanted me to listen and try to get their license plate numbers or any phone numbers. He wanted to know if I thought they liked me."

"Typical government worker. Wants you to do his job."

"Remy, this charade is getting too complex. I fear making a mistake," Uschi's voice echoed a plea.

"There's nothing to worry about, *ma chèrie*." Remy paused in the middle of the staircase and gazed at her. "Uschi, of all my lovers, you were the most memorable. Your breasts belong in the 'istory books. You do things other men only dream their woman would do. *En France*, they would call you *le pétard* – the firecracker. Because the explosion you cause the man is spectacular. I ask of you one more thing," Remy sounded sincere and heartfelt.

"Anything for you," she told him with a sense of desperation.

"Pray for me."

As he completed the sentence, a muffled shot was fired from a darkened corner of the 2nd floor walkway. The bullet came from a Remington model 700 tactical rifle with a silencer. The .308 caliber bullet was also a subsonic round to further minimize the sound. The bullet ripped through the right atrium of her heart after lifting her off her feet, sending her 10 feet backward, bouncing her body against the metal wall, and then sending her down to the concrete. She was dead before she hit the floor.

Remy and Brockman both slowly looked in the direction of the bullet's origin.

The sniper pulled the bolt back on the rifle and an empty shell ejected that he snatched with one hand. His voice came out of the darkness.

"Somebody owes me a beer."

The voice belonged to Kevin Camballa, 21 years old, of Philipino descent, 5 feet 6 inches tall, 140 pounds, with minimal body fat. His hair was jet black and his moustache had a penciled look. What he lacked in stature, he made up for in cold-bloodedness. Kevin was a master in the art of the assassin. He specialized in difficult sanctioned targets and never left a contract unfulfilled. He completed his 1st assignment at the age of 13 when a witness to a drive-by shooting needed to be silenced.

Kevin was dedicated to his craft. He was constantly researching any and all developments in technology that he could utilize for his profession, or that he needed to foil, to achieve the desired result.

"Kevin," Remy said, "when was the last time you saw Erhardt and Stryker?"

Kevin answered as he descended the metal staircase.

"I left Erhardt in a freezer in Amsterdam and Stryker is in the trunk of a car that's in a junk yard in Helsinki."

"EMILE," Remy yelled down to the far end of the building. Emile appeared wearing a dirty t-shirt, jeans, and an open welder's mask. "Get a tarp. Bring it down here. Have one of the guys get a mop and bucket. Tell'em all to wear gloves." Emile looked at Remy. "NOW!" Remy screamed.

Remy's raised voice caused a flurry of activity. Two men appeared, both wearing gloves, one carrying a tarp, and the other wheeling a mop bucket and mop in Remy's direction. The man wheeling the mop bucket was Pike. He was in his mid-50s, white hair with a ponytail, beard, and a slight paunch. He had a hulking stature and his expertise was the plasma torch, a tool that allowed for more precise cutting stability with less electrode use and power consumption than a regular torch.

The man carrying the tarp was Hazz, whose named rhymed with 'jazz' and it was actually short for Hezekiah. He was an Israeli munitions expert and his proficiency was creating, detecting, and overriding collapsible circuits. These were circuits that are designed to detect a failure in a circuit system, say if it was cut, and act on it so the desired result could still be achieved.

As they approached, Remy took a pair of latex gloves from his pocket and put them on. He picked up Uschi's purse and removed the keys to her car.

"Hazz," Remy said as he tossed her keys to him, "go get her car and bring it in here." He then turned to Kevin Camballa, "Can you follow him up to Orange County to ditch the car?"

"Sure," Kevin replied.

Then Brockman added his voice to the mix. "Maybe you could stop at Disneyland and see if you're tall enough to go on the rides?"

Kevin shot him a daggered glance.

"Maybe I could just stay here and learn science from a comic book?" Kevin's voice dripped sarcasm.

Kevin and Brockman had an intense dislike for each other because neither thought the other was as good as Remy believed them to be.

Brockman stood to address Kevin. "First of all, I don't read comic books, they're graphic novels. And I studied electrical engineering. So, why don't you go tell Remy how hard it is to pull a trigger," Brock's voice oozed with bitterness.

"Maybe studied it, but no degree. Can't finish what you start. I'll have to ask your girlfriend about that. If ya had one," Kevin said with an icy gaze. "Com'on. Now, tell Remy to stand up for ya."

"There's nothing cuter than a midget acting tough. Can you dance? I bet that would be entertaining. Someday you'll be able to play with the big boys," Brockman's voice was dismissive while attempting to set Kevin off. "Now, let the grown-ups talk."

Kevin made a move toward Brockman that was stopped by Remy.

"THAT'S ENOUGH!" Remy's voice boomed throughout the building. He gave both Brockman and Kevin a primal stare. The rhetoric in the room calmed after Remy's explosive roar.

Hazz pulled into the building with the car and he backed up to the area where Uschi's body lay. He and Pike opened the tarp and lifted Uschi's body onto it. They wrapped the body and placed it in the trunk of the car.

"Does her car have GPS?" Remy asked Hazz, referring to a global positioning satellite system.

"No," Hazz replied.

"Go leave it up in Orange County," Remy told him. "Nothing fancy. I want them to find it. Don't take anything. It's not a robbery. It's a message."

"What about her phone?" Hazz asked.

"Throw it in the ocean up there," Remy said.

"Why don't you leave it?" Brockman told him. "I can do somethin' with it."

"You got enough to do," Remy proclaimed. He then looked around at all of them. "Focus, gentlemen."

Remy ascended the staircase, Brockman returned to his computer screens, and Kevin and Hazz began their trek to Orange County.

CHAPTER 14

The Midway area of San Diego is located at the northern end of the Point Loma peninsula, just northwest of downtown San Diego. It is primarily comprised of commercial and industrial buildings with pockets of residential development and commercial service establishments.

One type of service establishment found in the Midway area are the gentlemen's clubs. There are a variety of topless and bottomless female entertainment venues that are available to anyone of age who can afford the cover charge or the drink minimum.

The flesh establishment also draws clientele that are willing to pay extra for sex with their dream date that they lusted after onstage. There are also young ladies who simply walk the streets hoping to be picked up for a quick and illegal carnal act.

Dana Barton had been turning 'tricks' for nearly a year. She moved to San Diego from Madison, Wisconsin three years earlier with dreams of escaping snow, living on the beach, and a high-paying internet job for her boyfriend that never materialized. Her boyfriend died after going to a party and trying a 'Sherm Stick,' which is a marijuana joint that is dipped in PCP or phencyclidine. He ran out onto interstate 5 and was struck by three cars and a tractor trailer before falling down dead. Without his financial support, Dana sold off his possessions and started to live out of his car.

She was 28 years old, beautiful once, scarred by methamphetamine use, anorexically thin, and had totally abandoned any hope of improving her station in life. At one point, she thought about becoming a high-end prostitute, but those dreams faded after her second abortion. She was told that she was HIV positive and if she continued to ply her trade, she would be charged with assault in addition to solicitation and prostitution. It made no difference to Dana.

Monday nights were slow and she had to avoid the main streets like Rosecrans and Midway Drive because vice cops liked to set up stings on a regular basis. She knew that she had two outstanding warrants, so she had to dodge anyone suspicious to avoid incarceration.

She sashayed along Riley and Hancock Streets trying to look sexy, but instead coming across as rather pathetic. She wore a red tube top with a loose-fitting, unbuttoned jean jacket and a short, pleated skirt.

As the night progressed, she noticed a 1996 Oldsmobile Cutlass Ciera, 2-door, slowly following her. The car pulled up to the curb, making sure that it did not stop under a street light. Dana walked up to the passenger window and the driver lowered it.

"You lookin' for a party?" she asked.

"How 'bout we go for a ride?" the driver suggested.

"Okay," she responded, then opened the door and stepped into the vehicle.

The man driving the car was Chuck Arango, a 66-year-old retiree, who spent 35 years on the San Diego Police force as a patrol officer, a field training officer, and a detective. He weighed approximately 280 pounds and wore a white t-shirt, shorts, and flip-flops. He had a bushy mustache, unshaven face, and reeked of body odor.

"So, you wanna party?" Dana asked.

"Are you a cop?" Chuck's voice was deadpan.

"No," she responded with histrionic flare at even a remote thought that she could be a police officer.

"Let me see your bush," Chuck demanded of her as they cruised down Sports Arena Boulevard.

"What?" she said, rather startled by the question.

"I know how this works," Chuck advised. "I was a vice cop for 5 years. If you're a cop, you can't show me. If you're a pro, consider it advertisement."

Dana lifted her skirt and raised her rear end up to slip her thong down. While stopped at a light, Chuck gazed at her pubic area.

"You got a forest goin' on down there."

"You wanna party or what?" Dana gave him a quick retort. She was ready to walk away from this potential sale.

"All right. I know a place, just down the block, it's not well lit."

Chuck pulled into a parking lot for an Audi repair service station and drove around to the back of the building. Lights could be seen off in the distance from establishments several blocks away.

"So, what do ya want?" Dana asked.

"What do you charge?" Chuck asked.

"You want regular, it's $40 with a condom, 80 without."

Chuck pondered her prices before making a decision.

"If I go 80, will you use your mouth to get me going?"

"Sure. I need to see the cash first."

Chuck pulled out his wallet and removed four twenty dollar bills. Dana reached her hands into his lap and it was necessary for him to reposition himself to allow her room to lower the zipper on his pants and then manipulate his rolls of fat, so that she could perform her business.

"Back when I was working this area, we'd call the girls who went down on cops 'Badge Bunnies' and 'Holster Humpers.' Do you do cops?"

Dana did not respond to his question.

Outside the vehicle, a tall, thin man with a black hoodie stood outside the Cutlass at the rear, driver's side of the vehicle. His gloved hand pulled a 9 millimeter Berretta with a suppressor or silencer attached to it from his waistband. As Chuck fidgeted with his pants, the man fired two shots through the driver's side, rear window directly into the back of Chuck's head.

Inside the car, Dana had been fidgeting with Chuck's zipper and moved her head in close for the task at hand. At first she heard what sounded like firecrackers, simultaneously with the sound of glass cracking, and she felt moisture spray on the nape of her neck. She reached her hand to the back of her neck and realized it was blood. She sat up to see a chunk of Chuck's forehead and right eye socket blown out. Dana let out a quick, short scream. Thinking quickly, she feared that she was next to be shot, so she opened her door and set one foot out. Before stepping out of the vehicle, she turned back to Chuck and took the $80 from his hand. She sprinted from the car and Chuck's dead body.

Before the shooter walked away, he took a business card out of his pocket and slipped it between the glass and the weather-stripping at the bottom of the driver's window. The card was from Dexter Frye, the Litigation Guy.

CHAPTER 15

Lester Abrams acquired a habit of brushing his teeth twice before leaving for work in the morning. He used a Sonicare toothbrush and the process took two minutes to cycle through all of his teeth. He would brush immediately upon rising and then a second time after he was fully dressed; right before walking out the door.

Diane awoke later than Lester and rested her clothes within arm's reach. She heard Lester brushing his teeth and from the bed she could see that he was fully clothed.

"Lester," she called out. "Lester!" she tried again with a raised decibel level. He did not acknowledge her until his toothbrush shut off and he rinsed out his mouth.

"Okay, I gotta go. Have a nice day." His tone sounded rote and mechanical. He was not even looking at her while he spoke.

"LESTER!" Diane boosted her voice, not quite a scream, but it left an echo in the room.

"What?" he responded as if bothered by her voice.

"I need a ride to physical therapy today. I told you yesterday, my sister can't take me today."

"You're kidding? When did you tell me?" he demanded.

"Yesterday, after you put on the little show with the vacuum cleaner."

Lester shook his head and let out an exasperated sigh.

"Look," he took out his wallet, removed $40, and handed it to her. "Call a cab."

"We have stairs in front. How am I supposed to get down 'em?"

"Hop," Lester asserted as if it was no big deal. "One step at a time."

"Forget it," Diane told him. Lester knew from her tone that she was beyond pissed.

"I'll take you," he said. "I'd rather be late for work than have the drama."

"Just bring me and I'll find a way home," Diane wanted to keep peace in the house. "Can you help me to the bathroom?"

Lester approached Diane's side of the bed as she scooted closer to the edge.

"You should think about changing your name to Eileen," Lester exclaimed to her with disdain as she put her arm around the back of his neck and she stood up.

"What? Why?" she responded indignantly.

"You know, 'I-lean.' Get it?"

"That's not funny."

Lester kept his mouth shut. He thought about being in a courtroom and Roger Legion telling him, "Don't let your adversary get to you. That's what they want. It's a sign of weakness. Stand silent, bide your time, and wait for the opportunity. When it arises – pounce!" Lester decided to change the subject.

"When are you going for an amniocentesis test?" Lester wondered.

"Why would I get that? I'm not over 35." She spoke as she hobbled.

"You don't want a kid with birth defects," Lester's voice had a forced seriousness.

"You don't want a kid at all. Get your hands off me." Diane pushed Lester away. "I can make it the rest-a the way."

At this point, they were in the doorway to the bathroom and Diane leaned against the doorway, allowing Lester to step back. She took one hop into the bathroom and appeared unstable as if she may fall.

"Let me help you," Lester told her.

"No."

She pushed him away again and this added to her instability. It was in that moment that Lester saw his opportunity. As she hopped forward, Lester put his foot in front of her leg and gave her a soft push forward. It was enough for her to lose her equilibrium. She let out a scream and her head struck a 90 degree corner of the vanity where the sink was located. Once her head hit the faux granite, she dropped to the floor like a dead weight.

On the tiled bathroom floor where her head lay, the grout lines created a conduit for her blood. As Lester watched, the grout lines overflowed and a pool of blood began to surround her head.

"Diane?" Lester called to her in a cold, normal tone. "Diane?"

Lester walked back to Diane's side of the bed and retrieved her crutch. He brought it to the bathroom and laid it down next to her.

He left the house and headed to work. As usual, Roger Legion's admonition proved it had a practical application.

CHAPTER 16

Roger Legion emerged from the 24th floor conference room and saw the receptionist, Nina, had arrived and was answering calls. He wore a blue, pinstripe suit and mauve, striped tie. Nina wore a blue skirt with a white top and matching sweater.

"Nina," he called out for her attention. She ceased all her activities to focus on him. "I have some visitors in the conference room. I'm going back to my office for a few moments. Let me know as soon as Lester Abrams gets here. If I'm on the phone, send me an e-mail or come and get me. And don't tell him I'm looking for him."

"Yes, Mr. Legion."

Roger walked back to his office, entered, and before sitting down, he picked up the telephone receiver from his phone and scanned his phone directory to the name, Glenn Edgarian. Glenn was a private investigator; not the type that carried a gun, but rather, a much more dangerous individual because of his ability to obtain information. Glenn knew everyone and who or what he didn't know, he could find out. His proficiency in the skill of information collection always impressed Roger. Roger considered Glenn the best private investigator in the city of San Diego because he always understood the objective and always exceeded expectations.

Roger pushed a button to dial Glenn's number and he answered on the 2nd ring.

"Hello," came his voice.

"Glenn. It's Roger Legion."

"Roger, how are ya?"

"Good. Ya keeping busy?"

"I'm keeping busy, but, you know, nobody pays like you. I'm not feelin' the love."

Roger always made it a habit not to scrutinize Glenn's bills that closely and he made sure they were paid immediately.

"Listen, I've got a little project for ya. Do you have some time that you can come over and we can discuss it?"

"How's this afternoon?" Glenn asked.

Roger quickly pulled up his electronic calendar to review it for any appointments.

"2:30?"

"I'll be there," Glenn responded.

"Okay. I'll see ya then. Thanks, Glenn."

Roger returned the telephone receiver to its cradle and sat in his chair, gazing forward. He then picked up the phone and dialed two numbers.

"Yes, Mr. Legion," the voice answered.

"DeAnna, is Lester Abrams covering for anyone today?"

Roger was inquiring of the firm's calendar clerk if Lester was substituting for any other attorney for any event outside the office.

"Not that I'm aware of," she replied.

"Thank you."

As soon as Legion returned the telephone receiver to its cradle, the phone rang. It was Nina.

"He's here."

"Very good."

At that moment, if someone had been in the room with him, they would have heard the wheels in Roger's mind moving at unfathomable speed.

CHAPTER 17

Lester Abrams was beginning the morning as he had every day that he was in the office. He reviewed e-mails to determine which ones he could delete immediately and which ones needed additional attention. He also had a list of telephone calls that were received the day before, but his intention was not to return any of them. As he was taught by Roger Legion, if someone wants something from you, make them come and get it. That way they will understand the value of it.

Lester had deleted approximately 25 e-mails when Roger appeared in his doorway. His presence caught Lester off guard, because whenever Roger wanted to speak to one of the attorneys, he would dispatch an e-mail that simply said: Come to my office. ASAP. He would use the same e-mail over and over.

"Roger. How's it goin'? Still waitin' on your jury?" Lester queried.

"No. I settled it. Ya got a minute?"

"Sure. You wanna go down to your office?" Lester wondered.

"No. This is fine," Roger stepped through the doorway and closed the door about three-fourths of the way. "I've got a personal question that I want to ask you."

"Go ahead," Lester told him becoming more relaxed with the situation.

"You know, you're my go-to guy around here." As Roger spoke, he sat down across from Lester. "Like I said, this is personal. I've got a business opportunity. I don't want to go into detail, but do you know where I might be able to get some cocaine?"

Lester worried about the question and worried even more about the answer.

"Roger, that's a tough one. Can I have some time to think about it?"

"Well, do you know what an ounce of cocaine would cost?"

"No," his voice had no expression at all.

"All right," Roger remarked as he stood up. "If you could help me out, I'd really appreciate it."

"Let me make a phone call or two and I'll let you know."

"Be sure it's a reliable source. Did you hear what happened to Jill Burdick?"

The name set off a flare in Lester's mind.

"What?"

"She was pulled over for an equipment violation and right out on the console, she had an ounce of cocaine."

"No kiddin'," Lester knew he had to remain cool, "What happened to her?"

"All I know is that it's necessary that we distance ourselves from it." His voice had a placid intonation.

"I had nothing to do with it," Lester blurted out.

"Now, why would you say something like that?" Roger quizzed.

"Just in case you heard something, it's not true."

"Why don't you tell me what is true." Roger's countenance was moving from serious to petulant.

"There's nothing to say," Lester pleaded. His abject denial was unpersuasive. He started to rise from his chair.

"Don't get up, because I'll knock you down." Roger's certainty stopped Lester.

"Listen," Lester advised, "take it easy. Let me explain."

Roger was about to allow Lester to testify, but the verdict had already been rendered.

CHAPTER 18

"She came to me," Lester told Legion attempting to keep the atmosphere halcyonic. "She asked me if I could get her some coke. I thought it was a rainmaking opportunity. That's it. I did it for the firm."

"A rainmaking opportunity?" Legion inquired. "Selling dope? You know how many sharks out there are gunning for me? What do you think would happen to this place if any of 'em found out you were selling dope to a client?" His voice left a deadly pall over the room.

Legion's eyes locked on to Lester's eyes like a missile guidance system.

"It was just for a little recreation," Lester said trying to mitigate its import, "a little socialization."

Legion looked down on him from the front of the desk.

"Are you taking stupid pills, because if you are, they're working. Drugs are not for recreation. Drugs are not for socialization. Drugs are for self-destruction. Period. No discussion. Save your bullshit for the courtroom. Somebody might listen." Legion continued his gaze. "Did you do it with her?"

"No."

"You should work on lying, because you're not good at it. Now, I want you to tell me, straight up, that you sold Jill Burdick an ounce of cocaine, but you didn't use it."

Lester became sullen and took a deep breath.

"I sold Jill the cocaine. I never used it. It won't happen again."

"Where'd you get it?"

"One of the runners downstairs."

"Who?" Legion's questions were quick and sharp.

"Her name is Jodi Deep."

"Get her up here. Now."

Lester picked up the telephone receiver and pressed two numbers.

"Hey, it's Lester Abrams." Lester spoke as he stared at Roger. "Would you send Jodi to my office. Now. It's important." Lester then hung up the phone.

"How are you able to get a specific runner?" Legion asked.

"I called DeAnna."

Legion then picked up the receiver of the phone and pressed two numbers.

"Louise, it's Roger. Would you please come to Lester Abrams' office and bring DeAnna with you. Right now. Thank you."

As he hung up the phone, there was a knock at the door and a young girl, 23-year-old, brunette, with short, cropped hair and wearing a green, cotton A-line dress entered. She froze in place when she saw Roger Legion.

"What's your name?" Roger asked with a gaze that could melt an iceberg.

"Jodi Deep." Her voice was slow and terror-filled.

"Did you sell Mr. Abrams some cocaine?"

"No! Did he say that?" She turned to Lester, "You are such a liar. Tell him the truth."

"I'm askin' you. You tell me," Legion demanded.

"One day I brought him some documents that were delivered by a special courier and he asked me if I knew where he could get some blow. I think the guy's a skeeve," referring to Lester. "I mean, he looks at ya like he's a pervert. At first I told him 'No', and he said he could make life easy for me here if I helped him out. So, I told him I don't know anybody, but my boyfriend might know a guy. I gave him my boyfriend's number and my boyfriend connected him up with somebody. I don't know who. All I know is my boyfriend was told he's a real good customer." Jodi looked at Legion in despair. "Mr. Legion, I need this job, I wouldn't do anything to jeopardize it." Jodi looked at Lester with repulsion. She asked Legion, "Can I hit him?"

"No," Roger told her. "If I ever hear your name and drugs in the same sentence, you will be fired immediately. Understand?"

"Yes, Mr. Legion."

"If anyone at this firm ever makes an inappropriate comment to you, you tell me and I will deal with them. Now, get back to work."

As Jodi left, Louise and DeAnna stood in the hallway.

"Com'on in," Legion told them as if he was welcoming them to a party.

DeAnna was in her mid-50s, long, blond hair, and cute face. She wore a flowing light blue, button shirt and dress slacks. Louise was in her late-60s, glasses, short, white hair, and her Liz Claiborne dress had a floral pattern. Both ladies were approximately 5 feet, 7 inches tall.

"DeAnna, what's your job title here?"

"I'm the calendar clerk." As she spoke, her fear was evident.

"Do you assign runners?"

"No, Mr. Legion." Her face was expressionless.

"Don't do it again." DeAnna appeared to be frozen in place. "You can go."

DeAnna and Louise both exited the room. Roger gyrated his focus to Lester.

"Just once, huh?"

"She's bullshiting you to save her ass," Lester retorted as he raised his voice.

"Maybe so." Roger's face looked relieved. He turned his head toward the door and said, "Keith, com'on in."

The man who entered the room was in his early 50s, thin, approximately 5 feet, 10 inches tall, with black, wavy hair, glasses, and a moustache. His suit was cheap compared to those seen at Legion & Associates. He looked at Lester with disgust.

"Lester," Roger said relishing in the anguish and shock on Lester's less than stern visage, "this is Lieutenant Keith Bremer from the Narcotics Section of the San Diego Police Department. Tell Lester your nickname down at the county jail."

"Hard-ass."

Lester was flummoxed by these events. Legion reached into the breast pocket of his suit coat and removed a small digital pocket recorder.

"Here's his confession," Roger said as he handed the recorder to the Lieutenant.

"I heard it," Bremer told Legion. He then turned to Lester. "Son, you're under arrest for felony possession of a controlled substance, felony possession of a controlled substance for purposes of sale, and sale and trafficking of a controlled substance." Bremer then turned to Legion. "Do I need to give him his *Miranda* rights?"

"No. He knows them and he understands them."

"Roger, what's wrong with you? Why are you doing this?" Lester pleaded.

"I'm an officer of the court. I can't stand by while a crime is being committed. And now I have to make sure you lose your law license." Legion's eyes seared into Lester. "And you've got a helluva nerve. I gotta clean up your mess because you wanna peddle dope in my shop. If there's any blowback, it's gonna be on you, not me."

"I know you're not gonna let him take me outta here in handcuffs, because God forbid, there might be some negative press for the almighty Legion & Associates."

"SHUT UP!" Legion's voice reverberated against the walls. He then went to the door and yanked it open. "Nina!" he commanded in a raised voice.

Nina stood up from her seat and stepped into the hallway. "Yes, Mr. Legion."

"Would you please ask the two gentlemen in the conference room to come in here?"

"Sure," she responded.

Within a few moments, two large, Samoan gentlemen entered the room. They were not just large, they were hulking. They gazed at Lester as if they were prepared for hand-to-hand combat.

"Lester, these gentlemen are from a drug rehabilitation facility in Coronado, called Coronado Paradisio or Cor-pare. You're gonna go with them."

"Why would I go with them?"

"To deal with your substance abuse problem."

"I don't have a problem," Lester's dissent was definite. "I'm not going with these guys," Lester's anger was rising.

"You're in denial. That's a problem," Legion told him. He turned to the Samoan gentlemen, "Would you mind waiting for me in either the conference room or the lobby? If you'd like something to drink, just tell the receptionist and she'll get it for you."

Legion thanked them as they exited the room. He closed the door and looked down at Lester from the front of the desk. Closing arguments were about to begin.

CHAPTER 19

Legion's disgust of Lester was growing exponentially.

"There is a condition in order for you to avoid being arrested. You're gonna tell this cop where you got that cocaine. You're gonna be his Judas goat. You know what that is? That's the animal that leads the others to the slaughter. You either roll over on your supplier, or you're going to jail. Choose. Now."

"I am not doing that," Lester spoke with stern indignation. "The Constitution protects me from self-incrimination."

"Well, I'll be God damned," Legion boasted with a smile, then turned to Bremer. "Hard-ass, did you know you were gonna get a lesson in Constitutional law today?"

Bremer stared at Lester and shook his head from side to side. Roger stopped smiling.

"Let me see your gun," he told Bremer.

Bremer pulled his Smith & Wesson semi-automatic 9 millimeter from his shoulder holster and handed it to Legion, grip first. Roger took it with his right hand and pulled the slide on the gun back slightly to see if there was a live round in the chamber. Lester watched Roger to see what his next action would be. Roger pulled the hammer back on the gun.

Legion was now behind the desk within 4 feet of Lester. He took one step toward Lester and within a blink, he was able to grab Lester's tie with his left hand, wrap it once around his fist, and pull it up like a noose with his body dangling from it. At the same time, Legion took the gun, with his finger on the trigger, and pressed the muzzle of the gun into Lester's temple.

"Now tell me," Legion demanded, "I wanna know, right now, how the Constitution protects you in this situation." Lester was silent. "Com'on! Tell me!" Roger commanded.

"What's wrong with this boy, Roger?" Bremer asked. "I guess he doesn't understand theory versus practice."

"What he doesn't understand are the rules of a criminal enterprise. Hard-ass, tell him the first rule."

"You don't shit where you eat," Bremer uttered it in a cold, calm manner without missing a beat.

"The second rule is that you trust no one except the guy in the mirror," Legion advised. "And the third rule is that when the grenade goes off, make sure you're not in the blast zone."

"I'm impressed," Lester replied with a sarcastic tone.

"So, what should I do with you, Lester?" Legion pushed the gun harder into his temple. "What should I do?" Legion demanded an answer.

"Pull the trigger." Lester's comment was emotionless.

Legion unwrapped Lester's tie from his fist and lowered the gun's hammer down. He handed the gun back to Bremer, grip first, and Bremer re-holstered it.

"I knew there was a reason I hired this guy," he told Bremer as he shook his finger at Lester. "That's the answer a man would give. You think I wouldn't pull the trigger? You think I'm afraid?" Legion asked rhetorically. "I just don't wanna pay to clean up the mess." He then turned to Bremer. "Tell him what's gonna happen next." Legion walked around the desk and stood with his arms crossed.

"We're gonna book you in the county lock-up," Bremer began to speak. "Because you're a lawyer, you'll be classified as high profile. Alotta the inmates blame their lawyers for being there. So, you'll be placed in segregation. Tomorrow morning, there's a shift change at 6 a.m. The new shift is gonna find you hanging in your cell from a bed sheet." Bremer paused so Lester could absorb what he said. "That's how we handle troublemakers. So, my advice is that you should listen to Mr. Legion."

Lester realized there was no way out of this situation. He wasn't going to win any verbal jousting. He went for the sympathy card.

"What about my wife? With the accident, she needs me and she's pregnant," he said and all the while, in the back of his mind, hoping that she and his unborn child were dead on the bathroom floor.

CHAPTER 20

The two Samoan gentlemen from Cor-pare, the drug rehabilitation facility, re-entered the room.

"Gentlemen," Legion said, "I apologize, I didn't introduce you the last time you were in here. Lester, this is Kono and Tiki."

Lester, now with his clothing disheveled, gazed at them and they returned his stare.

"I'll make sure your wife is taken care of, you don't have to worry," Legion told him.

"What about the files?"

"We'll take care of them."

"What about my bills?"

"I'll keep you on the payroll. The people at Cor-pare will get your mail if you need it."

"What about my car?"

"Cor-pare will take care of it." Legion turned to Kono and Tiki. "He's ready to go."

"Sir," Kono addressed Lester, "you have to surrender your cell phone and anything else in your pockets. You can do it here or at the facility."

"I need my cell phone." Lester was adamant.

"It's not allowed." Kono's voice was calm.

"That's bullshit," Lester spewed.

"It's my phone, give it to me," Legion demanded.

Lester removed the phone from his pants pocket and tossed it to Legion. He then removed his wallet, keys, and change from his pants and placed it on the desk.

"Let's go," Kono told him. Lester walked around the desk and stopped. He stared at Legion.

"Roger, you are making a mistake. One you can't afford. You will regret this."

"May we restrain him, if necessary?" Tiki queried.

"Absolutely," Legion told them. "You won't need to. He's foolish, not stupid."

All the men walked into the lobby. Legion shook hands with all of them except Lester. Nina was trying not to pay attention, but she was enjoying Lester's comeuppance, even though she did not know the full extent of all the facts. She felt a twinge of schadenfrude.

Tiki, Kono, Lester, and Bremer entered an elevator and the last thing Legion saw were the two elevator doors closing in front of Lester. Legion turned to Nina.

"Nina, Is Marty Hannah here?" She nodded affirmatively.

Marty Hannah was one of the seasoned lawyers in the firm. He was an excellent writer and handled nearly all complex motions.

"Ask him to meet me in my office now. Also, will you call Roy and have him come to my office."

"He's in with Mr. Cordel."

"Thank you."

Roger walked down the hallway on the western side of the building to Luke Cordel's office. All of the offices had a nameplate outside of their entranceway and the nameplate for Luke had not yet arrived. When Legion arrived at the doorway, Luke and Roy, the information technology person at the firm, were going over the various computer functions, telephone functions, and Luke's new law firm smartphone. Roger was right about to knock when Luke noticed him.

"Good morning, sir," Luke proclaimed with a beaming smile.

"What's up, Mister 'L'?" Roy asked.

Roy was in his late 20s, slightly heavyset, balding, wore glasses, and a blue, striped shirt, no tie, with Dockers slacks.

"Roy, this is Lester's cell phone. It's password protected. I wanna know the password. I also want his wife's cell phone number." Roger handed the phone to Roy.

"No prob-lem-o," Roy told him. "Can I finish with Mr. 'C' first?"

"Sure. Luke, we're going to court this afternoon. One-thirty. Be sure you're here. I'll come and get you."

"I'll be here," Luke advised.

Legion proceeded to his office and saw Marty Hannah in the hallway. Marty was in his mid-30s, short, bald, and weighed approximately 250 pounds. In addition to the traditional Legion garb, he wore suspenders. Legion started to speak as soon as he saw him.

"I want you to go through Lester's files right now and make sure nothing's on fire. Then we're gonna re-assign them. Get a list together. Anything within 120 days of trial assign to me. Get me the list of everything else and I'll see if we can give it to Luke, the new guy."

"What's going on with Lester?" Marty innocently inquired.

"Long story. We're gonna have a meeting on it."

"Okay." Marty accepted his response and retreated to his office.

Roger entered his office and before he sat down, he picked up his telephone receiver and pressed two numbers on the keypad.

"Louise, will you please get Lester's wife on the phone for me? Thank you."

Legion returned the phone to its cradle. He stood for a moment and surveyed the ocean. He pondered Lester's comment about regretting his course of action.

CHAPTER 21

The Tierrasanta neighborhood of San Diego is perhaps the only community in San Diego that is not bordered by another community. The name is Spanish for 'holy land' and it is surrounded by a park, a freeway, and the Marine Corps Air Station Miramar, which was once the home of the famous TOPGUN training program.

This neighborhood grew at an expeditious rate over the past 30 years and it attracted an eclectic demographic from various financial strata.

Chester 'Chet' Wulsifer and his wife moved to Tierrasanta in 1987 with their 3 children. At the time, they considered their 1800 square foot, two-story home to be a castle. Now, the children had moved away, but the memories would not allow them to downsize. Chet spent 12 years with the San Diego Police Department, primarily as a patrol officer. After that, he spent 25 years selling real estate before retiring 2 years ago. When he retired, Chet and his wife purchased a 28-foot recreation vehicle and planned 3 trips a year with the hope of eventually visiting every state and country on the North American continent.

Chet was 5 feet, 10 inches tall, 175 pounds, with a full head of gray hair, and in good shape for a 64-year-old man.

On Tuesdays, Chet's wife went grocery shopping and he enjoyed working around the house, cutting grass, and other assorted 'honey-do' projects.

Chet had just returned from the local Lowes Home Improvement store where he purchased a variety of light bulbs and decided that today was the day to replace the blown out bulbs. Also, once a year, he would change the 9-volt batteries in the smoke detectors, not because they needed a battery, but because he wanted to avoid the low battery signal they would give off, usually in the middle of the night.

When Chet entered his kitchen from the garage, he set the sundries he had just purchased on the kitchen table and made a quick pit stop in the bathroom. Chet's prostrate was more active than most volcanos. He always made sure that a bathroom was within earshot.

As he began to wizz in the bathroom, his doorbell rang. He endeavored to complete the task, knowing that he would probably have to go again in a few hours. He once again heard the doorbell.

"All right. I'm coming," he yelled toward the door. Chet didn't know if he should be upset at his visitor, the doorbell, or himself because of his condition.

When he reached the door, he looked through the peephole. He saw a tall, slender man, wearing sunglasses and blue coveralls with a box in his hand and a clipboard under his arm. Chet noticed he was wearing driving gloves.

"Who is it?" Chet asked through the door.

"I got a delivery for Chester Wulsifer. Somebody's gotta sign for it."

Chet unlocked the door and slid the security chain off its secured position.

As the door began to open, the delivery man unzipped his coveralls approximately half the length of the zipper and reached inside them to pull out a 9 millimeter Berretta with a silencer. It was the same gun that was used the night before on Chuck Arango when he had an unlucky encounter with a prostitute.

Before the door was fully opened, 2 shots were fired, point blank range. They were fired so quickly that his body had not fully responded to the first bullet when he was struck by the second bullet. His body slammed back into the tile entryway. His hands were moving, either from nerve impulses or survival instinct. The delivery man took 2 rapid steps into the house and instantaneously aimed at Chet's forehead and pulled the trigger.

The delivery man placed the box that he brought squarely on Chet's chest. Then he reached into his pocket and took out a business card. As with the shooting the day before, it was the business card of Dexter Frye, The Litigation Guy.

CHAPTER 22

Detective Skylar Stubbs and Detective Jeff Elkins of the San Diego Police Homicide Division sat in a booth at an In-N-Out Burger restaurant located on Camino Del Rio East in the Mission Valley section of San Diego. In addition to drinks, In-N-Out Burger had only 4 items on the menu: hamburger, cheeseburger, Double-Double, which was essentially a double cheeseburger, and fries. For anyone who loved the basics, In-N-Out was like crack to a junkie.

 While they waited for their order numbers to be called, they deliberated on the events of the last 18 hours. They were assigned to investigate the Chuck Arango killing and when the second Dexter Frye card was identified, they inherited the Chet Wulsifer murder.

"What do you think is gonna be in the box?" Skylar asked.

Skylar Stubbs was 32 years old, 5 feet, 6 inches tall, with the body of a long distance runner. He had blond hair, a clean-shaven, boyish face, and generally would ask questions until he was stopped by Jeff. He approached his job the way he approached his Mormon faith. He was a zealot, whose faith in the Lord and the truth could be tested, but not shaken. When he was assigned a case, he would live, breath, and sleep it. That was one of the reasons that he had risen so quickly within the department. In less than eight years, he was a homicide detective.

Skylar wore a long sleeve blue shirt with the cuffs folded up approximately one-fourth of the length of his arms. His light, blue tie was loose around his neck and he wore dark, blue, Haggar slacks. His shoulder holster carried a Glock 19 pistol chambered in 9 millimeter on one side and 2 additional magazines on the other.

"I don't know. Probably nothin'. Killer just wanted to slow us down," Jeff suggested. "It's a good thing the bomb squad didn't blow it up."

The first officers on the scene at Chet Wulsifer's murder contacted the Metro Arson Strike Team Bomb Squad to check out the box left by the killer. After x-raying the box, it was determined that its contents did not contain any explosive material. It was collected by the crime lab technicians along with the Dexter Frye card, three spent bullet casings, and various fingerprints they lifted around the doorway.

"They were both cops. You think there's a link?" Skylar queried.

"Come on, is this your first day on the job?" Jeff asked rhetorically. "There's gonna be a link, and it's probably this Dexter Frye guy."

Jeff Elkins was 54 years old, a 31-year veteran of the San Diego Police Department, who spent the last 12 years as a detective, 9 of which were in the Homicide Division. Jeff was 5 feet, 9 inches tall, 225 pounds, with thinning black hair, and a moustache. He wore a white shirt, gray pants, and a loose-fitting, red, striped tie. Jeff carried his .40 caliber Smith & Wesson semi-automatic weapon on his belt. He has been married for the past 25 years and has two children. He treats his job as just that – a job. At the end of the day, he turns it off until he returns for his next shift.

"You know what was bothering me?" Skylar said. "The telephone number on those cards had a 7-1-4 area code with a San Diego address. Seven-one-four is Orange County."

"I know the answer. I called my father-in-law," Jeff told him. "The San Diego area has only had the 6-1-9 area code since the early 1980s. Prior to that, San Diego was in the 7-1-4 area code."

"Did you ask your father-in-law about Dexter Frye?"

"He said the name sounded familiar, but he didn't know. Some days, my father-in-law is more on the ball than others."

Just then, Skylar and Jeff's order numbers were called. Skylar stood from the booth and began his trek to the pick-up area.

"Sky, get some ketchup," Jeff bellowed and Skylar shook his head in acknowledgement.

Skylar returned to the table with 2 trays. On Skylar's tray, was a cheeseburger without a bun, wrapped in lettuce, referred to as a 'protein burger.' On the table in front of him was a bottle of water. On Jeff's tray was a Double-Double burger, French fries slathered with melted cheese and Thousand Island dressing, known as 'animal fries.' In front of Jeff was a milkshake that was half chocolate, half vanilla.

Even though In-N-Out had a bare bones menu, they also had a secret menu of delights, of which Jeff had a keen awareness.

Skylar stared at Jeff's lunch.

"That stuff can't be good for you," Skylar proclaimed.

"Don't worry about it," Jeff said as he unwrapped his Double-Double. "You sound like my wife. You know what her deal is? She is a very high-functioning crazy person. She doesn't inflict pain, she denies pleasure. You know my wife: 5 feet 2, 105 pounds. She's still got a pretty smokin' body for a 54-year-old. So, that denial of pleasure thing is a perfect offensive weapon. If the government studied her, they could put a Disneyland in the Middle East."

"I bet she doesn't even know she's doing it."

"I can't argue that. But maybe it's her subconscious or something, because if I was with her right now – first of all we would never be at this restaurant – she has to go someplace that has salad. And I want red meat. But I learned a long time ago, shut your mouth and let her talk, eventually it stops."

"So, eat a hamburger someplace else."

"Sky, you're a newlywed. You're still in the honeymoon phase. I'm sure when you walk in the door at night, it's a triple-x throwdown. Newsflash! It won't be happening forever. Enjoy it while you got it. A marriage is like a car. You hope it won't break down before they plant ya in the ground. But it does fall apart and need repair along the way."

"Jeff, you sound bitter."

"Sound bitter? I am bitter."

"Why stay in a marriage if you're not happy?"

"I didn't say I wasn't happy. I'm challenged. Maybe that's a good thing. My wife likes to complain. She never shuts up. She could take a hard-on off a piece-a steel. Her head hurts, her feet hurt, her back hurts, her legs hurt, her clothes hurt, her hair hurts. Ya get dizzy after a while," Jeff was attempting to be comedic. "But, maybe that's a good thing. I've known her for 40 years. Now, don't get me wrong. There are days when I want to call an ambulance from a mental hospital and have her committed, restrained, medicated, and observed. But then, I say to myself, I don't know what I would do without her. I don't have the interest or the energy to chase another woman. I'm okay with the cards I was dealt."

"So, you are happily married. You just like to complain about it. You are so fulla crap," Skylar declared with a wide smile and a finger point.

"Well, it is fodder for conversation." Jeff's response also included a tacit agreement of Skylar's observation.

As Jeff finished his sentence, his cell phone rang. He put on his reading glasses, looked at the Caller ID, and answered it.

"Yeah," a moment passed. "We're on our way."

"Do we have to go?" Skylar asked.

"Not until we finish lunch," Jeff was resolute.

"Who was it?"

"The crime lab has some preliminary info for us."

"Shouldn't we get going?"

"I don't care if they find Jimmy Hoffa in Amelia Earhart's airplane, we're not goin' anywhere until I finish my lunch. And you can't do anything about it, because I have the keys to the car. So finish your," Jeff looked at Skylar's burger, "whatever that is."

Skylar smiled and gave thanks for his food. He chuckled lightly at Jeff's curmudgeonly style and the Jimmy Hoffa – Amelia Earhart comment.

CHAPTER 23

As Roger Legion and Luke Cordel ascended the escalator from the 2nd to 3rd floor of the downtown San Diego Superior Courthouse, Roger shared tidbits of information that he had gleaned over the years from the plaintiff's law firm that they were about to oppose. They were heading to court for a motion hearing to disqualify the plaintiff law firm after that firm had retained a forensic accountant as an expert for a case, who was originally approached by Legion and Associates to represent their client.

The Legion firm never had a formal agreement with the expert and they never retained him because the insurance company that hired Legion thought the expert's rates were too high.

"This law firm," Legion told Luke, referring to the plaintiff firm they were trying to disqualify, "Asunder and Holtz, their nickname is 'Assholes' and they earn it every time they open their mouths. The old man, Lionel Asunder, is an incompetent codger. How the hell that guy ever passed the bar exam is beyond me. He won't be here today. He's a money man. He only shows up to swap numbers at a settlement conference. If you can get through to him, you can close a deal. He can be reasonable when he stops being an asshole for 2 seconds."

"The opposition to our motion was done by a guy named Larry Barnsten," Luke stated.

"He carries bags for Asunder. Works off a script. Trip him up and he's down for the count. He's another one that went to law school for the legally-challenged. If he approaches you about a deal, you know you got him. Then, finish him."

Legion's words echoed with Luke. Court was not a rote billing exercise, but rather a duel of warriors played out in a legal arena. The concept evoked in Luke a kind of patriotism for Legion and Associates. He had to make sure Legion and Associates were the victors.

Legion and Luke sauntered to Department C-60 and reviewed the afternoon calendar that was posted on a corkboard immediately next to the courtroom doors. There was only one other case on the afternoon docket and a handwritten note next to it indicated that it was continued to another day.

As Legion and Luke scanned the calendar, they were approached by a heavyset man, mid-40s, glasses, bald, with a face that looked something like a chipmunk. He was squinting as he approached them and wiped an oily shine from the top of his head with a handkerchief.

"Are you from Legion and Associates?" he queried.

"I'm Luke Cordel. This is Roger Legion." Luke extended his hand to him.

"Sorry, I've got a cold. And it's allergy season. My name is Larry Barnsten from Asunder and Holtz," he informed him while refusing to shake Luke's hand. "I was wonderin' if I could talk to you before we go inside."

"Sure," Luke responded. His nice guy demeanor had totally evaporated and he had no plans to take any prisoners.

"Listen, we really wanna keep this case. I don't think this motion has any traction. I think that's clear from the fact we're having an oral argument on it. The judge coulda just issued a ruling."

"I think the judge is pissed that you made us bring this motion in the first place. There's a case right on point and it's cited in our brief. He probably wants to sanction you guys, in particular, the lawyer who shows up."

"Listen, why don't we talk settlement?" Larry's request sounded more like a desperate plea. He pushed up his glasses, scratched his face, and adjusted his tie. "Forget about experts."

"Are you the guy who can make decisions on this case?" Luke asked.

"I can negotiate it. I just have to make one phone call when we get to a final number."

Luke stared at Larry. Legion's stare at Larry was stern, hard, and icy.

"All right, but don't tell me a seven figure number, because that's an easy decision to make."

Luke was mimicking Roger's words that he used in his conversation with Hilly Geisser at Dobson's Restaurant.

"How close can you get to seven figures?" Larry wondered.

"I can't even get to 6 figures. We did a 9-9-8 for one penny shy of a hundred grand. Take it or we can argue the motion."

Luke was referring to the California Code of Civil Procedure section 998, which is a statutory offer to compromise. If a verdict comes in less than the amount in the offer, the plaintiff would be responsible to reimburse the defense for their post-offer costs. If the verdict exceeded the offer, the defense would be responsible to reimburse the plaintiff for their post-offer costs.

The reason the offer was one penny less than $100,000 was because the insurance claim handler would have to do additional paperwork if the offer was at $100,000 or above.

"Has the 9-9-8 expired?" Legion interjected.

"He still has 2 days," Luke answered while continuing to stare at Larry.

"Let me make a phone call," Larry told them as he walked away and called someone on his cell phone.

Legion knew at that moment that the case was settled. He saw a bright future for his new novice, but he felt that Luke needed to amp up his lust for blood.

CHAPTER 24

As Detective Jeff Elkins and Detective Skylar Stubbs cruised down the Interstate 163 freeway in their unmarked Chevrolet Impala patrol car, traffic moved at a brisk clip. Their destination was the downtown headquarters of the San Diego Police Department. It was located on Broadway, approximately 12 blocks to the east from the America's Finest City Building.

"So, you think that box was empty?" Skylar asked, but in his mind wondering why a killer would leave an empty box.

"I don't know," Jeff lamented. "Maybe the killer wanted to slow us down. You know, with the bomb squad and the hoops we gotta jump through to get the info from the crime lab."

"Something about it," Skylar wondered. "It doesn't pass the smell test. If it was nothin', wouldn't they tell us that on the phone?"

"Not necessarily. They probably know that you will have a million questions for them, so they don't wanna give you any extra time to think up more."

"Very funny. I'm thorough."

"Well, I'm old."

"I can tell by the way you're driving. If you push down on the gas pedal, it'll go faster," Skylar's voice made a poor attempt at sarcasm.

"What are ya, in a hurry to get killed?"

"No, I just want to get to the station before dawn. And how come you always drive?"

"Sky, I told you the first day they made us partners, if anybody's gotta be chased, you're the guy out the door. 'Cause, I don't chase people. I'll send one a my bullets after them. You were a track star, right?"

"High school state record in the hundred yard dash."

"Utah?"

"Wyoming," Skylar proudly admitted.

"Same thing. Well, you're an exception. Those Mormons are all pent-up, super horny, so they're focused on gettin' a wife. Sports take a back seat."

"You're a very strange man," Skylar told him with egalitarian enthusiasm.

"You have no idea."

"*Reversal of Fortune.* 1990," Skylar blurted it out as fast as he could like a game show contestant racing against a clock.

"Nice snag on that. Our record on movie trivia remains outstanding." As Jeff finished his statement, Skylar's cell phone rang.

"Hello." A moment passed. "Where?" Another moment passed. "We're on our way." Skylar ended the call.

"What is it?" Jeff inquired.

"They just picked up Dana Barton. CHP nabbed her up by Pendleton headin' outta town."

Dana was stopped on Interstate 5 near Camp Pendleton, the marine base in the northern section of San Diego County.

"Let's go see what she's gonna say."

With that, Jeff accelerated, racing to have a conversation with a prostitute.

CHAPTER 25

When Legion and Luke returned from court and emerged from the elevator, Glenn Edgarian was sitting in the law firm's lobby returning e-mails and text messages. He arose to greet Roger and Luke.

"Glenn," Roger said extending his hand, "how are ya? This is our newest attorney, Luke Cordel."

"Nice to meet ya, Luke," Glenn told him with a strong handshake.

"Nice to meet you, Glenn."

"Luke, if you ever need a private investigator, this is your guy. Best P-I in the city. Any other P-I in this town is a hack," Roger proudly declared.

"Roger, I gotta hang out with you more often," Glenn's devilish smile indicated that he enjoyed the accolades.

Glenn was 56 years old, 6 feet 2 inches tall, 205 pounds, with a lean, muscular build and short hair, feathered back with gray slowly overtaking the brown. If it wasn't for his hair, you would think he was 15 to 20 years younger. He had a fondness for the gym, sports, and large-breasted women. Anyone who ever saw him pump weights in the gym could regale you with stories of Glenn's herculean strength. But he never advertised it. He found humor in every facet of life and you felt safe to be in his company. His charm was disarming and he was admired for speaking like a man instead of a politically correct eunuch.

"Luke," Roger said turning his attention, "you do the report to the insurance company. At the end of the dictation, put a note that says, 'Roger needs to approve.' The secretaries will run it by me before it goes out the door."

"All right. See ya around, Glenn." Luke hastened a retreat to his office.

"Come on back," Roger told Glenn as he escorted him to his office.

They entered and Roger closed the door.

"Have a seat," Roger told him as Glenn sat and Roger proceeded to the other side of his desk. His chair was rolled slightly away from the desk.

Glenn quickly scanned the ocean view and placed his left foot over his right leg. Roger rested his elbows on the arms of his chair. His elbows were at a 90 degree position and the tips of the fingers of both hands touched each other. Their eyes locked.

"Somebody is trying to hijack some insurance accounts from me. I wanna know who the architect of the plan is," Roger's tone was nefarious.

"You think it's local? Alotta national firms would like a piece of your action." Glenn's observation was spot on.

"I know they're gunning for Acitu Mutual. Acitu would never go with a national firm. They've been burnt too many times. They know the judges here treat outta town firms like carpetbaggers. They don't have a level playing field."

"You got anybody in mind?" Glenn wondered.

"Yeah. But I want you to tell me if I'm right or wrong."

"You wanna give me any special instructions or restrictions?"

Roger's visage took on a hardened gaze.

"Scorch the earth."

Glenn understood what was being requested and nothing, including the law, should get in his way. The one person he would never disappoint was Roger Legion.

CHAPTER 26

Dana Barton sat quietly in a first floor interrogation room of the San Diego Police Headquarters. She wore a black skirt and the same red tube top, but now it was covered by a mauve windbreaker. She placed her jean jacket in a dumpster when she noticed it had some blood splatter on it. Her hair was parted differently and it was dirty.

Dana gazed forward craving a cigarette. She thought the room was clean, but boring. It was too sterile. Detective Skylar Stubbs entered followed by Detective Jeff Elkins.

"Well, Dana, how are you?" Jeff inquired in a loud, robust voice.

"I'm fine," she answered with a soft response.

"Where have you been the last 24 hours?" Skylar asked.

"I wasn't finished with my small talk." Jeff stated in an irritated tone. "We'll start again. Dana, what have you been up to?"

"Nothin' much. A little a this and a little a that."

"According to your arrest record, you've been busy engaging in the crime of solicitation and prostitution."

"What do you wanna talk to me about?" Dana asked with frustration.

Jeff turned to Skylar. "Begin," Jeff told him like a general about to unleash a blitzkrieg.

"Where have you been for the past 24 hours?" Skylar's seriousness was evident.

"Is this about the guy who was killed over on Sports Arena Boulevard?" Dana wondered.

"You tell us," Skylar said.

"I don't know anything about it," her voice was cold and unattached.

"Dana, Dana," Jeff uttered shaking his head in a negative fashion. "The best type of evidence we can have, short of a confession, is a suspect's fingerprint in the victim's blood. The inside of that car had blood splatter all over it. Now, how do you think we found you? See, on paper, it looks bad for you."

"I was with that guy," Dana's tune changed, "but he was wound tight. He was concerned that I was a cop. He picked the place where we stopped. I was helping him with his pants and I heard the glass crack."

"What about the gunshot?" Skylar asked.

"It wasn't loud. Musta been muffled. I saw the holes that were blown out of the front of his head, so I assume it was hollow point ammo."

"How are you so sure it was muffled?" Skylar posed his inquiry.

"You ever been to Wisconsin?" Dana asked. "Nothin' to do there but drink and shoot guns. I know what a gunshot sounds like. The shots that killed that guy came from a gun that had a silencer or somethin'."

"What did you do after your john was shot?" Skylar re-focused.

"I took off. I ran as fast as I could, but I was wearin' platform shoes. I did look back once."

"Did you see the guy?" Skylar inquired.

"I saw him walking away. He disappeared around the corner of the building."

"What did he look like?"

"He was tall, thin, wore a hoodie with the hood up."

"Did you see his face?"

"No."

"Where did you go after you got out of the car?

"Detective Stubbs," Jeff's voice stopped the tempo of the inquisition. "We're done."

"But," Skylar telegraphed that he had more questions.

"We're done." Jeff turned to Dana. "Dana, thanks for your time. With your knowledge of firearms, you should think about joining the force."

"Does it pay well?"

"Nah," Jeff replied and shook his head. "Let's go," he told Skylar. Then, turning to Dana one last time, he said, "We'll send somebody down for ya."

Jeff and Skylar were off to a meeting with a crime lab investigator.

CHAPTER 27

As Roger Legion perused correspondence that came in that afternoon, he recalled that he had asked his secretary to contact Lester Abrams' wife. He pushed 2 numbers on his office phone keypad and lifted the receiver.

"Louise, did you ever get ahold of Lester's wife?"

"I tried every number that I have and left messages. She hasn't called me back. I know she's friends with Nina. You want me to ask her?"

"No. I'll talk to her. What's their address?" Roger asked as he opened his desk drawer and removed a post-it note pad.

Roger wrote down the address and placed the piece of paper in the inside breast pocket of his suit coat. He arose from his chair and proceeded at a hastened gait down the hallway toward the lobby. When he reached Nina, he slowly walked around in front of her.

"Nina, I've been trying to get ahold of Lester Abrams' wife. She doesn't answer her phone. Could you try her on your cell phone?"

"Sure," Nina acknowledged reaching into her purse to retrieve her cell phone. Legion stood there as Nina called Diane Abrams' number and voice mail picked up.

"She has a tough time getting around. Maybe her phone isn't within reach."

"What's her first name?"

"Diane."

"Thanks. If you do hear from her, tell her I'd like to speak with her," Legion told Nina with a pensive look.

As he began to walk back to his office, he stopped for a moment and realized that someone should check in on her. He proceeded to Luke's office and stood in the doorway.

"Luke," Roger said, getting his attention, "what are you doing?"

"Reviewing the correspondence I dictated earlier."

"Come on, we're gonna take a ride."

Luke stood and grabbed his suit coat from a hanger on the back of the door. He put it on as they walked down the hallway.

"Call me on my cell if you hear from Diane," Roger told Nina as they passed her.

"Okay," Nina responded.

An elevator was available as soon as Legion pushed the call button and he and Luke stepped in. Legion started to speak as soon as the door closed.

"Whenever you have to deal with a female on a one-to-one basis, like an interview, a meeting, anything, unless it's in a public place, you bring another guy with you. That's a safeguard against any accusations of impropriety. Women see these suits and they think you got money in your wallet. That puts a target on your back. And if one guy gets hit, we all bleed. Understand?"

"Yes, sir," Luke acknowledged him and began to appreciate more and more Legion's principles, which he considered valuable life lessons.

"You enjoying it?" Legion wondered, referring to the past 2 days.

"I am," Luke told him with a smile.

"Did Louise go over the billing program?"

"She did," Luke told him. "I noticed she calls you Roger?"

"She's been with me from the beginning. She's earned it."

The elevator stopped at the first parking level. They walked through the elevator waiting area into the parking garage. Legion turned to Luke.

"I've gotta make a phone call. You drive."

"You wanna go in my car?" Luke asked in a bewildered tone.

"No. You drive my car," Roger told him.

Legion advanced to his late model, black Cadillac CTS-V. Legion unlocked the doors using his keychain fob. Both men entered the vehicle and Luke adjusted the rear-view mirror and fastened his seat belt. Legion and Luke looked at each other.

"Let's go," Legion told him while wondering what was holding him up.

"I need the keys."

"It's a keyless start. Which reminds me," Legion mentioned as an afterthought.

He opened the glove box and found another keyless remote fob.

"I gotta remember to give that to my wife."

Luke pushed a button and the car started immediately.

"Ritzy." Luke was impressed with the luxury and power of the vehicle.

"We're going to North Park. Are you familiar with that area or we can put it in the G-P-S?" Legion asked referring to the car's global positioning satellite system.

"I use to live up there. What's the address?"

They exited the parking garage and proceeded to the North Park section of San Diego to check in on Diane Abrams.

CHAPTER 28

As the sun waned on the Deus X Machine Shop, inside, Remy Kalm stood over Bob Brockman as Brockman pointed to various volume calculations on one of the flat screen monitors in front of his computer table. Brockman wanted to be certain that Remy understood the basis for the calculation and the impact caused by any modification. Remy was a quick learner and Brockman only had patience for him.

Their discussion was interrupted by an internal alarm, which again sounded a computerized voice that repeated the phrase, 'PERIMETER COMPROMISED.'

"Bring it up," Remy told Brockman.

With several keystrokes, the six screens in front of Brockman displayed the video images from cameras located outside the building. One of the screens showed a green, 1999 Ford F-150 pick-up truck pulling into the lot. The truck parked in a marked space and the driver stepped out. He was tall and thin with a flat top military haircut. He wore jeans, a black t-shirt and cowboy boots.

"Is that him?" Brockman asked.

"He looks like the guy Sweeney described." Remy looked at his watch. "On time. Like a good cop starting his shift. Kill the alarm."

Brockman shut off the computerized voice. Then a buzzing sound announced their visitor's arrival.

"Kevin," Remy called out to the darkness of the second floor walkway.

"Ready, Freddy," Kevin's voice emitted from the darkness.

"Let 'im in," Remy told Brockman and with three keystrokes, the lock to the door clicked, and Alton Burchesky was allowed to enter.

He slowly sauntered in while attempting to contemplate his surroundings.

"How ya doin'?" he asked. "You Remy?"

"Yes I am. Are you Sweeney's friend?"

"Yeah." As he spoke, Remy put out his hand to stop him.

"Let me ask you a few questions, before we begin. Normally, I would have to find out if you were a cop, but, in this instance, I guess I don't have to worry about that." A smile came across Remy's face.

"Nope," Alton told him.

"Are you wearing a wire?" Remy inquired.

"No."

"Do you have a recording device on you?"

"Yeah." Alton reached into his pocket and removed a digital recorder approximately the size of a cigarette lighter and held it up. "I can use it to record audio on traffic stops."

"Do you mind if I hold it while we talk?"

Alton shook his head and tossed it to Remy. Remy caught it with an overhand grab.

"No cell phone?" Remy asked.

"Left it in the truck."

"Mr. Brockman," Remy spoke while continuing to focus on Alton, "does he have anything else on him?"

Once again, Brockman poked several keys on one of his keyboards and a thin wall of high powered light from overhead scanned across Alton from back to front. Alton's silhouette appeared on one of Brockman's screens. Brockman studied the screen.

"He's got one item on him that's emitting a power source," Brockman told them. Based on the level, I'd say it's his keychain fob to unlock the doors of his truck."

Alton reached in his pocket and held up the keychain identified by Brockman.

"You wanna hold this, too?" Alton asked Remy.

"No, thank you, sir. How can I help you?"

"I'm lookin' for a torch," Alton said.

"So, you want somebody to drop a match; sell it back to the insurance company?"

"Not quite," he answered without emotion.

"Residential or commercial?" Remy inquired.

"Residential."

"Give us the keys and it's done."

"It's not that simple. There's a guy I want to burn with it."

Remy chuckled and shook his right index finger.

"You are an interesting man, Alton. Do you prefer Alton or Al?"

"Makes no difference," Alton replied.

"I like Alton. Americans like to give everyone a nickname. They're either too lazy to pronounce the name or they're ashamed of where they come from."

"Isn't Remy a nickname? I thought it was short for Rembrandt?" Alton wondered.

"No. Remy is the name on my birth certificate."

"So, do you do this kinda work?" Alton was anxious to move the process along.

Remy looked at him and paused for a moment.

"PHILIPPE," Remy yelled out, loud enough to be heard in the back of the building.

A young man appeared from behind the wall that separated the machine shop activities from the administrative portion of the shop. He was 28 years old, 160 pounds, wearing a dirty, white t-shirt and a baseball cap, with both arms fully tattooed.

"Tell our friend where you went to school," Remy commanded.

"Michigan State University," Philippe answered.

"Tell him what you studied there."

"Fire Science." Remy turned his attention to Alton.

"Can you believe that? A whole curriculum devoted to the flame."

"So, you can handle this?" Alton wanted an answer.

"I specialize in difficult situations. This job is not difficult."

"I should add one more piece to the puzzle. They know you're comin'. They'll be waitin' for ya."

"Who?"

"City cops."

"How do they know?" Remy was baffled by Alton's statement.

"I told 'em," Alton's voice was nonchalant. "I gave them a list of everybody I was going to kill and this guy we're talking about is next on the list. Now, what's something like this gonna cost me?"

CHAPTER 29

The North Park neighborhood of San Diego is located just north of Balboa Park, home of the San Diego Zoo, museums, and the world class San Diego Old Globe Theater. The main type of home found here is referred to as a California Bungalow. The homes are smaller, quaint, but they have character that is lacking in most modern tract homes. Most homes date back to the turn of the century and the area is an eclectic mix of culturally diverse boutiques, restaurants, and trendy watering holes.

Lester Abrams' home was a 1200 square foot single story structure with wood shingled exterior and a front porch that ran the length of the street side of the building. There were 6 concrete steps that you needed to climb to reach the front door.

Legion and Luke approached the front door and rang the doorbell. They both looked through the dining room window and neither saw any activity.

"See if there's a side door or a back door," Legion told Luke. "If you can get in, announce yourself, and then come and get me. His wife's name is Diane."

Luke found a side door on the driveway side of the building that was locked, but not closed completely. He was able to push the door open. Luke entered and called out to Diane with no response. He went to the front door and opened it for Roger.

"Diane?" Roger called out, also not getting a response.

Roger and Luke looked in Lester's home office and saw nothing but dust and clutter. When they walked out of the office, Roger again called out.

"Diane?" Roger said in an amplified voice.

Then, a voice, sounding like it was gasping for breath, could be heard.

"Heh, heh, help me." It trailed off as the word 'me' was spoken.

Legion and Luke raced into the bedroom and saw the tip of Diane's foot sticking out of the bathroom door. Legion dashed to the doorway and saw Diane on her side with a gash in her forehead and dried blood in her hair, covering her face. Parts of her hair appeared to be glued to her forehead with her blood. A pool of blood, more than a foot in circumference was adjacent to her head.

Roger immediately knelt down next to her and felt her throat. Her pulse was weak.

"Luke, let's lift her and put her on the bed."

"I can do it," Luke agreed, springing into action, to scoop her up in his arms.

"Wait," Diane uttered in a faint voice, "I wet my pants."

"It's all right. Don't worry," Legion told her.

Luke picked her up and set her on the bed. Her eye, under a forehead cut, was black and blue and her lip appeared to be bulging at the point where it struck the vanity.

"Get some water," Roger told Luke as he took out his phone and dialed 9-1-1.

Luke returned with a bottle of water from the refrigerator and an ambulance was now en route. Luke took the cap off the water and helped Diane sit up to take a sip.

"An ambulance is on its way," Legion advised.

"Come here," Diane asked, motioning for either Roger or Luke to come closer.

"Can you help me change my underwear, please?"

"Sure," Roger said expeditiously. "Where are the clean underwear?"

"The top drawer," she said pointing to a nearby dresser.

Luke retrieved a pair of her underwear and removed her soiled panties to replace them with a clean pair.

"Do you want to change your shirt?" Luke asked.

Diane was wearing a nightshirt, which was essentially a long, large t-shirt. The front of the shirt, around the neck, was covered with dried blood.

"No. It's all right," she answered in an exasperated manner. "There's my phone," she said pointing to a cell phone on the nightstand next to her bed. "Call my sister, let her know what happened."

Luke grabbed the cell phone and pulled up the contact directory.

"What's her name?" he asked.

"Patty White," she uttered. A moment passed. "Who are you guys?" She pointed at Roger. "You look like Roger Legion."

"I am Roger Legion. We came to check on you."

An ambulance could be heard in the distance.

"Did they arrest him?" Her voice was limp and powerless.

"Who?" Roger asked.

"Lester. He did this to me."

Roger could not believe what he just heard. His revulsion of Lester was now complete.

"Don't worry about Lester," Legion told her. "I'll take care of him."

Emergency Medical Technicians entered and immediately began to tend to Diane. Luke explained the situation to Diane's sister, Patty, over the phone and Legion watched the EMTs as his face displayed abhorrence at Lester's actions.

CHAPTER 30

Alton looked at Remy and assumed he was thinking of a price to charge him to burn down a home with the occupant in it.

"You ever heard the term, *Quid Pro Quo*?" Remy asked.

"No," Alton responded shaking his head.

"It's Latin. Means 'something for something.' So, I thought we could make an arrangement." As he spoke, his index finger moved back and forth from Alton to himself.

"What do you want?" Alton wondered.

"I am looking for a place in 'istory." His French accent dropped the 'h.' "I aspire to be something greater than a punk who can drop a match or pull a trigger. History remembers two kinds of people: the famous and the infamous. When I die, I want my obituary read and my face seen in every news outlet on this planet. I want you to help me do that."

"What can I do for ya?"

"You work for the California Highway Patrol, no? Some of the things they do is take care of the freeways, bridges, and manage traffic. On the Coronado Bay Bridge, there's a maintenance walkway under it. I need to get on that walkway."

"Why?" Alton's curiosity was evident.

"We're gonna take down the bridge."

Silence. Alton did not know how to respond.

"You're kidding, right?"

"No," Remy assured him. "I am very serious. You are looking at the new face of terror. And San Diego is about to be brought to its knees." Remy's tone was as serious as cancer. "But our portfolio is, how do you say – light. We have a benefactor, who is willing to fund us, on a limited basis. So, now we have to develop our reputation."

"Why this bridge?"

"If you want the world to listen, you gotta talk loud," Remy paused for a moment to allow Alton to soak in his comment. "It's the third most recognizable bridge in the United States. And it's not a suspension bridge. It can be taken down from under the water. My team has expertise in underwater demolition." The insidious comments brought a smile to Remy's face.

"I don't care. What timeframe were you thinking?" Alton asked.

"Before the end of the month."

"You'll take care a my thing first?"

"Sure. Get me the address and whatever anchor information you have on this guy and we'll take care of it."

Alton extended his hand to Remy. Remy walked toward him and they shook hands.

"Deal." Alton said with a smile. "You know, Sweeney never told me your last name."

"Kalm," Remy replied. "Like the condition before the storm."

This was the first and last time that Remy's plan would ever be shared with an outsider.

CHAPTER 31

Diane was taken to Scripps Mercy Hospital on 5th Avenue in the North Park section of San Diego. Roger rode with her in the ambulance and Luke followed them in Roger's car. Roger met Diane's sister, Patty, and advised her that if there was anything Diane needed, she should contact him and he would take care of it.

Roger also explained Lester's drug abuse problem to Patty and revealed that Lester would be at a drug rehabilitation facility in Coronado for an undetermined period of time. Roger would make sure Lester had no contact with Diane.

Lastly, Roger received assurances that Diane and Patty would not call the police. Roger would have Lester's paycheck sent directly to Diane and he would also pay for a nurse attendant if Diane wanted one.

Two hours after they arrived, Roger and Luke returned to Roger's vehicle.

"You're doin' a good job driving today, why don't you keep it up." Roger told Luke. "I wanna go to Coronado. Orange Boulevard."

They both got into the Cadillac and traveled South on Interstate 163 to Interstate 5. From there, they were able to traverse the Coronado Bay Bridge to Orange Avenue then Orange Boulevard.

The Coronado Paradisio drug rehabilitation facility or Cor-Pare was located in a magnificent, refurbished home off Orange Boulevard, also referred to as Mansion's Row, within walking distance of the Pacific Ocean. It was a high-end facility that allowed the affluent to convalesce in paradise, while keeping prying eyes at a safe distance.

Luke pulled up right in front of the building and he and Legion walked up to the front door. They entered into a lobby area that had a lone security guard sitting outside of a secured entrance to the facility.

"Sir," the guard said to Roger, "visiting hours are over."

"Is Bruce Bergon here?" Legion asked.

"Hold on. Let me check." The guard dialed an extension and shortly thereafter, through the secured door, appeared a short, thin Vietnamese gentleman wearing a Ralph Lauren shirt.

"Mr. Bergon sends his apologies, Mr. Legion," the gentleman said. Then in a cold, distant voice, he told the security guard, "Let him in."

As Legion entered through the security door with Luke, he had one final question for the man who greeted him.

"Do you know what room Mr. Abrams is in?"

"One twenty-six."

The interior of the facility was plush yet sterile, like a 5-star hotel. There was a main hallway that branched off into smaller hallways that led to the rooms. The building had three levels, so guests stayed throughout the structure.

Legion was in a hurry to get to room 126. He opened the door without knocking and caught Lester, standing near the bed, by surprise. Lester was actually happy to see him.

"Wow, Roger. I'm glad you're here. I've been thinking about the situation and I think I've got a way out of it," Lester spoke with a hurried cadence. He then noticed Luke. "Who is this guy?"

"This is Luke Cordel. Our newest attorney." Both Roger and Luke had an austere appearance.

"Nice to meet you," Lester told Luke. He then turned to Roger and said, "He's not replacing me, is he?"

"We just went to see your wife," Roger said.

The blood drained from Lester's face. He prepared for a performance.

"How is she?" he asked sheepishly.

"She wanted us to tell you something." Legion said. The expression on his face remained unyielding.

"What?" Lester asked, attempting to be innocent.

Roger spoke to Luke without turning his head.

"Tell him," he spoke in a terse, emotionless tenor.

Luke walked up to Lester, looked him directly in the eyes. Like a lightning bolt from a storm that was never expected, Luke's left fist hit Lester's jaw with a roundhouse punch that was so hard, at the moment of impact it appeared that his jaw separated from his skull. Lester was coldcocked by the blow and hit the bed on the way down to the floor. The sound of his body hitting the floor was like a sack of potatoes crashing into the ground from a second story window.

Roger walked over to a desk in the room and picked up a pitcher of water that was sitting on top of it. He stood over Lester and poured it out over his head. Legion kicked his leg and saw him start to move.

"You ever touch her again like that, next time I'll tell you what she said." A moment passed. "And if anything happens to that baby, I'll be back."

Roger and Luke left the room. Luke shook his left hand as they walked to shake off the throbbing caused by the blow to Lester. On the way out, they passed an area where employees were congregated, like a nurse's station. Residents could make special requests and have their needs fulfilled by the staff, all according to a strict regimen.

As they passed by, Roger spoke up.

"Mr. Abrams needs a compress and a bandage." He did not miss a step.

"And maybe a dentist," Luke added.

Roger was more pleased with Luke's performance than anything Luke could ever do in a courtroom. Roger was convinced that before you can become a lawyer, you have to become a man.

Part 2

CHAPTER 32

10 Days Later

Roger Legion studied the flat screen monitor on his desk as he reviewed accounts payable invoices from various vendors. He had to make sure that items that should be charged to a file were done so correctly. Anything that he questioned was returned to the accounting department requesting an explanation. Nothing at Legion and Associates was paid without Roger's authorization.

The time display in the corner of his computer screen read '8:47 AM.' It was then that the telephone rang. He swiveled in his chair and pressed a button on the phone.

"Yes?" he inquired.

"Patrick Madore of Newford Casualty is on line 3," Nina told him.

"Thank you." He immediately pushed the flashing line 3 button.

"Hello, Pat," Roger answered with a robust, welcoming voice.

Patrick Madore was a claims representative at the San Diego office of Newford Casualty Insurance. Pat was new to the office, but he was loyal to Legion and Associates. He worked at various independent adjusting firms and always directed clients to Roger.

"Roger, how ya doin'?" he asked. "You keepin' busy?"

"Always. How's everything at your place?"

"I'm drowning in files, but I haven't had any new ones lately. I'm told we got a bunch on their way."

"Sounds good. So, what have ya been doin' for fun?" Roger asked, continuing the small talk.

"Well, that's why I'm callin' ya. Eddie is standing over me right now. I didn't want to bother you, but I told him my situation and he says, 'Call Roger.' I feel kinda foolish."

Eddie was the claims manager in the office. He was older, but enjoyed drinking with the younger attorneys and going to topless bars. Roger always sent at least two attorneys with him, so that there was a designated driver. He supplied the law firm with plenty of work, especially when they allowed him to 'go wild.'

"Never," Roger told him. "You tell me the situation. I like to help friends out."

"You know my son, Jason?"

"The twelve-year-old?"

"That's him," Pat acknowledged. "He's been on my back to go to a monster truck event at the stadium." As he spoke, Roger took notes. "I told him we were gonna go and I thought my brother-in-law was also gonna go. You know I got that macular degeneration and I can't drive at night. Now, my brother-in-law says he can't go and I don't know if there's any tickets left."

"You know, we've got an attorney here, who likes that kinda stuff. He's the new guy, Luke Cordel. I'll have him give you a call. You guys can have dinner and check out the monster trucks."

"But, I don't know if there's tickets available," Pat's tone was somber.

"My secretary is excellent at locating tickets. Tell your son, he's gonna see monster trucks. Now, what about your wife?" Roger wondered.

"She doesn't like that kinda thing."

"Does she like the theater?"

"Yeah," Pat responded sheepishly.

"Well, I will have my secretary contact you and let you know what's playing and she'll arrange for dinner and a show. We'll get a limo to take you there."

"Roger, this is too much."

"No, it isn't. I told you, I like to help out friends and I appreciate the work."

"I don't know what to say," Pat was flabbergasted.

"Just enjoy it. Let me know how it was."

"Thanks, my friend," Pat was genuine in his response.

"You're welcome. I will have Luke and my secretary call you."

"Okay."

"Take care." With that Roger ended the call. While he still had the receiver in his hand, he dialed two numbers on the phone.

"Louise, I need you to get three tickets to a monster truck event at the stadium, I assume it is this weekend. When you get 'em, give them to Luke Cordel."

"Does he need dinner reservations?" she asked.

"No, but I do need you to set up a full theater package for Pat Madore at Newford, including a limo."

"Any play in particular?" she inquired.

"No. Give him a choice. Ya got it?"

"Yes," she answered.

"Thank you." He disconnected the call.

Roger turned to his flat screen monitor and brought up his e-mail inbox. He pulled up a sent e-mail that he forwarded on a regular basis. He addressed it to Luke Cordel. It simply stated, 'Come to my office. ASAP.'

CHAPTER 33

Remy Kalm gave a pensive stare out the window of a Boeing Business Jet 3 flying at an altitude of 41,000 feet along the California coast. This airplane would cost approximately $93 million new and was intended for the very privileged executive. The interior was hygienic. It was intended to carry 8 passengers within its 1,120 cubic feet of interior space and included an office, conference room, living room, bedroom, bathroom, complete with shower, and a passenger area for passengers to sit during take-off and landing. The plane had a range of 5,495 miles, which is the approximate distance from San Diego to London, where this plane's itinerary had originated.

Remy wore a blue, striped, Ralph Lauren shirt with the top button open. His apparel also included black slacks, wingtip shoes, and a sand colored sport coat. His face sported a slight stubble that was neatly trimmed.

An elderly gentleman with a black suit and white gloves walked up and stood in the aisle at the end of the row where Remy sat. He had white hair that was combed over the bald top of his head and a moustache.

"Mr. Kalm, would you follow me, please?" His English accent was distinct.

Remy unclasped his seat belt and picked up a small briefcase that he had under the seat in front of him. He followed the man to the conference room and as they reached the door, he turned to Remy.

"They're waiting for you, sir."

Remy opened the door and in the center of this small room was a rectangular shaped conference table that allowed 2 people to sit on each side and one person at each end of it. On the wall, at the far end from where Remy entered, was a large, flat screen monitor. Two men sat on the windowed side of the table.

The man at Remy's far left was Sir Basil Crumpton. He was 81 years old, with thick, white hair and a handlebar moustache. His suit appeared to be slightly large on him, but was of fine quality. He wore a bowtie and a vest.

"Remy, my boy, it's good to see you," Basil told him with a smile. His moustache was so large, you could not see his full smile.

"It is my pleasure to see you, Sir Basil," Remy beamed as he shook Basil's hand.

"I hope you don't mind if I don't stand. Bloody turbulence. This is the price we have to pay for priv-icy. I try to stay off my feet as much as possible."

"No problem," Remy said.

"You know my lawyer, Mr. Farnsworth?" Basil gestured to the man sitting to his left.

Farnsworth was in his late 40s, slender, with a finely appointed black suit and perfectly coifed, jet black hair.

"We've talked before," he told Basil and turned to Farnsworth. "Nice to meet you." Farnsworth acknowledged him with a nod and a latent handshake.

"Sit," Basil told him. Remy took a seat opposite Farnsworth. "How is the weather in San Diego today?"

"It's nice. Low 70s."

"Years ago, after the war, my family went on holiday there. I found it to be most lovely. We stayed at the Del Coronado. Oh, the beach was pristine."

"It's still there. And the beach is still very nice."

"Can I interest you in a spot of tea and a biscuit, perhaps?"

"No, thank you," Remy told him. "I'm fine."

"I was talking to an Arab sheik yesterday and when I told him I was coming to San Diego today, he said I should try the," Basil stopped to think. Then Farnsworth spoke up.

"Fish tacos," he filled in with a slightly less distinct British accent.

"Yes. Quite. Have you ever had these fish tah-coses, Remy?"

"It's peasant food," Remy shrugged dismissively.

"Perhaps that explains my ignorance on the topic." Basil assessed. "I understand that you have a presentation for me."

Remy removed a laptop computer from his briefcase and began to connect cords to it to allow for an exposition on the flat screen monitor that hung on the wall. The details of the plan were about to be totally unveiled.

CHAPTER 34

Luke Cordel arrived at Roger Legion's office door within 60 seconds of receiving Roger's e-mail.

"Did you want to see me, sir?" he asked.

"Come on in. Have a seat," Roger told him.

Luke sat and smiled.

"Have you ever been to a monster truck show?" Roger inquired.

"No," Luke answered and shook his head.

"Would you like to go?"

"Sure. You going?"

"No," Roger said, shocked at the thought. "Patrick Madore is a claim rep for Newford Casualty. They give us a nice chunk of work. Pat has macular degeneration – he's unable to drive at night. He's also got a 12-year-old son and they want to go to the monster truck show at the stadium this weekend. So, you take 'em. I figure it'll be a good rainmaking opportunity and they'll get to meet you."

"Okay. So, just give him a call?" Luke wondered.

"Louise is gonna get the tickets. Take 'em out to eat. Ask Pat if he or his son have a favorite place. If it's a place that takes reservations, have Louise do it. She gets priority at places all over the city. Be sure you have cash on ya. If the kid wants a soda, a hot dog, ice cream, t-shirt, or a souvenir, buy it."

As Roger finished his sentence, his phone rang.

"Hold on," he said as he lifted one finger up and pressed a button on the phone.

"Yes?" Roger asked.

"The San Diego Police Chief is on line 5," Nina told him.

Roger and Luke looked at each other. Roger shrugged his shoulders.

"Put him through," he told her.

His phone rang again and Roger picked up the receiver and pressed line 5.

"This is Roger Legion."

"Please hold for the Chief," a woman's voice said.

"Hello, Roger," was uttered by a calm, friendly voice.

"How are you doing, Bill? It's been a little while."

William Piersol had been the San Diego Police Chief for 12 years. Prior to that, he worked with Roger on a variety of civil litigation cases as the police liaison for the collection of information to assist Roger in defending the police department. The Chief credited Roger in assisting with his rise to become Chief because Roger always credited his assistance for the excellent results Roger achieved.

"It has. Are we gonna see you at the police charity auction this year?" Bill inquired.

"I wouldn't miss it," Roger told him.

"We would miss your checkbook if you didn't show up. And if they force me to golf this year, you're gonna be in my foursome, right?"

"Absolutely. We're both so bad, we make each other look good," Roger acknowledged succinctly.

"That is true, my friend. Listen, would you have some time to come down to my office to discuss an investigation that we have going on? You might be able to help us out," the Chief's voice turned serious.

"Sure. You tell me when," Roger answered.

"The sooner, the better."

Roger looked at his flat screen monitor and pulled up his calendar.

"I can be there in 30 minutes," he told him.

"I really appreciate it, Roger. I'll let the front desk know that they should expect you. Thanks, a lot."

"I'll see ya, shortly," Roger assured him.

Roger's face had a pensive demeanor. He pivoted his head to Luke.

"What are you doing now?" Roger asked him.

"I was gonna go over some interrogatory responses and see if we needed to send out another set of rogs based on the answers we got."

"That can wait" Roger asserted. "Get your coat. I want you to come with me."

Luke hurried out the door to grab his suit coat. Roger cogitated about the nature of the Chief's phone call.

CHAPTER 35

"Can we lower the shades?" Remy asked and Farnsworth stood to close the six shades within the airplane's conference room. He then dimmed the lights and reclaimed his seat next to Sir Basil Crumpton.

The first slide simply stated 'Ponte Curvo.' It is Italian for 'curved bridge.'

"I'm pleased that you utilized my suggestion for the name of the operation," Basil said, "I visited a lovely little E-talian town by that name, back in '65, shortly after Churchill died. The people were most gracious, even though they did have these Maa-fia hooligan types. Disgusting rubbish," he acknowledged and shook his head. "Please. Proceed."

"The Coronado Bay Bridge," Remy began as the next slide of the complete bridge appeared, "also known as the San Diego – Coronado Bridge, first opened in 1969. It is a little over 2 miles long and at its highest point, it is approximately 200 feet over the water. It sweeps down into Coronado at a 90 degree angle. It's built with a curve to allow Navy ships to pass under it. It is relatively basic: prestressed concrete and steel girders. All the braces and stiffeners are contained within a box girder design," Remy told them as he used a red laser pointer to spot out areas as he described them.

The next slide was an aerial view of the bridge.

"It has 5 lanes of traffic with a moveable median, called a zipper, to allow an extra lane to accommodate traffic congestion. Generally, in the morning there are 3 lanes heading westbound and in the afternoon, 3 lanes heading eastbound. About 80,000 vehicles a day pass over it."

"Is it a toll bridge?" Sir Basil asked curiously while twisting his moustache.

"No. It was originally, but they stopped taking the toll in 2002," Remy told him.

Remy moved on to the next slide, which showed a view of the bridge from ground level.

"There are 30 concrete pylons or towers that hold it up. They are all specifically numbered and the numbers are written on the inside of the bridge railing."

"How high is that railing?" Sir Basil inquired.

"It's 34 inches," Remy replied.

"My word. No wonder everyone jumps off the bloody thing. It's easy to scale," Basil sounded flabbergasted.

"Tower number 19 is the highest tower." Remy once again used the pointer to locate it. "That one is 200 feet over the water. We are focusing on Tower 18 and Tower 20."

The next slide was an animation of the bridge above and below the water line.

"At the base of those towers, near the floor of the bay," Remy told them as he circled the laser pointer at the bottom of two support towers, "we began a drilling process to cut through the base of those towers – straight through," Remy spoke with proud aplomb and looked over at both men for their reaction.

"You have made a swath all the way through the base of two towers?" Basil's voice indicated that he was amazed. "Explain to me how you accomplished that."

"Not all the way through. I spent a year working on an oil rig in the Gulf of Mexico. I learned about underwater robotic drilling systems. I developed a portable system. We core test the concrete and we know from old video taken during the construction, the configuration of the rebar system used to strengthen the concrete. The system drills straight through the concrete, pulls the bit out, it moves down along a horizontal plane and does it again. Once we get to a piece of the rebar, we do a tensile test. Then, we bring in a plasma torch and cut through it like a laser."

"They don't have any perimeter surveillance on these towers?" Basil wondered.

"They do. Above the water."

"You're able to operate uninterrupted?"

"We've done it every night for the past 3 months. We set up a camouflage shield above our work area, so if you look down from a boat or helicopter, it looks like the rest of the ocean."

"How do your men get out to the job site?" Basil inquired, again twisting the ends of his moustache.

"We have a boat that allows us to offload from a compartment under the boat. No one sees us get on it. No one sees us get off it. We also have a device called a tool sled that allows us to transport our tools to our underwater location."

"Once you cut through the base, doesn't the weight of the bridge just keep it in place?" Basil queried.

"We want the top of the tower to be close to free flowing from the bottom. We also inject a reinforced non-explosive demolition agent at various points along the cutting line. This ensures that the top of the tower won't settle tightly into the base."

"This work is complete? Don't they ever check this bridge for structural cracks?"

"It's complete on Tower 18 and approximately 85% complete on Tower 20. It will be done within the next 2 weeks. As to your question about the bridge being checked, that process is done every 5 years. It was just done in March of this year. We were able to read the report and watch the video of their inspection."

"Magnificent. Continue."

"Based on the size and strength of the concrete and the rebar, my team has calculated the amount of explosive necessary, depending on the explosive. The explosive will be placed into a reinforced steel container. It will be lowered from underneath the boat using a winch. We will then bolt the container to the land side of Tower 18 and Tower 20. The explosives detonate off an electronic harness that works on a collapsible circuit system. Once it's online, it can't be stopped."

"How do you control the direction of the blast?" Basil asked.

"The container is steel reinforced. It will be open to the side that abuts the bridge. The explosion will follow the path of least resistance. When it goes off, the towers will sweep in toward Tower 19, the highest tower, taking those 2 towers off the base and pulling the roadway down."

"Those roadway girders may be a problem, Remy," Basil warned.

"We're gonna help them out," Remy told him and turned to an overview shot looking down at the bridge. "I mentioned earlier that there are 5 traffic lanes on the bridge. Each lane is approximately 12 feet wide. We have 2 trucks for each direction of the bridge," Remy proudly expressed. "The trucks will be long enough to create a perpendicular blockade of traffic on the bridge."

"In the eastern direction, the lead truck will stop at a pre-determined point between the 17th and 18th tower. The second truck will create a blockade at a pre-determined point between the 20th and 21st tower. We follow the same procedure for the westbound traffic. We allow all the cars to pass, then the lead trucks also take their positions, engine-to-engine, to create a blockade. The bridge is then totally blocked off from the 17th tower to the 21st tower."

"Minimum casualties?" Basil inquired.

"That's what you asked for," Remy affirmed.

"I think it's the right thing for this operation. Blood can be very expensive."

"The trucks will be loaded with explosive. The body of the truck will be reinforced and the bottom of the truck will be weakened. That's how we control the direction of the blast. We will chain the trucks to each other and to the bridge. All the explosives on the bottom of the bridge and the top of the bridge will be on the same circuit. They can be detonated on-site or remotely."

"Would you mind if we took a break?" Basil asked. "I need to visit the loo."

"Go right ahead," Remy told him.

Basil stood, assisted by Farnsworth, and began a shaky trek towards the airplane's bathroom as his ultimate destination.

"Don't get old, Remy. If we hit some turbulence, I may go arse over tit," Basil advised. He stopped for a moment and thought about what he said. "I must admit the image of that is quite jovial." He slowly sauntered out of the room.

Remy leaned back in his chair and gazed at Farnsworth.

"You don't talk much," Remy said.

"I prefer to listen," Farnsworth advised.

CHAPTER 36

When Roger Legion and Luke Cordel arrived at the San Diego Police Headquarters, they were escorted to the 6th floor office of Police Chief William Piersol. The police headquarters was located on Broadway, the same street where the America's Finest City Building was situated, which housed Legion & Associates. The main difference was that the offices at Legion and Associates all had spectacular views, while the view from the Chief's office was rather mundane, lacking the 'awe' factor, as it presented the viewer with a snapshot of city life that, at times, would rather be forgotten.

The office was quite large, almost cavernous, compared to the cubicles occupied by most officers. The walls were loaded with photographs and awards and in the center of the room sat a large, oak desk with a glass-covered top. In front of the desk were 2 leather chairs and a matching couch rested against the wall behind the chairs.

"Feel free to have a seat," a uniformed female officer instructed Roger and Luke after walking them through the Chief's outer office.

Both Legion and Luke looked around at the various photos and awards and Luke found one with several different gentlemen, including Roger.

"This guy looks familiar," Luke told Roger with a smile.

"That was some political benefit, probably 10 years ago," Roger said as he reflected about the photo's location and date. A voice stopped Roger's train of thought.

"Roger Legion, as I live and breathe!"

The voice belonged to Chief William Piersol. He was 68 years old, 5 feet 10 inches tall, snow-colored hair, slightly above his normal weight, and wore a complete police uniform, including tie, badge with a black stripe across the number, and weapon. On his blue uniform collar were 4 stars on each side, which proudly denoted his rank. His greeting to Roger was accompanied by a wide smile.

"Bill, how are ya?" Roger asked as he extended his hand.

"I'm fine. How's the lawsuit game?" the Chief wondered. As he shook Roger's hand, he patted Roger on the shoulder.

"Loaves and fishes. It never runs out. I wanna introduce you to our newest attorney," Roger said while pointing, "Luke Cordel."

The Chief and Luke exchanged a handshake.

"You're gonna keep this guy honest, right?" the Chief posed the question to Luke.

"Absolutely," Luke concurred.

"You're gonna learn from the best," the Chief opined, referring to Roger. "I hope you appreciate the opportunity."

"I do, sir," Luke replied.

"I would love to go to lunch one a these days, Roger, but you know how busy I am."

"It's no problem. We'll catch up at one of the many charity events."

"Why don't you guys have a seat," the Chief offered, "and I'll call in a couple of officers. They're in charge of an investigation and they have a few questions."

Both Roger and Luke sat in the chairs in front of the Chief's desk and gave a quick nod in agreement. The Chief walked around his desk to his chair and pressed one number on his phone.

"Please have Captain Shood come in with Detectives Elkins and Stubbs." He returned the phone receiver to its cradle.

"City council's trying to put the screws on the budget again," the Chief told Roger with a sardonic tone. "I might need you for a little comment on that."

"Just tell me when," Roger advised. His answer seemed to include a tacit acknowledgement of unceasing support.

Luke wondered what was meant by the term 'comment.' It was then that a knock on the door was heard and 3 men stood in the doorway.

"Come'on in," the Chief told the men.

Detective Skylar Stubbs entered and gave a smiling nod to the Chief. He was followed by his partner, Jeff Elkins, and Captain Russ Shood, who was in charge of the Homicide Division. Russ was 54 years old, 5 feet, 10 inches tall, physically fit, with wavy, salt and pepper hair color. He had been a member of the San Diego Police Department for 26 years. His accoutrements included a sport coat, loose-fitting tie, and slacks that did not match his coat.

Detective Skylar Stubbs wore his trademark, white shirt with the sleeves folded up several turns. His apparel also included black pants and a solid, blue tie.

Detective Jeff Elkins was dressed in a red, striped shirt with vertical stripes and a red and blue diamond tie. He also wore black, Haggar slacks.

There was an awkward moment of silence and the 3 men, that entered the room, looked to the Chief for guidance.

"Well, you wanted to talk to him, here he is," the Chief's voice was cold and unattached.

Luke thought it was odd that the Chief did not introduce any of the men who entered the room.

CHAPTER 37

Sir Basil retraced his steps from the bathroom back to the conference room chair all while trying to retain decorum and poise. Remy stood and closed the door once Basil was seated.

"So, tell me, Remy, what is your escape plan?" Basil inquired.

"Once everything is online, we jump off the bridge," Remy told him.

"I hope your men are trained in that sort of thing," Basil added.

"They are. There will be a boat waiting for us and everyone will see us board it. We will quietly slip off it through the bottom compartment and the boat will take off at a high speed, presumably being chased by the Coast Guard or the Harbor Patrol. We let them catch it, board it, and we blow it remotely. My crew and I want to put as much distance as possible between ourselves and the bridge because when it blows, the water displacement will be extraordinary. Any boat in that channel will be flipped over."

"Who actually detonates this thing?" Basil wondered.

"One of my crew at the machine shop. Once he hears from me that we are in the clear."

"Oh, at your gare-raj (garage)? Makes sense. Now, let me play devil's advocate. What about the authorities? I assume this bridge is very well surveilled. Do you expect any problems?" Basil cautioned as he began to play with his moustache.

"No. The plan from start to detonation should take approximately 12 minutes. By the time they figure out what is going on, we'll be off the bridge. In addition, we're gonna take away their eyes. We will control all the cameras on the bridge. So, only my man at the machine shop will know what is going on," Remy's voice had a sound of finality to it.

"Remy, I must say, your attention to detail is most refreshing. Now, what time of day do you believe this little drama will play out?"

"I plan on 3:30 in the afternoon, so it can be on the 5 o'clock news."

"Ah, yes. Accommodation for the telly. Anyone who doesn't like it can piss off," Basil said while hammering his fist into the table. "Remy, you came into my life at a time when I was forlorn of hope regarding my future. As I told you once before, I am a simple arms dealer. If my name was Berretta or Glock, they would build statues bearing my distinctive visage. But the younger generation doesn't respect the landed gentry. They treat me like a pariah, an outcast, because they take is-sue with what I do to preserve my station in life. All I want to do is keep the traditions of the past alive. I simply want to continue what is my birthright. You can help me achieve this. Because now, in addition to weapons and hardware, I can offer logistics. That, my friend, will be a very valuable commodity. And this bridge will be the perfect calling card," Basil gazed at Remy for a moment. "Young people must understand that if they will not respect me, then they will fear me." His voice was serene and his words were succinct.

"I am your man, Sir Basil," Remy acknowledged.

"Good. Have you ever been to Abu Dhabi?"

"No."

"There is much work there for an enterprising, young man like you."

"I look forward to it."

Basil glanced at Farnsworth.

"Are we done?"

"No. We have to discuss the type of explosive he needs," Farnsworth advised.

"I'd like a snack first. Tell them to bring us something," Basil told Farnsworth. "Remy, you've been talking quite a bit, you must be parched. Name your poison."

"Vichy water," Remy relayed.

"I can assure you that it is from Vichy in France," Basil said.

"*Trés bien*," Remy acknowledged.

It was obvious that Remy and Basil were quite adept at pleasing each other.

CHAPTER 38

Captain Russ Shood and Detective Jeff Elkins took a seat on the couch behind Roger and Luke in Chief Piersol's office. Jeff carried a large, yellow envelope and Detective Skylar Stubbs walked around to the side of the Chief's desk, so that he could face Roger.

"Mr. Legion," Skylar began, "you must be a very busy man."

"I am," Roger replied with a stern countenance and his eyes were locked on Skylar.

"My partner," Skylar said pointing to Jeff, "and I have been to your office no less than 3 times and you're never available. We have also called and left messages at least a half dozen times, but never a return call."

"My days are always full, so that's why it's best to make an appointment," Roger told him. "I don't return calls if I don't recognize the name or they don't tell me what it's about."

"Do you get a lot of calls from police officers?" Skylar wondered.

"I get alotta calls from telemarketers, who will say whatever is necessary to get me on the phone."

Skylar looked at Legion and nodded.

"Is this what you called me down here for?" Roger quizzed. "You're interested in my telephone answering habits?"

"No. But before we begin, can you tell me who this guy is?" Skylar inquired and pointed to Luke.

Luke saw Roger raise his right palm of his hand slightly off the arm of the chair. Luke understood that it meant not to speak or move.

"He's my lawyer," Legion retorted.

"You brought a lawyer?" Skylar's shock was evident. His immediate reflex when anyone "lawyered-up" was that they had something to hide.

"He's a lawyer that works for me," Legion's response echoed annoyance.

"Well, I don't know if the Chief told you, but we wanted our conversation with you to be," Skylar hesitated for a moment, "confidential. Maybe, your friend should wait outside."

Luke looked to Roger in the event Roger told him to leave. Roger remained stoic and focused on Skylar.

"He'll keep his mouth shut." Roger advised.

"He can stay," the Chief blurted out, putting an immediate end to any discussion on the topic.

"Captain," Skylar focused on Captain Shood, "would you get the door?"

Russ stood quickly, clicked the door closed, and regained his seat. Skylar reached out his hand to Jeff, who handed him the yellow envelope. Skylar opened the envelope and removed a Ziploc bag that contained a single business card.

"Mr. Legion, does this look familiar?" Skylar inquired and handed him the plastic bag.

The business card contained a cartoon graphic of a nicely-dressed man at a podium and in the center of the card it read

'DEXTER FRYE.' Under the name were the words 'The Litigation Guy,' along with an address and phone number. Roger looked at it for a little over a moment and returned his gaze to Skylar.

"I haven't seen one of those in a long time." Roger's voice was sullen.

"About 12 days ago, that was found at the murder scene of a retired police officer in the Midway district."

Roger looked at Skylar providing him with a tacit response of 'So, what?'

"The next day, another retired officer answered the door at his Tierrasanta home and somebody shot him 3 times. Same gun at both homicides." As Skylar spoke he again reached into the envelope, "At that crime scene, this card was left."

He handed a 2nd Ziploc bag to Roger with the same business card. Roger examined both sides of the card through the Ziploc bag and returned it to Skylar.

"Do you have a question for me?" Roger wondered.

"Why don't I tell you what we know and maybe you can fill in the blanks."

"Go ahead," Roger answered accepting Skylar's proposal.

"Those 2 cards that I showed you: according to our forensic document examiner, the card stock dates back to the late 1970s, as does the ink. In addition, there's a union mark on the cards and that would also date the cards back to the late 70s. On both of those cards is a fingerprint from Dexter Frye. On one of them, it appears that he probably touched a stamp pad and then touched the card. On the other card, we have his fingerprint, but it didn't come directly from Dexter Frye. It's a bio-metric transfer. Are you familiar with that term, Mr. Legion?"

Legion responded without missing a beat.

"It's when the bio-metric marker did not come from the original source. The marker is lifted from an original source and placed onto a secondary source."

"Very good, Mr. Legion," Skylar feigned that he was impressed. "So, we don't think Dexter Frye is our gunman. But I would like to ask you: Do you think Dexter Frye is alive?"

"I don't know. If he is, I haven't heard from him in 33 years. Neither has anyone else that I know."

"Did you consider him a close friend?" Skylar asked.

"I considered him my best friend."

"After the incident on the bridge, you completed or finished work on the remainder of his files, right?"

"Yes, I did."

"Did you make a lot of money from that?"

"What does that have to do with the death of 2 cops?" Legion responded incredulously.

"Probably nothing, but we're flying blind here. That day on the bridge, Dexter Frye killed a cop and it's presumed he killed his wife that evening, but we cannot find a piece of paper within this department that has his name on it. No file, no murder book, no nothing. We got his prints from his application for a concealed weapons permit. So, Dexter Frye and all his records have disappeared. Do you know anything about that?" Skylar's voice pulsed disbelief.

"I have no control over the files of the San Diego Police Department."

"Let me throw something else in the mix. At the last murder scene, the killer left a box. Inside the box was a section of the _San Diego Union-Tribune_, dated approximately 8 years ago, that had a story about the 25th anniversary of Dexter Frye's jump from the bridge. A lot of it seemed to deal with innuendo and possible scenarios about what happened." Skylar spoke and removed a photocopy of the article from the yellow envelope. He handed the copy to Legion.

Roger glanced at the pages quickly and handed it back to Skylar.

"I remember this article," Roger told him.

"I noticed that you didn't contribute to it," Skylar commented.

"I had nothing to say," Roger's dictum was answered like a defense lawyer protecting a client. "Why don't you talk to the guy who wrote the article?"

"He died 4 years ago. Mr. Legion, if you look at the article, there are 5 people, not including Dexter Frye, who were alive at the time it was written. This killer is targeting those 5 people and you are one of them."

Legion moved his eyes from Skylar to the Chief when Skylar spoke up.

"Can you tell us about the *Necioro* case?" Skylar inquired.

At that moment, Roger became contemplative. He had not thought about the *Necioro* case for decades. Roger turned his gaze to the Chief, who gave him a slight nod, as if granting permission to discuss it. He was about to tell the story of the case that took down Dexter Frye and what really happened the night Dexter jumped off the bridge and into history.

CHAPTER 39

Remy, Basil, and Farnsworth each selected a snack from a tray of scones, teacakes, sweet crisps, and petticoat tail shortbreads. Remy drank Vichy water and Farnsworth drank from a bottle of water he had brought in with him when the meeting commenced.

"Where is my tea?" Basil uttered in a perturbed tone.

"I'll check," Farnsworth told him and arose from his seat. Just then, the attendant who escorted Remy to the conference room entered with a tray that contained a tea service.

"About time," Basil said with disgust. "Is it Taylors of Harrogate?"

"Yes, sir," the attendant answered.

"Damn well better be," Basil replied in disgust. "Remy, would you like another refill on your drink?"

"I'm fine."

"Let's talk about the final is-sue," Basil continued. "From the beginning, I've advised Mr. Farnsworth to obtain for you every item you requested, without consideration of cost. I plan to continue that course of conduct to the conclusion of this project. The final item has some unique considerations, which merit discourse. Mr. Farnsworth, why don't you explain."

Farnsworth opened a manila folder that sat before him. He began speaking as he opened it.

"As you are aware, your volume calculations, based on the various explosives, are all quite substantial. The problems that we face involve obtaining those volumes and then getting them to you. Your operation is being conducted in a place that is surrounded by 3 military bases and one of the busiest border crossings in the world. So, the police presence there is quite extraordinary. Nevertheless, we believe that we can muster the resources necessary for you to conclude your activities."

"I appreciate that," Remy told him.

"The first explosive is Octanitrocubane," Farnsworth pronounced it slowly. "This material is like trying to obtain moon rocks. Highly accountable and made under strict government supervision," Farnsworth informed him. "To obtain the volumes you require would entail some brazen larceny. And I don't think you want to raise your profile at this point."

"I agree," Remy submitted. "Octan is perhaps the most powerful non-nuclear explosive on the planet. United States doesn't want anybody getting their hands on it. But if any of it ever comes your way, I'll take as much as you can get."

"The next is," Farnsworth looked at a sheet of paper in front of him for the next explosive to discuss. Remy spoke up.

"Why don't we just discuss the ones you can get to me."

"Very well. Dynamite, TNT, C-4, and Semtex."

"I always thought dynamite and TNT were the same thing?" Basil interjected.

"They are not," Remy advised. "Dynamite is an absorbent mixture dipped in nitroglycerin and compressed into a cylindrical form. TNT is a specific chemical compound. Let me ask: Where are they manufactured?"

"These both come from Nevada," Farnsworth said.

"Commercial or military?" Remy asked.

"The dynamite is commercial. The TNT, we can obtain either one."

"I don't like dynamite for underwater projects. I find it can lose its stability. The military TNT is a possibility. What about the C-4 and the Semtex?"

"We can get military for both of those."

"Where is the C-4 manufactured?" Remy asked.

"China."

"I'm not comfortable with that. I don't trust their quality control. I've had problems with it in the past. What about the Semtex?"

"The Czech Republic," Farnsworth noted after glancing down the sheet of paper.

"That's acceptable." Remy thought for a moment. "Let's go with the Semtex."

"Very well. I need to make some phone calls," Farnsworth said as he stood from his chair. "I still have some details that I have to finalize for it."

"How long before you will know for sure?" Remy inquired.

"I'll know by the time we land," Farnsworth assured him. "I'll have the delivery instructions within 24 hours. Is your e-mail still cloaked?"

"Yes. The IP address changes every 72 hours," Remy disclosed.

Remy was referring to the Internet Protocol address assigned to every computer providing it a unique point of origin.

"Where does it trace back to?" Farnsworth asked.

"A public computer, like a library or school."

Farnsworth walked around the table and Basil spoke up.

"Mr. Farnsworth," Basil's voice stopped him and he turned. "While we are together, Remy, I just wish to inquire as to your shed-yool (schedule) for conclusion of this matter?"

"Two weeks or less," Remy told him.

"Smashing. Within a fortnight," Basil said and his look at Remy took a hardened gaze. "I know you won't disappoint me."

"You have my word," Remy told him.

For a moment, Remy felt uneasy, but Basil's smile, under his thick, handlebar moustache, returned as did Remy's confidence with it.

CHAPTER 40

Inside Police Chief William Piersol's office, Detectives Skylar Stubbs and Jeff Elkins were awaiting the gospel according to Roger Legion regarding the _Necioro_ case. This lawsuit was referenced in the newspaper article that was left at the 2nd crime scene. Jeff Elkins leaned forward as Roger began to speak.

"In the late 1970s, lawyers were just starting to advertise. Dexter thought that was going to be the way of the future. He wanted to give everybody access to justice, not just those who could afford it. So, he advertised heavily on television and radio. He had a catchy, little jingle, so everyone knew his name."

"We heard the jingle," Stubbs told him. "One of the retirees directed us to a guy who saves all that kinda stuff."

"Well, back in the late 1970s, it was all over the radio and TV. Mrs. Necioro, her husband and their 9-month-old baby lived in the South Bay. One night, Mr. Necioro drinks a little too much tequila and fires a handgun into the air. When the police get there, they believe he's armed. He's also holding his 9-month-old son. People are screaming back and forth. The police in English and Mr. and Mrs. Necioro in Spanish. If you take the newspaper article out," he motioned to Skylar, "it may be easier to follow."

"The first 2 officers on the scene were Arango and Adams," Legion continued as he pointed to their pictures on the newspaper article.

Both Skylar and his partner, Jeff, were extremely interested because Arango had been murdered in the Midway district 12 days earlier. Adams was listed in the newspaper article as deceased.

"They called for back-up and a captain, and 2 officers, named Barkley and Wulsifer, responded," Legion once again pointed them out in the newspaper article.

Wulsifer was killed 11 days earlier when he answered the door at his Tierrasanta home. Barkley was also deceased.

"What happened next is up for debate, but by the time the captain arrived, a guy named Kyle Bober," who Roger again pointed out in the newspaper article. He was still alive. "Mr. Necioro and his 9-month-old son were dead. They were both hit with a bullet from Arango's gun and Adams' gun."

Skylar and Jeff looked at each other.

"I believe we've found a nexus," Jeff proclaimed to the group.

"So, I guess," Skylar quizzed, "Mrs. Necioro sued the city?"

"She tried, but no one would touch her case. Then, she called the Litigation Guy and Dexter was more than willing to represent her. This was the kind of case he wanted," Roger told them. "One thing you should understand is, whatever you think about lawyers who advertise, Dexter didn't need to do it. He was an excellent attorney. He knew how to win a case. And that's what he was gonna do with the _Necioro_ case."

"How was he going to do that?" Skylar inquired.

"At the time her husband and baby were shot, a relative was in the house calling the police emergency line. On the tape of the call, you can hear the shots fired and Mrs. Necioro screaming over and over to the police officers, '*¡Tengo la pistola!*' Do you speak Spanish?" Legion asked Skylar.

"I have the gun," Skylar translated.

"She did have the gun, but someone – Dexter alleged it was the police – placed a drop gun right in Mr. Necioro's hand. His prints were all over the gun, but no prints on the bullets. That was tough for the police to explain.

"In addition, Dexter found a witness who saw Arango and Adams, shortly before the incident, drinking at a dive bar near the airport," Roger paused and looked at Jeff and Russ on the couch before turning back to Skylar. "So, when you look at the totality of the circumstances, Mrs. Necioro hit the lottery."

"Once again," Skylar lamented, "there was no information at the courthouse except for the date the case was dismissed. So, why was it dismissed?"

"We settled the case," Legion told him.

"What's interesting about that is," Skylar observed, "if Mrs. Necioro 'hit the lottery' and sued the police department, any settlement would have to be approved by the city council. We checked the city council records for 1980, 1981, and 1982 and there is not one mention of the name, Necioro."

"If we had this conversation sooner," Legion opined, "I could have saved you some time. In those days, any settlement over $25,000 required council approval."

"So, you settled her case for less than $25,000?" Skylar was flabbergasted.

"No. We settled it for $250,000. We simply arranged for 10 payments of $25,000 to my law firm and I paid Mrs. Necioro. We essentially kept the settlement under the radar."

"Why was it necessary?" Skylar pried.

"The goal was to avoid any further embarrassment to the department. The part of the story we haven't discussed is that somebody went rogue and wanted to frame Dexter Frye for the murder of his wife. Earlier in the evening, on the night he jumped, he came home to find his wife strangled. As he found her, the cops busted through the door to arrest him. The plan was to shoot him on the spot, but like plans that are not thought through, Dexter escaped, with 8 police cars in high pursuit. So, that's why Dexter was on the bridge that night."

"Mr. Legion, do you know this information for a fact, or is it conjecture on your part?" Skylar retorted.

"I know it because another officer, off your list, named Luther Cosgrove, was the lookout while his partner, Gordon Votnage, went in and strangled Dexter's wife. He was willing to rat everyone else out. He gave me a sworn statement the day before he stepped in front of an Amtrak train."

"Chief, did you know about this?" Skylar was astounded at the degree of complexity of this cover-up.

"What if I did?" the Chief posed inquiry.

Skylar had no response. Luke Cordel was bewildered at this case study of law enforcement working with the legal community to condone and cover-up murder.

"Detective Stubbs," Roger calmly evoked his attention, "you've got to understand that for a long time, San Diego has been a city with growing pains. It was looked upon as a military town that was the bastard sibling of Los Angeles. It had a reputation as a good time for a card game and a prostitute when you were on shore leave. At the time of these events, everyone involved believed there was no point in perpetuating that myth."

"Was there any internal action taken against the officers?" Skylar's voice was now slow and pensive.

"No," Legion responded bluntly. "If you refer to the list of people in the newspaper article, the judge, named Gene Garubo, was an assistant district attorney at the time. He wrote a report stating that all the officers at the Necioro shooting followed police protocol."

Skylar turned away from Legion and gazed out the window. He looked aimlessly at the street in the distance. The wind was out of his sails. This whole story literally left a bad taste in his mouth.

"What happened to Mrs. Necioro?" Skylar asked.

"She moved to Sucre, Bolivia shortly after the incident," Legion informed them. "My understanding is that she died about a year ago."

"So, Mr. Legion," Skylar paused and pivoted from the window to look Legion directly in the eyes. He began to get a second wind. "Why now? Why are these people being killed now?"

"I don't know. I don't know why."

"Whoever it is, we're gonna catch 'em. Because, we know the targets. From where I sit," Skylar cautioned, "you're one of 'em. We want to provide you with police protection."

"That's not necessary. I wasn't adversarial to Dexter Frye," Legion reminded him. "I helped him. Whoever it is, they won't target me."

"Are you kidding me?" Skylar was incredulous. "You just sat here and told us how you conspired with the police department to get away with murder."

"I told you what you needed to know," Legion declared.

"Will you let us put an undercover man in your law firm?"

"No. I've got clients coming in and out of there all day sharing confidential information with us. I don't think they'd be too forthcoming, if they thought there was a cop around."

"We'll put him in a suit. Let him stay in the lobby."

"No," Roger's voice echoed finality. "Do you have any other questions or are we done here?"

"Would you be willing to take a polygraph test?"

Immediately, the Chief sprung up from his chair.

"Roger, don't answer that!" the Chief's imperative reverberated in the room. He focused on Skylar. "Mr. Legion is here at my request as a friend of the department. I will not allow any activity to go forward that might besmirch his reputation."

"Chief," Skylar pleaded, "he's a material witness in a double murder investigation."

"Skylar, he's here voluntarily and he's answered all of your questions. Don't develop tunnel vision. Move on."

Skylar let out an exasperated sigh.

"All right. Mr. Legion, thank you for your time."

Roger looked to Skylar and nodded.

"I'd like to talk to Mr. Legion alone," the Chief told the crowd.

Russ, Jeff and Skylar moved toward the door. Roger turned to Luke.

"Wait for me in the outer office."

Luke left his chair to follow the crowd out of the room.

"Russ," the Chief called out to Captain Shood. He raised his hand and with one finger requested his return.

Captain Shood re-entered the room and walked up to the desk. The Chief looked at him directly in his eyes.

"Contain him," the Chief told Russ.

"Yes, sir," Russ answered followed by an about face, whereby he exited the room again and closed the door behind him.

CHAPTER 41

In the San Diego neighborhood of Normal Heights, a 1988 Ford F-350, with a stake-bed body pulled up in front of the home of Vincenzo Fiorito. Vincenzo's nickname was Jimmy Flowers. He was the proprietor of an Italian restaurant in the Little Italy section of San Diego called the Bagheria Bedda. The restaurant's name is from a Sicilian dialect and it means 'Beautiful Bagheria.' Bagheria is a town located just outside of Palermo, Sicily. A town that, over the years, had developed a reputation for producing individuals who were quite skilled in the organized crime arts.

In addition to being a simple restaurant entrepreneur, Jimmy was a San Diego crime boss. He was involved with gambling, loan shark operations, truck hijacking, and adult entertainment. But the real cash cow of his empire was prescription drugs. He wanted nothing to do with street drugs or marijuana. He had a sophisticated distribution system utilizing legitimate individuals and sold high quality, prescription drugs to the affluent in places like La Jolla, Del Mar, and Rancho Santa Fe. People who lived in these areas could afford outrageous amounts for their vices and, if necessary, they could afford high-powered attorneys to deal with any 'problems.'

Jimmy kept an extremely low profile and operated his empire for the past 35 years unabated. He had never been arrested and his name had never appeared in the newspaper associated with any crime. He received an MBA from Stanford University and he had been married to the same woman for 39 years.

His house was an old, ranch-style structure, with a one-car garage and 3 bedrooms. Like all the other houses in the neighborhood, it was weathered by the sun.

The 4 occupants of the Ford truck were there to cut the grass and maintain the yard at the property. On the door of the truck, it read, 'Jimenez Landscaping.'

An older gentleman, in his mid-60s stepped out of the passenger side of the cab. The driver, and 2 men riding in the bed of the truck, began to unload 2 lawnmowers and various tools to commence their activities.

The older gentleman wore black slacks that were worn at the knees and a blue, buttoned shirt. He also wore a Mexican cowboy hat, made of palm straw. He walked up to the front door of the house and rang the doorbell. The front door opened and an occupant pushed open the screen door.

"Javier, my friend, *hola*," Jimmy Flowers told him with a welcoming smile. "Com'on in."

"Jimmy," Javier answered, "*mi amigo*." Javier entered and they shared a firm handshake.

Jimmy Flowers was 6 feet tall, with a thick frame, 240 pounds, and solid for a man in his early 60s. He wore blue slacks, and a green, Polo shirt with all 3 buttons buttoned to his neck.

Javier Jimenez serviced the drug clientele that Jimmy avoided. They often worked together and shared information they gleaned from their various sources. Their activities rarely crossed paths and they were always able to resolve any business concerns that may arise. Both men respected the business acumen of the other and they always avoided allowing any personal feelings to intervene.

"Have a seat," Jimmy offered and Javier made his way to a Barcolounger and sat down. Next to the Barcolounger was a small magazine table. Next to that was an upholstered chair. Jimmy took his place at that seat.

"Joe," Jimmy called out to his wife, Josephine. "Bring us something to drink."

As if she had anticipated his request, she emerged from the kitchen with 2 glasses of ice tea. Jimmy put down 2 coasters and his wife set the drinks on them. Josephine was in her late 50s, slightly heavyset, but you would never notice it, because she had a smile that flooded the room. She wore a summer dress with a floral pattern and a teal colored sweater that was unbuttoned.

"How are you, Javier? How's Corina?" Josephine asked.

"She's fine, Josephine. She sends her regards."

"Tell her she's got to come over some time and we'll have coffee. I've got some biscotti cooling right now for you."

"The tea is enough for me, thank you." Javier gratefully acknowledged.

"Okay. Well, Jimmy, I'm gonna bring some cookies down to Mrs. Flannigan," Josephine told Jimmy and turned to Javier. "Her husband broke his ankle and he's diabetic. The bones take longer to heal."

"Do you want me to drive you?" Jimmy asked.

"It's 3 houses down," Josephine said as she pointed her hand with an open palm down the street. Josephine again turned to Javier. "I don't drive, so he always offers. I'll see you boys later. Don't forget to tell Corina: Coffee."

"I'll tell her," Javier promised.

Josephine returned to the kitchen and exited the house through a side door that led to the garage. Jimmy waited for the door that she exited to click closed.

"Any problems, my friend?" Jimmy inquired.

"Not with you, Jimmy," Javier's ebullient voice became sullen. "I give my children everything I never had," Javier twisted in the chair towards Jimmy and leaned forward. "You and I realize the value of things because we know the cost. My son is lazy and he thinks he's a gangster, like in the movies. I tell him that's exactly what you don't want to be. I tell him the reason that image is popular is because it draws attention. I tell him you need to assess your environment and develop a skill set to accommodate that environment. But does he listen?" Javier paused and Jimmy could sense his anger. "I should send him to the North Pole to handle business. He has a problem now and this is why I've come to see you."

"Share it with me," Jimmy told him.

Javier reached into his pocket and removed a small, folded piece of college-ruled paper. He placed it on the magazine table and slid it over to Jimmy. Jimmy picked it up, unfolded the paper, and perused it. For a moment, he was contemplative as he pondered the information written on the paper. A smile came to his face and he turned to Javier.

"Consider it taken care of, my friend," Jimmy proclaimed.

"What do I owe you?" Javier wondered.

"No charge for this one," Jimmy remarked. "Friends help friends."

"*Señor* Jimmy, you are my friend." Javier's voice echoed sincerity.

As the sounds of lawn mowers crept closer to the house, Javier and Jimmy tapped their ice tea glasses together and wished each other good health.

CHAPTER 42

Detectives Jeff Elkins and Skylar Stubbs returned to their 3rd floor cubicles within the San Diego Police Headquarters followed by their Captain, Russ Shood. They were almost at their desks, when Jeff spoke up.

"So Sky, you think the Chief is filling out papers for your promotion right now?" he chuckled before he finished his sentence. *"Chief, did you know about this?"* Jeff feigned an impression of Skylar. "Sky, I thought you were gonna arrest the Chief right on the spot."

"Shut up," Skylar responded in irritation.

In the cubicle located next to Jeff, sat Detective Margaret Byrne. She was in her early 40s, slender frame, with petite features and medium-length, brown hair in a cute bob. She wore her badge on a lanyard around her neck. Her proficiency with a firearm was legendary in the department. As she typed, her face emanated calmness and serenity. Those attributes were rare among police officers. She was recently divorced and when often asked how she remained in such a good mood, her canned response was that she merely reflected those around her. And every police officer and perpetrator knew that was a blatant lie.

"Hey, Maggie," Jeff spoke up to get her attention, "Sky's gunning to be the next Chief. We just had a meeting with the Chief and I was waiting for Sky to turn to me and say, 'Put the cuffs on him.' I was lookin' for the door. You know, 'Check, please!'"

"Was the Chief giving you a tough time?" she asked rather surprised.

"No. It was somebody that you know," Jeff told her.

"Who?" she wondered.

"Roger Legion," Skylar answered.

"You're kidding? You got him to come down here to talk?"

"The Chief did," Skylar said.

"I've got no use for that guy," Margaret said in disgust.

Eighteen months earlier, Margaret's partner at the time was killed in a shootout in the conference room at Legion and Associates. In addition to Margaret's partner, 10 other people died in that shootout. Margaret and another attorney, named Michael Eiffert, were able to end the madness through sheer fire power. Roger Legion was in the middle of it all, but he walked out the way he walked in: without a scratch. It was claimed that the killer's animosity toward Legion was the catalyst for the events that day.

"Well, we're not gonna start a fan club for him any time soon," Jeff let her know.

"Jeff, Skylar," Captain Shood's voice called out from inside his office, "come in here."

Jeff and Skylar made their way to Russ Shood's office and Skylar closed the door once they entered. The office was small, cluttered, and sterile. The walls were filled with photos and commendations, but they appeared to belong more in a nameless corporation than a police station. Jeff and Skylar sat in the chairs across the desk from Captain Shood.

"We're gonna keep moving forward with this Dexter Frye stuff," Russ declared. "I've authorized 2 patrol units for round the clock surveillance on Kyle Bober."

Kyle Bober was the police captain at the Necioro shooting.

"As you know, he's got stage 4 lung cancer that's metastasized into his lymph nodes. He's not very mobile or very lucid. He doesn't have any family in the area, but he does have hospice that comes in. I suggest that you have a man stand a post outside the bedroom door and check on the guy periodically. Have the other unit sweep the premises and the yard on a varied timetable. We'll also beef up patrols in the immediate area. I want you guys to go out to his house now and organize it. I'll find out who they're sending and let you know. Take a marked patrol unit, so you can move around faster."

Jeff and Skylar stood to leave and trekked to the door.

"Skylar," Russ said, "you're doin' a good job."

Skylar smiled and nodded. They left the room on their way to the parking garage.

CHAPTER 43

As the afternoon commenced, Luke Cordel looked out the window of his office and thought about the story of Dexter Frye that unfolded. It caused him mixed feelings about Roger Legion; yet, it was so far in the past, Luke believed it was better to develop his opinions about Roger based on his personal interactions with him. It was then out of the corner of his eye, Luke caught a glimpse of someone, within a fraction of a second, which caused him to lose his train of thought.

People passed in front of Luke's door constantly, so he wondered why this person caused him to hit the brakes. He got out of his chair, walked to the doorway, and stood over the threshold. He looked up and down the hallway and saw no one. Perhaps it was an apparition, or wishful daydreaming, but Luke decided to go down the hallway in the direction of the wraith-like entity.

When he reached the lobby, he spied a set of elevator doors closing and he quickly moved toward them to see if he could identify the occupants. He reached a vantage point within a millisecond of the doors closing. Who he saw was Karla Mulry, arms filled with folders, as she looked down to the floor in the moment that she noticed Luke. Karla rode the elevator with Luke and Legion from the 23rd floor to the 1st floor on Luke's first day of work.

Her visage stopped Luke in his tracks. She wore a dark suit with a white blouse and her skin was flawless. She was a vision of class, style, and refinement. She appeared academic, not in a preppie way, but in a well-mannered, intellectual presence. She radiated a kind of perfection that was not sexy, but elegantly beautiful. He had heard her speak only a few words that day, but he was able to play her voice, like a recording, in his mind. He was spellbound, yet amidst his hypnotic, mesmerizing, fascination with her, he felt disconnected from her. He thought she was probably betrothed or in a relationship, so his hope of getting to know her would probably be dashed.

He made the sojourn back to his office, walked over to the windows, and stared at the horizon for a moment of introspection. Luke thought about his time in the Marines and he could hear the cries of death of his fellow comrades. Why did he survive when so many others died? He closed his eyes tightly and the sounds stopped. He preferred listening to the sound of Karla's voice, which now occupied his mind.

Luke opened his eyes and did an about face, moving at a quick gait directly to Roger Legion's office. When he arrived at the doorway, he was about to knock, when he saw Roger was on the phone. Roger also caught sight of him, waved him in, and pointed to a chair for him to sit. While Roger continued his telephone discussion, Luke scrutinized the various photos on shelves, tabletops, and those hanging on the walls. He was amazed at the number of photos that included Dexter Frye. He recognized him from the newspaper article shown to Roger by Detective Stubbs and in every photo, both Roger and Dexter emoted a brotherly bond.

Luke walked over to the shelves and then the walls to examine the photos in closer detail.

Roger's call finally ended.

"What's going on?" Roger asked with expressed interest.

"What was he like?" Luke posed his inquiry like he was asking for details about a legend.

"Who?" Roger wondered.

"Dexter Frye."

Roger reflected on his friend and smiled.

"He was the kind of lawyer that could make a good lawyer a great lawyer. He would help you reach his level. Most honest guy I knew. People liked him and he knew it. Before he picked a jury, he would take a walk, out on Broadway, and work the street like a politician. Just say 'hello,' shake people's hands, stop and talk to them. It was like he charged his batteries. Then when he picked a jury, as long as they smiled at him, he knew he owned 'em. He didn't care how shitty the facts of his case were, the guy had no fear. As long as it was a jury and not a bench trial, he knew he was gonna win. And he did. Christ, at the voir dire, you would have lawyers come in just to see him in action as he questioned the jurors. I will admit, in those days, I attended those sessions as often as I could."

"So that one case sunk his ship?" Luke wondered.

"Dexter had lofty goals. He wanted to change the way law was practiced. Back in the late 1970s, there was a Supreme Court Case that allowed lawyer advertising," Roger reminisced.

"*Bates v. State Bar of Arizona*," Luke piped in. "I had to know it for the bar exam."

"Very good. Dexter saw this as an opportunity to broaden his range exponentially. The sad part is he didn't need it. He didn't need the jingle, the Litigation Guy, the 'I don't ration the passion,' but he thought he could change the perception of lawyers. While that ambition was noble, it was also flawed. And unfortunately, he paid the price for it."

"Why did you let the police get away with what they did?"

"Over the years, you don't know how many times I've asked myself that question," Roger ruminated. "But I knew it's what Dexter would have wanted. After his wife died, I knew Dexter would never be the same. I didn't want his reputation to be sullied. The news coverage of it disappeared almost immediately and if you recall, Detective Stubbs said they couldn't find any files on Dexter Frye. Well, that was part of the settlement of the *Necioro* case. There would be no investigation into Dexter Frye in regard to the murder of his wife or the death of the police officer that night when he jumped off the bridge. All records were to be destroyed and the police were to forget about Dexter Frye."

Luke realized that the Dexter Frye saga was a plethora of secrets. Perhaps, he would be better off minding his own business.

"I did have a question for you that didn't involve Dexter Frye," Luke re-focused.

"Shoot," Roger quipped.

"Does the firm have any rules against fraternization with people on the 23rd floor?"

"You're the first guy to ask that question. Probably, the other guys would do it behind my back," Roger spoke matter-of-factly. "I've got no problem with it as long as it doesn't affect their work. It's a young lady, right? Don't tell me different." Roger's voice had an implied demand.

"It's a young lady," Luke told him.

"Same rules apply. She can't be on this floor without a reason – a law firm reason – and I don't care if you marry her and stay married for 50 years. As long as she works here, she calls you 'Mr. Cordel.' Understood?"

"Yes, sir," Luke acknowledged.

"Who is it?"

"That girl, Karla, that we rode on the elevator with, the first day."

"Did you find out if she has a boyfriend or husband?" Legion inquired.

"I don't know."

Roger looked at Luke for a moment.

"Let's find out. A successful mission requires good intel."

Legion lifted the receiver from his desktop phone and pushed 2 numbers.

"Louise, you have a young lady down there named Karla . . .," Roger looked at Luke.

"I think it's Mulry," Luke chirped in.

"Mulry," Roger spoke into the phone. "Do you know if she's married or has a boyfriend?" Roger paused for a moment. "Okay."

Roger returned the phone to its cradle and shared his findings with Luke.

"She doesn't have a husband. Louise is gonna let me know if she has a boyfriend."

As he finished his sentence, the phone rang. Roger again picked up the receiver.

"Yes, Louise," Roger listened for her response. "Would you send her up to my office, please? Thank you."

"Can I ask what you're doing?" Luke wondered.

"Helping out a fellow Marine."

Luke was becoming nervous and the butterflies in his stomach were extremely active.

Karla appeared at Legion's door, slightly out of breath, with a yellow pad and pen in hand. She knocked. Roger turned his gaze to her.

"Did you want to see me, Mr. Legion?"

"Come on in, Karla," Roger's voice was serious and all business. "Do you remember Mr. Cordel?"

Luke stood as she entered.

"Yes. Hello, Mr. Cordel." Her nervousness was evident.

"Karla, Mr. Cordel has been in the military for the past several years and he's a little rusty around the courthouse. I'd like you to give him a tour of the courthouses, be sure he knows where the business offices are, the larger courtrooms, and the walkway bridge between the 2 courthouses. You might as well take him to the federal courthouse, too."

"Yes, Mr. Legion," Karla acknowledged the request feeling relieved that it was nothing time-sensitive.

"Mr. Cordel," Roger spoke as he stood up from his chair in order to pull out his money clip, "if she does a good job, I want you to take her for a cup of coffee."

Roger removed a $20 bill from the money clip and handed it to Luke.

"Yes, sir," Luke responded with a smile.

"Would it be alright if I had a cold drink?" Karla queried.

"You can have whatever you want," Roger's response sounded as if he was perturbed at the question.

Karla and Luke headed to the door when Legion's voice interrupted them.

"Karla," Legion inquired as he pointed to Luke. "What's his name?"

She paused to think and nervously uttered, "Mr. Legion."

Roger's gaze was penetrating and he raised an eyebrow. Karla caught her mistake.

"I mean, Mr. Cordel." Her voice was apologetic.

"Don't forget it," Legion spewed his admonition. "Go."

With that, the odyssey of Karla and Luke commenced.

CHAPTER 44

Remy entered the Deus X Machine Shop and most of the normal sounds were stilled. Bob Brockman was exactly where Remy left him: perched on a swivel chair, hitting keys on more than one keyboard at a time, and his eyes moved around the various screens like a single player of a video game trying to kill as many zombies as possible.

"Brock," Remy spoke up to get his attention as he approached him, "where is everybody?"

"Kevin and Philippe went to take care of some details regarding that thing for our new cop friend. Hazz and Pike are in the clean room workin' on a harness. Emile went to get us somethin' to eat. Give me some good news: What did those guys get for us?"

"Semtex," Remy uttered the word with an ear to ear smile.

"Pure or with the plasticizer?"

A plasticizer is an additive to increase the fluid nature of the explosive, but it also reduces its power.

"Pure. It's military grade."

"Boo-yaa!" Brockman was ecstatic as he gave a hard fist pump in the air. "We're gonna set'em up and knock'em down! And take all the asshole pricks with us. When are we gettin' it?"

"Within 72 hours. Keep your eyes on the e-mails. It should come from something called Church of England. We should have the transit instructions tomorrow," Remy proudly proclaimed.

"I knew they were gonna get us either C-4 or Semtex. Hazz has been working on the circuitry and the harnesses. I think we can speed things up. It's gonna take him a little while to put in the slapper detonator. That's a 2 man operation because of the precision. Might as well put it on the trucks, too. When do you think you're gonna be able to get on the bridge maintenance walkway?"

"Is Kevin and Philippe gonna drop a match and get rid of that guy tonight?"

"That's my understanding," Brockman bemoaned, "unless Kevin shits his pants and somebody's gotta change his diaper."

"He's good at what he does," Remy was quick to defend Kevin.

"There's no talent in pullin' a trigger," Brockman opined.

"It's not about pulling a trigger, Brock. It's about following an order to a tee and paying attention to detail."

"Remy, that guy's smoke and mirrors. Without you backin' him up, he's a piss ant."

"Don't worry about him. If they take care of this thing tonight, I wanna see if I can get on the bridge tomorrow. All right?" Remy asked, still beaming with a good mood.

"I'm all in. Lock, Brock, and barrel, baby!"

"I'm gonna change my clothes. Call me when the food gets here," Remy requested.

"Kevin said he might call ya if he needs ya."

"I'll be here," Remy assured him as he alighted the stairs.

"I'm gonna call Emile and see if he can get some donuts. There's a 24-hour donut place next to that Italian restaurant that serves family style."

Remy raised his hand as he continued walking up the stairs indicating 'Good for you.' Before Remy reached the top of the stairs, Brockman's phone rang. He picked up the phone and looked at the number on the Caller ID. It was Kevin Camballa.

"Tiny's Short Man's Shop. Tiny speaking," Brockman answered.

"Where's Remy?" Kevin's voice was hurried. "Put him on the phone."

"Remy," Brockman called up to him on the 2nd floor walkway, "your short friend has some tall orders."

Remy did an immediate about face and hustled down the stairs. Brockman tossed the phone to Remy as he reached the ground floor.

"What's wrong?" Remy asked impatiently.

"Nothing, yet. There are 3 cop cars here right now. I've got a plan, but I need Philippe with me on the inside. Can you come over and assist with an exit plan, if necessary? I'm trying to avoid collateral damage involving these guys, but there's always a possibility things may get *rough*."

"All right. Wait for me. I'm on my way." Remy ended the call and handed the phone to Brockman.

"Make sure they save me something to eat. I don't know when I'll be back. Tell everybody: Maintain radio silence."

"We-we mon-sewer," Brockman's response was his attempt at a comedic moment.

Remy looked at him bewildered.

"Why is it that Americans always make such good assholes?" Remy inquired inviting a response.

"Because they enjoy shittin' on French people," Brockman followed his sentence with a wide grin.

"Get back to work," Remy told him as he headed for the door.

As the door closed behind Remy, Brockman pressed several buttons on one of the keypads. On all 6 screens, an American flag was seen waving in the wind and the music for _The Star-Spangled Banner_ filled the building. Brockman stood from his chair and sang it, along with the music, at the top of his lungs.

CHAPTER 45

As Karla Mulry and Luke Cordel waited for an elevator on the 24th floor of the America's Finest City Building, Luke just smiled and attempted to avoid the appearance of staring at Karla. Karla looked slightly perturbed and shifted her gaze in various directions, including the ground, but not in Luke's direction.

"Karla," Nina, the receptionist, called out to her. "Can you do lunch late one day this week?"

"I think so," she answered with a smile and looked briefly in Luke's direction, "unless I have to wash someone's car."

"This wasn't my idea," Luke told Karla as the elevator doors opened. She walked past him as she entered the elevator, as if she had never met him.

When the doors had fully closed, she commented.

"What is this, your pimp's idea?" she blurted out referring to Legion.

"Your what?" Luke asked.

"Pimp!"

"Wouldn't he technically be your pimp?"

"No!" She thought for a minute. "Well," as she thought, "maybe." Another moment passed. "He's pimping us both out."

"I don't think that analogy fits this situation," Luke told her. "How is he making money by sending us on a tour of the courthouse?"

"I don't know," Karla's voice evidenced her fluster. "You'll be smarter and you can bill more."

"Maybe," he acknowledged with a sincere smile.

Karla looked at him, sighed, and smiled.

"I'm sorry. Can we start again?"

"Sure. My name is Luke Cordel." Luke welcomed the opportunity to shake her hand.

"Nice to meet you, Mr. Cordel. My name is Karla Mulry."

"You can call me Luke," he assured her.

"No, I can't, Mr. Cordel. The law firm has a rule that prohibits it."

"All right," Luke told her, "if you're gonna call me Mr. Cordel, then I'm gonna call you Miss Mulry. Or would you prefer *Ms.* Mulry?"

"Either one is fine," she replied.

With that, the elevator doors opened and the 1st floor lobby was in sight.

"Lead the way, Miss Mulry."

Luke followed Karla out of the building and her accelerated gait caused Luke to stay conscious of keeping up with her.

The downtown courthouses of the San Diego Superior Court are located at 220 W. Broadway and 330 W. Broadway. They are situated next to each other on different blocks and connected by a glass walkway bridge that traverses Union Street on the 4th floor of each building. The 220 W. Broadway building was completed in 1961 and handles criminal matters, family law matters, and houses the Sheriff's Office that is responsible for providing bailiffs to courtrooms and security for the buildings.

The 330 W. Broadway location was completed in 1996 and handles civil matters, the kind which involve the lawyers at Legion and Associates. The District Attorney's offices and jury services are also located within this building.

Karla gave Luke a rather nonchalant, glossy tour of the 330 W. Broadway building and as they proceeded across the glass walkway bridge, Karla stopped in the center of it. She looked south in the direction of the city's Convention Center. Luke stood next to her admiring the view. Karla turned to Luke.

"Mr. Cordel, I want to apologize to you."

"Miss Mulry, there's nothing to apologize for. I'm enjoying the afternoon. I should apologize to you, if this tour makes you uncomfortable."

"It doesn't. I was just in a mood. You didn't really need a tour of the courthouses, did you?"

"No," Luke confessed, "but I did learn a lot about the stuff in the business office."

"Can we go get a drink?"

"Absolutely, lead the way."

"Let's go back through the new courthouse. I always try to avoid the old one. It has kind of a spook vibe."

As Karla's comfort level with Luke continued to increase, so did her communication skills. She spoke non-stop until they reached the food court located on the 1st floor of the new courthouse. They stopped at a Subway sandwich shop and Karla selected a bottle of protein water. Luke ordered a Coke fountain drink. She was hungry, and Luke offered to buy her lunch, but she refused. Instead, they purchased 3 chocolate chip cookies and she made sure that she did not eat any more of them than Luke did.

"You dress very nicely," Luke shared with her.

"It's one of the few things in my life I can control. I'm kinda clumsy."

Her attempt to be self-deprecating failed miserably.

"I don't get that impression."

"How did you end up at Legion and Associates?" she wondered.

"My uncle was a Superior Court judge and when I got out of the service, I called him for advice. He made a phone call and then Louise called me."

"So, you weren't even interviewed?" Karla was astonished.

"Well, I guess over the phone."

"Do you live with your uncle?"

"Not exactly. My aunt and uncle have a condo downtown. They're on a mission right now in South America. Their main house is in Del Mar."

Del Mar was located in the northern portion of San Diego County along the coast. It is the home of the famous Del Mar Racetrack.

"So, they just had an extra house they let you use?"

"I'm also watching their other house."

"What do you pay in rent?"

"They're not charging me rent."

"You know where I live?"

Luke shook his head.

"I live on Winona Avenue. It's out east off University Ave. between 49th and 50th. It takes me 1 ½ hours each way on the bus."

Luke didn't know how to respond.

"Where do you catch the bus?" Luke quizzed hoping to propel small talk.

"Across the street from the office," she said rhetorically indicating that he was stupid for asking it. Karla re-focused.

"Oh," Karla shook her head then rubbed her forehead like she had a headache. "I'm not upset, but I hear stories about people like you, I think about this thing my mother always used to talk about. She's in an assisted living facility, in a memory care place. But she used to say that there are some people in this world that just don't get a break. Those people don't win the lottery, they get traffic tickets, and they don't find husbands, or get the cute babies. Nobody ever helps them. They're not on the corner when the bus comes by. It's just not meant to be. If you accept that, you can understand why the world pees on you and craps on you. For some bizarre, perverse reason, they must deserve it. My mother would call those individuals, 'tissue people.' Because, like a tissue, once they're used, you throw them away. So, that's what you're looking at. A tissue person."

"That's awfully pessimistic," Luke confided.

"Does it make you uncomfortable?"

"No. I just don't think it's a healthy outlook on life."

Karla gazed at him for a moment but wasn't in the mood to talk anymore.

"Listen, you're not going to tell Mr. Legion that I called him a pimp?"

"No," he assured her.

"Thank you," she graciously replied.

"Roger was supposed to give me a tour of the 23rd floor, but he never got around to it. Would you like to give me a tour of it?"

"No," Karla answered decisively. "People will talk. In fact, I should go up now and you should stay here for a few minutes."

Karla stood from the table as did Luke to acknowledge her leaving.

"Thank you, Miss Mulry."

"You're welcome, Mr. Cordel."

Karla headed out of the courthouse and as she walked away, Luke had one thought on his mind to which he gave a laser's focus. He wanted to prove that Karla's mother was wrong.

CHAPTER 46

Outside the home of Kyle Bober, 2 marked police cars sat parked along the curb to advise any would-be assassins that they would be met with severe resistance and an army of police commandos was only a radio call away. Inside, an officer named Accendo, sat outside Kyle Bober's bedroom door, while another officer, named Rivers, made a periodic check of the rooms in the house and the yard. These officers would spend 4 hours of their shift on this detail before being relieved by another set of officers.

Kyle Bober was 78 years old and currently suffering from lung cancer and dementia. An oxygen tank was his constant companion. His wife died 3 years earlier and they had no children. His closest living relative was in Burlington, Vermont. A court had appointed a conservator for Bober, but due to his terminal condition and desire to be at home, he was allowed to live there with daily hospice care. The local hospice facility wanted to provide 24-hour care to Bober, but he refused and generally, at some point during the day, he would chase them away.

Kyle was provided police protection since the 2nd Dexter Frye-related murder. He liked the idea of 2 police officers providing him 24-hour protection. It made him feel important and he believed that he could 'boss them around.' The situation also made the hospice workers comfortable, knowing that he would not be alone.

Bober spent most of his time in his room watching television and would occasionally emerge to bark an order.

Detective Stubbs and Elkins had stopped by earlier in the afternoon to provide procedures that they wanted the officers on-site to follow. By mid-afternoon, they departed for a late lunch.

A mini-van pulled in the driveway with the words 'Cielo Hospice Services' on each side. This was the hospice company retained by Kyle Bober's conservator to provide comfort to him in his final days.

Out of the van stepped 2 gentlemen, dressed in blue hospital scrubs. They both looked around the area and proceeded to the front door. The lead person was Kevin Camballa, Remy's assassin, wearing black, horn rimmed glasses. He carried a medical bag and a stethoscope could be seen in his pocket. Behind him was Philippe, the member of Remy's crew who received a college degree in fire science. Philippe also wore a long sleeve t-shirt under his scrubs top to cover his arm tattoos. When they reached the door, Kevin rang the doorbell. Officer Accendo answered it.

"Hi," Kevin said. "We have a work order for Mr. Bober. We were gonna give him a sedative to help him sleep and a basic hygiene check."

"Com'on in," Accendo instructed them. As they entered, Officer Rivers appeared in the foyer. "Let me see your work order."

Kevin handed a piece of paper to Accendo, who read it.

"I gotta call to confirm it," Accendo advised.

From his cell phone, Accendo dialed the number located on the work order. He waited while it rang.

Back at the Deus X Machine Shop, Bob Brockman was cutting up a chocolate-glazed donut and placing the pieces on a slice of pizza. He then cut the pizza, so that each bite included a piece of donut. When he took his first bite, he savored it.

"Perfection – thy name is Brock!"

As he finished his proclamation, one of the cell phones on his desk began to ring. The Caller ID simply stated 'San Diego,' but he knew who it was.

"Brock and roll, baby," he proudly called out and answered it. "Cielo Hospice Services, may I help you?"

"I'd like to check on the status of a work order," Accendo requested.

"Can you give me the number, it should be in the upper right hand corner."

"3-2-8-1-6."

"May I ask who's calling?"

"This is Officer Accendo of the San Diego Police Department. It's in reference to Kyle Bober."

"Hold, please."

Brockman put the call on hold and returned to eating his pizza and donuts. Kevin and Philippe stood there looking at Officers Accendo and Rivers.

"I'm gonna have to check your bag," Rivers stated.

"You better frisk 'em, too," Accendo added.

Kevin handed the bag to Rivers, who looked through it, finding nothing out of the ordinary. He returned the bag to Kevin. Kevin and Philippe held their hands up, while Officer Rivers gave them a quick pat down. Kevin wondered what was taking Brockman so long. Brockman came back on the line.

"That work order is for a sedative injection, if necessary, and a personal hygiene check. Is there any problem?" Brockman asked.

"Do you normally send 2 people?" Accendo inquired.

"Not everyone is certified in administering the injectable meds. My understanding is that the hygiene check can be quite the project."

"Okay, thank you," Officer Accendo told Brockman as he ended the call.

"If you need to," Kevin suggested, "you can come in while we give him a shot. We usually try to give people some privacy for the hygiene check."

Accendo looked at Rivers.

"You might as well watch it," Accendo told Rivers. As he spoke, Kyle Bober appeared from the bedroom, wearing a bath robe, with his oxygen tank in tow.

"Hello, Mr. Bober," Kevin spoke immediately.

"It's captain. And where's your uniform?" Kyle demanded.

"They're here to help you," Accendo told him.

"Was I talkin' to you, rookie? And don't forget my rank. You there," he motioned to Rivers, "I can't find _Dragnet_ on the television. Help me find it."

"We'll help you find it," Kevin told him.

Kevin, Philippe and Rivers entered the room, with Kevin assisting Bober. He walked Bober to the edge of the bed and sat him down. Philippe entered the bathroom and looked in the toilet and then gave a quick look in the trash can. Philippe was able to see that Officer Rivers was bouncing back and forth between watching Kevin prepare to give a shot and going through the search function on the television to see if he could find the _Dragnet_ show.

Philippe reached into the back of his pants and removed a small, test tube-type vial from his anal cavity. He washed it off in the sink and went into the toilet area, where he cracked the vial. It emitted a horrendous smell, like boiled cabbage mixed with sulfur. He dumped the contents of the vial around the base of the toilet.

Philippe walked out of the toilet area and allowed the smell to permeate the air. He then flushed the broken portions of the vial.

In the bedroom, Kevin had Bober remove his bath robe and then he rolled up Bober's sleeve sufficiently to select an injection site. While wearing latex gloves, he opened an individual alcohol wipe and swabbed the area. From a small case, he removed a fully loaded syringe, like one used by a diabetic. Kevin massaged Kyle's arm to locate a vein for an intravenous injection. In less than 10 seconds, the syringe was emptied.

What Kevin pumped into Kyle's vein was Succinylcholine, a neuromuscular, paralytic drug. It causes muscular paralysis of all the muscles, including those used for breathing. Without some sort of ventilator support, a person would die from asphyxia. This drug has no sedative effect, so a person would be awake while the paralysis occurs, causing them to die a very slow, tortured death.

Philippe emerged from the bathroom.

"It's kind of a mess in here," he said as he waived his hand in front of his nose. The smell was beginning to waft into the bedroom.

"That does smell potent," Rivers exclaimed.

Kevin pulled the elastic on the back of Kyle's pajama bottoms, including his underwear.

"He soiled himself," he told Rivers, then turned to Philippe. "Go get the laundry bag."

Rivers left the room followed by Philippe. Kyle was already beginning to tense up from paralysis and started uttering unintelligible syllables. Kevin laid him down on the bed, took off his slippers, and placed the bed's covers over him, up to his chest.

Philippe moved quickly to the van and opened the back doors. Inside, there was a laundry bag approximately three-quarters full and Philippe grabbed another small, test tube vial, the same as he had used inside and cracked it open. He dumped the contents of the vial into the bag and closed it. He put the pieces of glass in an ashtray and hoisted the bag over his shoulder to carry it in the house.

When he entered, he asked Officer Accendo if he would like to search the bag. Philippe opened it and Accendo immediately told him to close it. Philippe explained that it contained soiled laundry from earlier visits to other hospice patients that day.

"Just take it in," Accendo told him.

Philippe lifted the bag with both hands, brought it in the room and closed the door.

Within 15 minutes, Kevin and Philippe exited the room.

"He should be set for a while," Kevin told Accendo. "Any problems, give us a call."

"Okay," Accendo said. "Take it easy."

With that, Kevin and Philippe exited the house and walked back to the van. Then, Kevin walked up to one of the police cars and looked through the windshield and slightly lifted the windshield wiper. When both men were back in the van, they backed out of the driveway and drove off to the west into the afternoon sunlight. Their plan was to ditch the van and rendezvous with Remy.

CHAPTER 47

Luke sauntered back to the America's Finest City Building and pondered the beauty of the weather and Karla. The temperature was in the low 70s and the bright sun made every object appear clear and crisp, like a neatly defined painting. In Afghanistan, he never thought about the weather; he only thought about making it through to the next day.

As he entered the building, the A.F.C. News caught his eye. He didn't really need anything, but he decided to stop in, say 'Hello' to Roux, and buy a pack of gum. Luke liked Roux and he understood why Roger Legion had a fondness for him. Roux was a man of simple pleasures and, in light of the problems he faced in life, he was the antithesis of Karla. He greeted everyone with a smile and a laugh.

Luke entered the shop and Roux's smile beamed like a cat knowing dinner is on the way. Roux wore a tan, cardigan sweater with his trademark black glasses and a slight stubble of beard growth.

"Roux, my friend, how are ya?" Luke called rather loudly.

"Is that Mr. Luke?" Roux wondered.

"You got it."

"Now, Mr. Luke, there's no need to raise your voice. I'm blind, not deaf."

"Sorry about that Roux." Luke apologetically replied.

"I'm just joshin' ya. At least I can understand you when ya talk. I get some people comin' in here – mumblin'- like they got marbles in their mouth. Hey, Mr. Luke, you wanna hear a legal joke?"

"Sure."

"What do an assignment and a girdle have in common?"

"I don't know?"

"They both got an ass-in-'er."

Luke sincerely chuckled.

"See that was a good joke and it didn't involve trash," Roux proclaimed.

"Can I ask: How'd ya get the name 'Roux'?" Luke wondered.

"A long time ago, I was a chef in the French Quarter down N'awlins. Right down on Dauphine Street. You like gumbo? I make a mean crawfish étouffée. You can't make a good étouffée without a nice roux."

"I'm gonna trust you on that," Luke told him. "Why'd you stop cookin?"

"Drink got the better a me. I lost everything and started hitching a ride. When I got to San Diego, I run outta road."

"How'd you connect up with Roger?"

"It's Mr. Legion in here." Roux was serious when he corrected Luke. "I use to sell newspapers in front of the old courthouse. I could still see a little bit in those days. I had real bad sugar – ya know, the de-be-tis (diabetes). Every day, Mr. Legion would give me a fi'dolla bill for a twenty-five cent newspaper. Five dollas. When I saw him, I knew I was gonna eat good that day.

Then the city said that I had to move and Mr. Legion said, 'No.' He get me a job. Made sure I had health insurance. Made sure I could pay my bills and made sure I got a ride to get here and a ride home every day. Without him, I'm sure I'd be homeless – no, dead. So, nobody says nothin' bad about Mr. Legion in here."

Luke understood Roux and now he started to understand Roger Legion.

"Thanks for sharing that story, Roux."

"You welcome. Now, don't forget, you see any cuties, you gonna send 'em my way, right?" Roux asked with a devilish smile. "Even though I'm oppressed, I'm not prejudiced when it comes to the ladies. Sometimes, they gotta have some cream in the coffee, chocolate in the milk. You like white meat or dark?"

"I like it all," Luke exclaimed with his own personal smart-ass charm.

"That's my boy."

"Roux, you are always a pleasure to talk with." Luke's voice was genuine.

"You take care now, Mr. Luke."

Roux held out his shaky hand and Luke embraced it with both of his hands as Roger Legion had done on the first day Luke was introduced to Roux.

CHAPTER 48

Detectives Stubbs and & Elkins finished lunch at a Chipotle Mexican restaurant in the Mira Mesa Mall. After that, they sat in their marked patrol car and each retrieved several voice messages from their cell phones. It was a rare occasion because Detective Elkins allowed Detective Stubbs to drive.

Skylar finished with his calls and waited for Jeff to finish. When he did, Jeff let out an exasperated sigh and shook his head.

"You gonna have kids?" Jeff asked.

"I hope so," Skylar told him.

"How many you think you wanna have?"

"It's not up to me," Skylar was matter-of-fact.

"Who's it up to?" Jeff asked with incredulous wonder.

"It depends on how many times Heavenly Father is willing to bless us."

Jeff looked at him with his mouth open.

"What the hell did they put in your burrito? I only asked ya because I have two kids and sometimes I think I'm in a constant life or death battle with them. I tell them to turn off lights. They never say no. But as soon as I walk away, the lights are on. It's like I never said it. My daughter just called and she asked for $40 to go to a concert. Now, I'd like to be a jerk, but I'm not, so I'm gonna give her the 40 bucks, but, I'm thinkin' to myself 'How 'bout getting' a job? Her and my son never say 'no' to that, but there are just some places they can't work. They're too good for it."

"I think they need some tough love," Skylar advised.

"I just think my kids are dedicated to my financial, physical, social, emotional, and spiritual destruction."

"You recognize Satan my friend, that's the first step," Skylar's voice was rushed. "Come with me on Sunday. I'll help you find the path to happiness and ever-lasting life."

"What are ya, a cult leader now? Wait till you have your 10 kids. Your wife better hide the gun at night."

When Jeff spoke, anything not related to police work, sounded funny to Skylar. He chortled at Jeff's comment regarding the gun. As he did, his cell phone rang.

Skylar looked at the Caller ID and it said 'BOBER, KYLE.' Any lighthearted moment, being shared with Jeff quickly evaporated. How would Bober, who they were supposed to be protecting, have Skylar's cell phone number? The color drained from his face. He answered it and pressed the speaker button. There was a moment of silence, and then music began:

> *If you get in trouble, my oh my,*
> *And all you really wanna, do is cry.*
> *Well, there's one thing that you oughta try,*
> *Tell 'em your lawyer is Dexter Frye.*

As the music started to play, Skylar and Jeff locked eyes.

"He's there. He must be in the house," Skylar's voice pulsed urgency.

"Let's go. Code 3," Jeff responded with similar urgency.

As soon as the car backed out of the space, Skylar turned on the siren and overhead lights. The car moved as fast as traffic would allow: on straightaways in excess of 80 miles an hour and 50 miles an hour around curves. The music continued:

Dexter will get you a settlement,
So you don't have to worry, about the rent.
You can afford him, wait and see,
'Cause Dexter works on contingency.

Dexter Frye, Dexter Frye, Dexter Frye,
The Litigation Guy.

It finished in less than 1 minute. Then, whoever was on the other end disconnected the call.

Kyle Bober's house was less than 4 miles from the Chipotle restaurant. Jeff and Skylar were in Bober's driveway in 3 minutes and 50 seconds. While en route, they tried to call Officers Accendo and Rivers without luck. Jeff called the police department radio dispatch and requested back-up at the house. Skylar screeched the tires on the car and did a slight fishtail maneuver as he pulled into the driveway. Officer Rivers was in his car talking on the phone. He immediately stepped out of his vehicle. Skylar stepped out of his patrol car and saw Rivers.

"Is anybody inside?" Skylar's voice was hurried.

"No. Just Accendo," Rivers replied.

"Has anybody been here?"

"A coupla guys from hospice were here to give him a sedative. We called hospice to verify it."

At this point, Jeff was out of the car. Neither Jeff nor Skylar were wearing their sport coats and Jeff was holding his Smith & Wesson service revolver.

"Check the back. Wait for my orders," Skylar spoke like a general in the heat of battle.

Skylar and Jeff raced to the front door and entered without announcing themselves. Accendo immediately stood up and placed his hand on his gun. As Skylar walked towards Accendo, he started to ask him questions.

"The guy from hospice, was he tall and thin?" Skylar demanded an answer.

"No," Accendo said bewildered. "One guy was short, Pilipino-looking. The other guy was blond, average height."

"When was the last time you checked on Bober?" Skylar's tone was no-nonsense.

"They left less than 10 minutes ago and he's supposed to be sleeping. I was right about to check on him." Accendo's comment sounded more like he was covering up for his lack of action.

Skylar walked up to the bedroom door, followed closely by Jeff and Officer Accendo. All three men had their guns drawn. Skylar pressed down on the handle and the door unlatched. There was a light on in the room and Skylar opened the door approximately 1 inch. He saw Bober on the bed, under the covers, with his eyes open, and mouth slightly open. His left foot was in a position that looked like he was trying to kick off the covers. There was a smell in the room of some type of petroleum product. The smell mixed with the putrid odor both officers were exposed to earlier.

Skylar raised his gun and turned and looked back to Accendo.

"Go around back and back-up Rivers."

Accendo nodded in acknowledgement and raced out. While Skylar spoke, Jeff examined the room through the one inch opening of the door. Skylar grabbed the door handle and was about to slam his shoulder into the door.

"STOP!" Jeff screamed suddenly. Skylar looked at him wondering what was wrong. "Sky, look."

Jeff pointed down to a thin, metal wire that ran approximately 6 inches from the door and 3 inches from the ground.

"That's a tripwire," Jeff told him. From their vantage point, they were unable to see the device to which it was connected. "Let's go check the sliding glass door."

Skylar sprinted to the backyard and saw Accendo and Rivers looking through the glass door with their flashlights. As he approached the door, he could see 2 lines of the same metal wire, parallel to the ground that ran across the sliding glass door and the stationary glass next to the door. The wires were located one-third of the way up the glass and two-thirds of the way up the glass. Another wire ran from the frame around the sliding glass door. If you tried to open the sliding glass door or break the glass, you would trip one of the wires.

Skylar cupped his hands around eyes and pressed them against the glass door. Jeff borrowed a flashlight from Rivers. Jeff followed one of the wires and recognized the attached device.

"It's a Claymore mine," he told Skylar. Rivers was standing behind him. Jeff glanced to Rivers. "Call the bomb squad." Rivers immediately radioed in his request.

A Claymore mine is an anti-personnel mine used by the military against enemy infantry. It contains the explosive C-4 and shoots a pattern of metal balls like a shotgun. The detonation of one mine would easily destroy anything in the room.

Approximately a half hour earlier, Kevin removed from the laundry bag and set 2 Claymore mines, one for the bedroom door and the other to handle any attempt at entry through the sliding glass door.

While Kevin was constructing the booby-traps, Philippe doused the floor with benzene, also brought in with the laundry bag. The smell of the benzene was masked by the stench of the liquid they brought into the house. He then took a lamp from one of the end tables that he kept turned on, removed the shade, and placed the lamp on the floor, next to the bed. On top of the hot bulb, he placed several pieces of cheesecloth. The cheesecloth would act as a delayed striker to start a fire. The cloth would eventually become hot enough to ignite and the gaseous benzene would burst into a fireball.

Jeff recognized the set-up on the lamp.

"We gotta find the fuse box and cut the power!" Jeff yelled and all the men scrambled to the side of the house. There was a lock on the fuse box and Skylar aimed his Glock to shoot it off. Before he could pull the trigger, the cheesecloth ignited. That fire detonated the benzene gas that filled the bedroom. A fireball erupted.

From the side of the house, the first explosion shook the entire structure and in less than a second, a second explosion went off from the 2 Claymore mines. That explosion caused all 4 men to be knocked to the ground.

Skylar looked around and stood up. His white shirt was covered in grass stains and mud. Jeff was moving slowly and Skylar helped him to his feet. They walked to the backyard and could see that the back of the house was completely blown out and most of the structure was on fire. Skylar viewed the bedroom area and thought about entering. Jeff knew what he was thinking.

"Forget it, Sky. He's toast."

"Accendo said one guy was short, the other average. No tall, thin guy. That means we're dealing with a team, a gang, a crew. Who would want these old guys dead for something that happened over 30 years ago?" Skylar paused. "I know Legion knows."

Skylar was angry. He blamed himself. In the distance, fire trucks and police cars could be heard racing to the scene. Skylar marched to the front of the house and surveyed it from the sidewalk. He turned away from it near Accendo's police car. This was the car that Kevin walked up to and lifted one of the wiper blades. Skylar saw what Kevin placed there. It was a business card from Dexter Frye, the Litigation Guy.

CHAPTER 49

At 5:40 p.m., Karla Mulry emerged from the America's Finest City Building and followed the crowd to the corner to await the crossing light's permission to traverse Broadway. When it was granted, Karla crossed the street and joined another crowd awaiting the 5:54 p.m. Route 2 bus. She stood out among the crowd, with a celebrity's glow, as she wondered if she needed to buy laundry soap. She didn't like to go out after dark, so laundry may have to wait for the weekend.

Over the flood of voices and the overabundance of noises, a single raised voice, halfway up the block, caught her attention.

"MISS MULRY!"

When she turned, there stood Luke Cordel. His smile evidenced his pleasure in seeing her. He started to walk toward her.

"MISS MULRY!" he screamed.

"I can't talk. My bus is coming," she yelled.

She knew he was not going to stop, so she started walking toward him. When they were within 10 feet of each other, she let out a frustrated inquiry.

"What?"

"I'm going to Winona Avenue. Can you give me directions?"

She turned away from him and realized that she missed her bus. Luke walked up behind her.

"Can I get those directions?" he asked.

An older gentleman, in his mid-70s, wearing a hat and a brown sweater watched the exchange between Karla and Luke. He approached Karla.

"You know this guy?" the old man asked.

"He's my ride," Karla told him with a tone of surrender.

She turned and gave a wise-ass smirk. She then looked at the line of cars parked along the curb up the block from the bus stop.

"Which one is it?" She rather politely asked.

"The Kia," he answered and pointed, while hastening his return to the car to open her door.

At that moment, Karla Mulry wondered if she would ever ride a San Diego city bus again.

CHAPTER 50

When Alton Burchesky awoke this Thursday morning, he felt a slight pounding in his head from excessive imbibing the night before at the Swing and A Miss bar in San Clemente. His clock radio read '7:15.' He heaved himself to a sitting position on the side of the bed in one motion and thought about what he should do next. The decision was that coffee would assist with his focus.

He wore boxer shorts and a white t-shirt. The hallway to the kitchen was approximately 12 feet. Alton began his trek and kept his right hand in front of him touching the wall for guidance. As soon as he entered the hallway, he heard the sound of a newspaper rustling. Alton reacted like he had just been hit in the face with a bucket of cold water. He was now fully awake and raced back to the nightstand, next to his bed, to retrieve his service weapon. It wasn't there. He tried to hastily recall the events of the night before in an attempt to determine the gun's location. He was stopped when a voice with a French accent called out.

"It's over here," Remy told him.

Alton quickly made his way to the kitchen where Remy was sitting at the kitchen table reading a section of the newspaper. Remy wore jeans, boots and a neat, button shirt.

"How'd you get in here?" Alton asked.

"Through the door," Remy completed reading an article and put the paper down. "You looking for this?" Remy held up Alton's Berretta 92FS 9 millimeter semiautomatic weapon. He then set it down on the table.

"What do ya want?" Alton asked.

"I wanna get on the bridge," Remy told him with a steely gaze.

"I'm not workin' today."

"When are you working?"

"Monday," Alton told him.

"Shit," Remy paused. "All right, Monday, you get me on the bridge."

"But," Alton began.

"No excuses," Remy shut him down. "You read the paper or see the TV? Everybody in that area called Mira Mesa knows we were there. I kept my end of the agreement."

"Listen, I can get you on the bridge on Monday, but I need a little more help."

"No. The original agreement was one guy. Roasted. We called the cop with the song and left the calling card. Now, two of my guys gotta keep a low profile because the cops over there saw them."

"This next guy, it's a real bitch. He's in the courthouse. It's fortified. Loaded with cops. You gotta help me," Alton desperately begged.

"Not my problem," Remy told him.

"Then I'm gonna go do it. Today or tomorrow. And if I get caught or killed, you find a way to get on the bridge."

Remy had serious doubts about Alton's chances for success. He had no interest in threatening him.

"When you plan for failure, it's easy to meet your objective. Why do you want these guys dead?" Remy asked curiously.

"It's none of your business." Alton told him bluntly.

"You're making it my business," Remy retorted. "Does it have something to do with this lawyer – Legion?"

"How do you know him?"

"I just read about him in your newspaper. The story with all the pictures."

The newspaper Remy was reading was the same one left at the 2nd crime scene and discussed in the police chief's office.

"He's not a problem. I can handle Legion," Alton assured him.

"You related to Dexter Frye?" Remy quizzed.

"Nope." Alton's response was cold and detached.

Remy stood from the table and stared at Alton.

"This is the last time that I am going to help you. But you're gonna get me on the bridge first. What time does your shift start on Monday?"

"Eight a.m."

"You come and pick me up at the machine shop at 8:30. There's two other things that I want. First: I want you to bring your patrol car over to the shop. We need to go through it for 30 minutes to get all the radio frequencies. Second: On the day my little event goes down, I want you to run a traffic break for the eastbound traffic on the bridge. The trucks are a little larger on that side and they need extra time to maneuver," Remy told him. "If you disappoint me from this point forward, they're gonna find you in the trunk of your cop car in pieces." Remy just stared at Alton. "What department of the courthouse is this guy in?"

"Department 63," Alton answered.

Remy walked out the kitchen door, which exited to the driveway of the house. Kevin Camballa sat in the driver's seat of a black, GMC pick-up truck waiting for Remy. Remy entered the vehicle and immediately put on his seatbelt. His anger was evident.

"Let's go back to the shop," Remy commanded.

"When it comes time to kill this guy, let me do it," Kevin shared with him.

"*Avec plaisir* (With pleasure)," Remy declared.

CHAPTER 51

In the courtyard of the Coronado Paradisio, various chairs and tables with umbrellas were set up to allow visitors to interact with residents. Around the perimeter of the courtyard was finely appointed landscaping that included bougainvilleas, birds of paradise, and canary palms. A food service was set up in the corner for hot and cold drinks and a continental breakfast. Waiters and waitresses served the guests and residents while they visited.

Roger Legion sat at one of the tables admiring the landscape and cleanliness of the facility. He wore a blue, herringbone suit, trademark, white shirt, and a yellow, silk tie with a slight red stripe inlay.

Within a minute, he saw Lester Abrams exit the building into the courtyard. Lester looked gaunt and his cheeks appeared slightly swollen. He wore a black t-shirt that said, 'COR-PARE,' and the same pants that he wore when he arrived. On his feet were orange Crocs. Roger raised his hand to get his attention.

Lester came over to his table and sat across from him.

"Hello, Lester," Roger scanned him as he spoke.

"Roger," Lester said with a slight lisp. He was unable to fully open his mouth.

"How's life in here?"

"Actually, not bad. But, I can only watch so much TV and I can't stand talking about my feelings."

"How are you?" Legion wondered.

"Not bad for a guy with a dislocated jaw. I can't yawn and this place is boring as shit. Oh, I also can't sneeze. That new guy better watch his back, 'cause I'm gonna mop the floor with him," Lester warned.

"No, you're not. You know I don't like it when people talk tough, but can't back it up."

"I'll sue the son of a bitch."

"No, you won't," Roger was definite. "Lester, what am I going to do with you?"

"Let me go. Fire me."

"And what would you tell your next employer? Why were you let go? You'd tell them Roger Legion wanted me to give cocaine to a client and I refused. So, he said 'hit the road.' See, I know you wanna be the good guy, the guy wearing the white hat, the saint. But you and I know the truth. About your drug use, your sale of drugs, and your attempt to murder your wife and unborn child." Roger paused and looked at Lester. "I need to control you. I can make a phone call and you will lose your law license. And you will be ineligible to practice law in the entire United States. So, I can't let you leave. Not yet."

"Can I come back to the firm and work?" Lester's voice echoed desperation.

"Do you think I'm gonna pay for you to be on vacation forever? You need to rebuild my trust in you. You're a good lawyer and you have the potential to be a great lawyer. But for some reason, you went off the rails. Now, you've seen firsthand, the muscle I have in this town. I suggest you avoid my wrath."

Lester realized that he had to live with his situation.

"Have you heard from my wife?"

"She's fine. I send her your paycheck."

"Did she say anything about a divorce?" Lester's voice was skittish.

"Not to me."

"Roger, in here, you have alotta time to think. You know what I was thinkin'? How did you and I get to this place?" Lester was sincere about his inquiry and wasn't talking about the Coronado Paradisio.

The question brought a smile to Roger's face.

"Years ago, when I first got out of law school, I interviewed with this old-time personal injury lawyer, big guy, reminded me of a mortician, who had an office down on 4th and Ash. When I went for the interview, the first question the guy asked me was, 'What kind of lawyer do you want to be?' Well, I thought I would keep it light and I said to him, 'The kind that charges a thousand dollars an hour.' His immediate response was, 'There's no such thing as a thousand dollar an hour lawyer, just thousand dollar an hour clients.'"

Roger allowed the concept to settle in with Lester before he continued.

"He was right. You've got to distinguish yourself from the pack. There are only so many dollars to chase. You and I didn't create the system, but we learned how to operate within it. So now, here we are. You and I both know that if someone needs a lawyer and they have a choice between one who's the nicest guy in the world or one who's a ruthless, no-holds-barred, blood-thirsty SOB, which one are they gonna choose? Don't blame me because you don't like the answer. That's how you and I got here."

Lester seemed to understand Roger's mindset and his success. Roger stood from the table and pushed his chair in. Lester followed suit.

"Three more days and then I'll come and get you," Roger told him.

Roger was not going to offer to shake Lester's hand, but Lester extended his hand to him. Roger shook it and left him with a final admonition.

"Don't throw away what you've worked for the past 10 years."

"I won't."

Roger wanted to believe him, but he knew that once a person goes down a dark path, the most applicable statement is: Once a junkie, always a junkie.

CHAPTER 52

At the Orange County office of the Los Angeles Division of the Federal Bureau of Investigation, Special Agent Oliver Love sat in his 2nd floor office and reviewed various reports dealing with cyber security and a Middle Eastern terrorist cell allegedly involved in swapping arms for drugs. Oliver was 33 years old, 6 feet, 3 inches tall, 215 pounds with the chiseled features of an athlete. He wore a white shirt with a blue tie and blue, striped pants that were part of his suit. His service revolver was a .40 caliber CZ P-06.

On this sunny afternoon, Special Agent Joseph Rossi, who was the Agent-In-Charge of the Orange County office, appeared in his doorway.

"Ollie," Joe called to him catching his attention. "Remember that lady you were telling me about, the bartender, she had some intel on radioactive material comin' in to the Port of L.A.?"

"Uschi Horton," Oliver told him. "They found her dead the next day. The info she told me didn't check out. One of the guys she mentioned was found dead a month earlier."

"Costa Mesa PD found her cell phone. Here's the report," Joe advised and handed a copy to Oliver. "They got some stuff off it, but they're sending it to us for a forensic review."

On the day that Uschi was shot and killed by Kevin Camballa, Remy told Kevin and Hazz to leave her car, with her body in the trunk, in Orange County. They were supposed to throw her cell phone into the ocean. They left her car in the parking lot of the South Coast Plaza and their travels never took them near the ocean. Kevin threw the phone into a dumpster behind a 7-Eleven convenience store. A dumpster-diving, homeless person found it and it subsequently made its way into the hands of the Costa Mesa Police Department.

"Let me know what they find out," Oliver replied.

"I'll have them copy you on the report," Joe told him.

Oliver was bored with the reports he had been reading and decided to peruse the report involving Uschi's phone.

According to the document, the call log on the phone had a variety of incoming calls made from either a public phone, like a payphone, library, or school or from a 'dead' number. A 'dead' number is one that is no longer in service. It appeared that she received a call for a minute then she would immediately return the call to the same number. This technique is commonly used by criminals to avoid telephone lines that might have traps on incoming calls. A trap line identifies the physical location of the call if you are calling from a landline.

The cell phone towers for Uschi's outgoing calls were located near the Swing and A Miss bar. The incoming calls pinged off cell towers all over San Diego County.

According to the 'Maps' app on the phone, the last address that was sought was on Sampson Street, in the Logan Heights area of San Diego. The Costa Mesa Police identified it as an auto repair shop. Their information was stale. It was actually the Deus X Machine Shop.

A copy of all the photos from the telephone's camera was contained within the report. Oliver went through the 72 photos. One photo in particular caught his attention. It was a group of people sitting around a table at a birthday party. Oliver had seen one of the men somewhere before, but the name and place were not clicking. He decided to run the photo through the FBI's Facial Recognition Database.

Soon, Oliver would have a name to go with the face.

CHAPTER 53

At 8:05 a.m., on one of the 6 screens that sat before Bob Brockman, he checked the image quality of a video camera that was located within a pair of glasses, which he wore. The glasses had clear lenses and looked like a pair of plastic, lightweight reading glasses that you could buy in a drug store. He took the glasses and continually checked the focus of the image from various distances.

"Remy," Brockman called out. "It's ready to go."

Remy entered the administrative end of the building from the workshop area. He wore jeans, work boots, a red and black checkered flannel shirt, a fluorescent, yellow vest with orange piping, and he carried a white hard hat with the Caltrans logo.

Caltrans is the abbreviated name for the California Department of Transportation.

"Let's run a test on these things," Brockman told Remy.

Remy set the hard hat down and put the glasses on.

"Come here," Brockman requested. Remy walked around the computer desk to see the screens. "The focus on it is pretty good. If there's any delicate work, you have to get within 12 to 15 inches of it."

"All right," Remy acknowledged.

"Here's the earpiece." Brockman handed him a small, sealed plastic bag that contained a device that looked like a petite hearing aid. "Let's check it for a sound level."

The device was actually a hearing transmission device. Brockman would be able to hear Remy's conversations and also speak to him through the ear piece. The device was checked in the clean room and Remy demanded that it be germ-free before he would place it in his ear.

Remy adjusted the device into his ear and gave Brockman a thumb's up.

"How does it sound, Remy?" Brockman quizzed.

Remy raised his thumb and Brockman adjusted the volume from his on-screen controls.

"How 'bout now?"

"It's good," Remy replied.

"Okay, now walk away and either talk to one of the guys or clap your hands."

Remy walked around the partition and Brockman had the same line of sight as Remy on one of his screens through the video glasses. Remy saw Pike washing his hands.

"Pike, how's the downstairs activity?"

"Good," Pike told him while drying his hands. "We should be finished with the drilling tonight. Then, the final Dexpan injections and camouflage, and it's ready to go."

Pike was referring to the drilling at the base of Tower 20 of the bridge. As explained to Sir Basil Crumpton, Remy and his crew were engaging in a drilling process at the floor of San Diego Bay to essentially allow the tower to be nearly free flowing from its base. The Dexpan is a non-explosive demolition agent that keeps the top of the tower from sinking tightly back into the base. Finally, to camouflage their activities, they placed an elastomeric coating over their work area and match the color and rough exterior to the rest of the tower. From a distance, their work was not noticeable.

"Excellent," Remy beamed. "Tell Philippe to recharge the air tanks and I'll go with you guys tonight for a final inspection. We'll also sink the bolts for the hold downs."

The bolts that Remy mentioned would hold the steel containers, loaded with Semtex explosive, sufficient to take down the towers.

"Consider it done," Pike told him.

Then, Remy heard a voice in his ear.

"Remy, get back here, we gotta finish this," Brockman demanded.

"How does it look and sound?" Remy inquired as he walked back to Brockman.

"El perfecto. I know we went over this before, but let's do it one more time."

Brockman opened a small, leather briefcase that sat on the computer table. Inside were various tools for precision work, such as small screwdrivers, wrenches, a drill, and cutting tools for piping, wires, and cable.

"This is the device: a splice hijacker." Brockman held up a small collar ring, not much bigger than a ring a person would wear with a small color indicator on the outside of the ring collar. "It's an optoelectronic device that controls and redirects the optical feed from its original source. I have it in three different sizes for you. All you need to do is splice it in. What you're gonna look for is the input on the video deck or transmission device. You understand?"

"Yeah," Remy told him while examining the various devices.

"The connector is basically a rigid cylindrical barrel surrounded by a sleeve that holds the barrel in its mating socket. The mating mechanism can be 'push and click,' 'turn and latch,' which is like a bayonet, or screw-in, which is threaded. A problem with the connection will cause a gap loss. That will affect the signal strength and I don't know if we'd be able to totally blind them."

"Once you get the device connected, you just place the power source and turn it on. Put it somewhere outta sight. It can be within 50 feet of the splice hijacker." Brockman was serious in his delivery.

"You got this now?" Brockman was sincere in his concern.

"I can do it," Remy assured him.

"You sure you don't want me to go?"

"No. Don't worry. I appreciate the offer."

Remy did appreciate the offer, but he knew that if Brockman was ever forced into a corner, he wouldn't be able to get out. He was more valuable in the shop performing his electronic wizardry.

Within the building, a computer voice filled the air, repeating over and over again: "PERIMETER COMPROMISED." Brockman pulled up the outside cameras on the screens and saw it was Alton in his police cruiser. He silenced the computer voice with several key strokes.

"Good luck, Remy. I'll be right there with ya."

They exchanged a handshake and Remy walked to the closest door, strolling out to the parking lot to meet Alton.

CHAPTER 54

Every morning since Luke Cordel brought Karla Mulry home, after their courthouse tour, he would arrive outside of her apartment at 6:45 a.m. to give her a ride to work. He also made sure that his work day was complete by 5:15 p.m., so he could give her a ride home. Each time, she told him that it was not necessary, but always took him up on his offer.

The ride was always quiet with Luke's never ending attempt at small talk. Something about the ride this morning was different.

"Are you working on any interesting cases, Miss Mulry?" Luke innocently inquired.

"No. Let's not talk about work, Mr. Cordel," she urged as she watched the various cars and people, wondering where they were going.

When his car stopped at red lights, Luke tried to avoid staring at her, but he found it difficult to do. She had not one hair out of place and her scant make-up highlighted what was already perfection. Her clothes were modest, yet she elevated them to a designer level. In Luke's eyes, she was somewhat of a paradox, because she made the clothes look beautiful, instead of the clothes making her look beautiful.

"I was wondering," Luke chanced, "do you have a driver's license?"

"Why? Do you think I'm stupid?" Karla responded with histrionic flare.

"No. I would have never asked that question, if I thought it would upset you. I was just wondering?"

"Well, I don't have one," her voice calmed. "I took the test twice and I flunked it twice. So, your little perfect girlfriend isn't so perfect."

At that moment, Luke did not care where he was or even if the car went off a cliff. The only thing on his mind was that in her dismissive tirade, Karla referred to herself as his girlfriend. All he wanted to do was think about her comment. An errant driver, cutting him off, brought Luke back to reality.

"Driving is overrated," Luke said. "Sometimes it's nice to be the passenger."

Karla continued her gaze out the window. Then, without provocation, she asked, "So, what do you do for fun?"

Luke wanted to have a snappy answer, but thought he should just play it cool.

"Not much. There are certain shows that I like on TV. I read and follow sports. Sometimes, I like going to a shooting range and target practice."

"A shooting range?" Karla's voice was curious.

"When I was in the Marines, I spent alotta time developing shooting skills, so I wanna make sure I don't get too rusty." Luke hoped she was not an anti-gun proponent.

"I'd like to try that sometime. When I was young, I had an uncle who was a hunter. He would take me along with all my male cousins out for skeet shooting. He taught me how to do trick shots, twirl a six-shooter, and re-holster it all in one motion," Karla's voice echoed pride.

"Now that is something I'd like to see. Are you available on Saturday?" Luke was hopeful.

"I'll have to check my busy calendar and let you know, Mr. Cordel," Karla retorted. "Perhaps, I could ask you a favor."

"Sure," Luke said, as he thought this day just keeps getting better and better.

"I've got to bring my dog to the vet on Thursday. I usually leave work early when I bring her, so I can pick her up before the vet closes."

"Miss Mulry, that's no problem at all. I look forward to it. What kind of dog do you have?"

"A West Highland terrier," Karla smiled.

"What's your dog's name?" Luke wondered.

"Sophie. It's a princess name."

"I look forward to meeting Sophie."

Luke was hopeful that the ice surrounding Karla was beginning to crack or, at least, melt.

CHAPTER 55

The ride from the Deus X Machine Shop to the employee maintenance entrance of the Coronado Bay Bridge took approximately 12 minutes. Both Alton and Remy did not say a word until their destination was in sight.

"Alton, listen to me," Remy demanded Alton's attention. "If anything goes sour in there, I'm gonna grab your gun. Don't fight with me. I won't kill anyone. I'm just gonna get out if I have to. If you have a safety on your holster, take it off. I'll make sure you get the gun back."

"Just make it look real," Alton retorted. "What's the name on your badge?"

"Steve Jones," Remy told him.

"You don't sound like a Steve Jones."

"I will." Remy's voice was certain.

Alton parked his police cruiser on the street near a fenced area that surrounded two solid doors that allowed entrance onto the interior structure of the bridge. Within the fenced areas were various Caltrans vehicles and tractor trailer sized containers used for storage of materials for repairs, painting, and electrical needs. Outside of the doors was a video camera and a keypad with a card swipe device to allow authorized individuals access. On the keypad was also a call button.

Alton pushed the call button twice and awaited a response.

"Can I help you?" a voice asked.

"This is officer Alton Burchesky. California Highway Patrol. I'm escorting a Caltrans employee for maintenance work."

"Someone will be right there," the voice again replied.

Within 60 seconds, one of the doors opened and a Hispanic man, approximately 45 years old, 5 feet, 8 inches tall, 180 pounds, with a dark complexion, glasses, and a thick moustache stood in the doorway. He wore jeans, a blue, flannel shirt, and the same yellow and orange fluorescent vest and hardhat as Remy. His face beamed when he saw Alton.

"*¿Cómo está usted, jefe?*(How are you, boss?)" his voice was exuberant.

"Hey, Romo, how's it hanging?" Alton asked.

"Low and lazy. Like a gringo watching a Mexican cut his grass," Romo bellowed. "Come on in."

Remy smiled as he was pleased with Alton's banter with his apparent friend, Romo. The California Highway Patrol guards both the top of the bridge and the maintenance area under it. Romo knew Alton from his various patrol visits to the bridge.

"What brings you over here?" Romo wondered.

"One of your fellow co-workers was workin' on some of the video stuff in the Control Center down at the station. Romo, this is Steve," Alton told him.

"How are ya?" Remy said, as he shook Romo's hand, without the slightest hint of an accent.

"Good. They usually let us know when somebody's coming," Romo told them.

"I was already down here and there seems to be a hiccup in the system. The picture quality is comin' and going," Remy replied.

"You shoulda called. We could probably take care of it here. What office are you from?" Romo asked.

Immediately, Remy heard Bob Brockman in his ear.

"Santa Ana."

"Santa Ana," Remy proclaimed.

"Let me ask you somethin', then," Remy thought he was going to ask him about a specific individual or situation in the Santa Ana office. "Do they pay you a shift differential to come down here?"

Brockman had an answer.

"Only after 8 hours."

"After 8 hours," Remy answered.

"Lousy union," Romo was disgusted. What are they good for?"

Brockman's voice filled Remy's ear.

"Collecting dues."

"Collectin' dues, I guess," Remy replied.

"Damn straight. How many years you got in?" Romo wondered.

"Eight," Remy answered.

"I got nineteen in this February," Romo proudly announced.

Brockman interjected, "Ask him if he's gonna pull the plug at 20."

"You gonna pull the plug at 20?" Remy asked.

"I gotta see what my bill situation is then. My lottery numbers haven't come in yet. You ever try to compute retirement prior to age 60? You gotta be a freakin' rocket scientist to figure that out. So, the answer to your question is: Maybe."

"I gotta get going," Alton said.

"Come on back to the electrical room," Romo told them as he open a 2nd set of secured doors. "Maybe I should call somebody?" Romo wondered and looked at Alton then Remy.

Brockman once again was ready.

"Tell him you don't have a work order for this. It just saves you another trip down."

"I don't have a work order for this. When I did the repairs at the station, they asked me to look at some of the bridge cameras where the picture jumped and lost image quality. I think it's a gap loss. Something is affecting one of the connections."

"*Très bien*, my student." Brockman was impressed that Remy shared the tidbit of knowledge with Romo regarding the gap loss.

"Between the wind and the bird shit, everything starts to fall apart," Romo concluded. "What do you want for 40 years? You know that bird shit is like acid. Come on, let's go back."

Romo escorted Remy and Alton to the electrical room and all three entered. The room was loud with a variety of circuitry control devices for the lights, cameras, and telephones used on the bridge. Because of the high propensity for suicides, a call box system existed throughout the bridge, complete with a direct line to a suicide hotline, in an attempt to discourage any would-be jumpers.

"These control the cameras," Romo said pointing to a portion of the southern wall that contained optical transmission devices, the circuitry for the cameras, and a main circuit breaker, with the words, "LEAVE ON,' under it.

Remy set his tool suitcase on the ground and opened it. Brockman began giving him directions. Remy took out a needle nose pliers and a regular small pliers and began his work.

"Got any inside dirt on anything goin' on at Del Mar?" Romo asked Alton. "That one you gave me on that horse, Sorta Sorta, was a nice payday," Remy proudly boasted.

Romo was referring to the Del Mar Race Track. Located in northern San Diego County, it is one of the pre-eminent thoroughbred horse racing venues in Southern California.

"Let's go outside and talk," Alton told him, acting as if he wanted to keep any tip information away from the other individual in the room. Romo and Alton left Remy alone in the room.

Remy followed Brockman's instructions precisely, including a step to avoid interruption in any video transmission, while the splice hijacker was installed. To those watching any video of the bridge at that time, it appeared as a simple black screen, and then the picture returned immediately. This would be a common sight when a bird would suddenly block a camera.

"Remy," Brockman's serious tone continued, "put the power source on the back of the telephone box to your right. It's held on with a magnet."

Remy turned on the power source and mounted it to the back of the telephone box. Brockman checked the system at his end.

"We've got a connection," Brockman told him. "There's only one final thing: You need to re-boot the system. Don't touch the circuit breaker; it'll take too long to power up the system. You need to find a re-set button on the video deck."

Remy searched for a re-set button without success.

"Ask Romo," Brockman told him.

Remy went to the door of the room and opened it.

"Hey, Romo," Remy interrupted their conversation. "Do you know where the re-set button is on the video deck?"

"If it needs to be re-set, they do it down at the CHP office?"

Remy could feel the acid in his stomach start to rise up. Things were going extremely well up to this point.

"Do you want me to call 'em?" Romo asked.

"It's gotta be done," Remy told him with an air of finality. He raised his hand and motioned to Alton to enter the room.

Romo took out his cell phone and dialed. Remy moved to the right side of Alton. He looked at Alton in the eye and then glanced down at his gun. Then, Remy heard Brockman's voice.

"Wait, Remy. There's another way."

"Hey, Judy. It's Romo. Let me talk to Karen."

"I just remembered something," Remy spoke up to gain Romo's attention. "I can take care of it here."

"You sure?" Romo asked turning away from his call. He then turned back to his cell phone. "Karen, we got it under control here. Thanks, anyway." Romo ended the communication.

Brockman's voice returned to Remy's ear.

"Essentially, we're gonna unplug it and plug it back in. Look at the bottom of the box."

Remy squatted and the bottom of the metal box was within Remy's line of sight and Brockman's via Remy's video glasses.

"The line on the left side is bolted in. That's the power cord. Use the drill to take the bolts off."

Remy followed Brockman's directions and removed the metal cover on the power cord.

"Pull the cord out," Brockman said, "and I'll tell you when to put it back in."

Remy pulled it out and after 3 seconds, Brockman told him to put it back in.

"Put the cover back on and get out." Brockman concluded his transmission.

Anyone watching the bridge cameras would have seen the cameras go black and turn back on immediately with a fleeting message that said, 'VIDEO INTERRUPTED.'

Remy re-installed the power cord cover and told Alton and Romo that he was done.

"You're all set," Remy proclaimed and shook hands with Romo.

"Thanks, a lot," Romo said and turned to Alton. "If you hear anything about what we were talkin' about, you're gonna let me know, right?"

"Absolutely," Alton acknowledged.

The three men walked out into the breeze of the maintenance walkway. Remy could not help but stop to admire the alluring view of San Diego to the right and the tranquil innocence of the Pacific Ocean to the left.

CHAPTER 56

On this Tuesday morning, Roger Legion sat at his desk reviewing new lawsuits that had been received the day before. Roger would generally handle all the Answers that needed to be filed, especially if they could be done from mere boilerplate language. He also made sure that any time-sensitive matters were handled immediately. Finally, he would determine which lawyer was best suited to handle a particular case, including himself.

As he turned the page on the pleading, his office phone rang and Nina's voice filled the air.

"Yes," Legion responded.

"Patrick Madore from Newford is on line 3."

"Thank you."

Pat was a claims representative from Newford Casualty Insurance. Roger had made arrangements for Luke to take Pat and his son to a monster truck event over the past weekend.

"Hello, Pat," Roger answered in an ebullient tone.

"Roger, how are you?" Pat's voice matched Rogers in enthusiasm.

"I'm fine. How 'bout you?"

"Wonderful. I just wanted to let you know that my son and

I had a great time with Luke on Saturday night. What a nice guy," Pat professed.

"How were the monster trucks?" Roger wondered.

"They were great, but earlier in the day, Luke brought us to a shooting range in Kearny Mesa. He's got one of those AR-15 rifles and he let my son shoot. I even shot it. We met his friend-young lady-real cute. He was teaching my son how to shoot correctly and my son couldn't get enough. If my wife knew, she'd probably say 'No,' but I just thought it was so cool."

Legion suspected that the lady friend mentioned was Karla Mulry.

"I didn't know about his talent with weapons, but he is a marine," Roger confessed.

"I was tellin' the claims manager, Eddie, and he said that he'd like to go sometime," Pat added.

"We'll make that happen."

"Roger, I got some files over here for ya. Four new ones. I was wondering if maybe Luke could handle 'em?" Pat inquired.

"Don't worry, Pat. We'll make that happen," Roger told him with a smile from ear to ear.

"You gonna send somebody over?"

"They're on their way," Legion confirmed.

"I really want to say thanks for everything, my friend," Pat sincerely stated.

"You need anything, you call me," Roger added.

"Will do. Take it easy." With that, the phone call ended.

Roger returned the phone receiver to its cradle and turned to his flat screen monitor. He forwarded his standard e-mail message to Luke, telling him to come to his office ASAP. Roger then picked up the phone and pushed 2 numbers.

"Louise, please send a runner to Newford. They have 4 new

files for us." Then after a moment, he added, "Thank you."

As Roger hung up the phone, Luke appeared at his door.

"You wanted to see me, sir?" he inquired.

"Come on in, Roger told him. He entered the office and stood in front of Roger's desk. Luke's stance was that of a military formation with his hands behind his back.

"Pat Madore is sending over 4 new files and he wants you to handle 'em. He said he and his son had a good time on Saturday night."

"He's a nice guy and his son's a good kid," Luke replied.

"Pat was impressed with your shooting ability. He also said your lady friend was cute."

"The facts are what the facts are, right?" Luke was wearing a mischievous grin. "But, she's not my girlfriend."

Roger stared at him for a moment with an awkward gaze.

"Did you fill out your expense report yet?" he inquired.

"Yes," Luke answered.

"Did you include the costs for the range?"

"No. That was my idea."

Roger stood from his chair and reached into his pocket as he spoke.

"This place is not a charity. You do something for this place, you shouldn't have to go outta pocket. What did you spend at the shooting range?"

"The ammo was 120 bucks."

"That was it?"

"Yeah."

Roger pulled a money clip from his pants pocket. He removed the clip and peeled off two $100 bills. He gently tossed them to the desk in front of Luke.

"I don't have change," Luke said as he picked them up.

"Keep it."

"Thanks," Luke acknowledged.

"Pat said that the claims manager, Eddie, wants to go shooting. If either of those guys ask you about it, make it happen. Whenever you do anything with Eddie, make sure you have one or more of our guys with you. Eddie likes to do everything to excess, in particular, eating and drinking. He also likes the girls. So, I don't suggest that you invite your lady friend. You have to make sure that one of our guys is a designated driver and make sure that Eddie gets home. Understand?"

"Understood."

"That's it," Roger advised as he returned to his chair. Luke started walking to the door.

"Luke," Roger said, requesting his attention. "Don't forget to bill for this inter-office conference."

"Are you kidding?" Luke inquired, because the conversation had nothing to do with any legal work.

There was no smile on Roger's face.

"No. Bill it to the file that you and I are going to go to court on this morning. The case management conference. It's a Newford file. That's what we have to do around here to keep everybody happy."

Rogers comment hit Luke like cold water from a shower. It was obvious that all of Roger's hospitality events came with a price and, as always, billing cast a dark pall on the practice of law. But it was the enigma of Roger Legion that continued to amaze him.

CHAPTER 57

At the Deus X Machine Shop, Pike continued to weld steel reinforcements on the bumper of a 32-foot straight-back or box truck. The box of the truck, where the payload was kept was 24 feet long. This would be the area filled with Semtex explosive. The Semtex would not be loaded until the morning of the bridge event.

There were 2 of this size truck and 2 trucks that were 20 feet long, with a box of 12 feet. These were the trucks that would be used to block the lanes of the bridge over the area where the 2 towers were set to be knocked down.

Philippe used a pneumatic paint brush and stencils to paint the name D-A-Go Trucking on all the doors of the trucks, complete with a palm tree logo. Hazz and Emile worked in the clean room on the final circuitry for the harnesses that would connect to the detonators for the Semtex. They tested each individual circuit to make sure it was collapsible. This meant that if the circuit failed for some reason, it would not stop the other circuits from sending a charge to the detonators.

Remy, Kevin, and Brockman were in the parking lot of the machine shop leering at a new, black Cadillac Escalade that had just been delivered. Each man took turns sitting in the driver's seat and passenger seat of the vehicle. The plan was for Remy and Kevin to be in this vehicle on the day of the bridge event. Brockman was especially disheartened by the fact that in approximately 48 hours, the vehicle would end up on the bottom of the bay along with a ½ mile chunk of the bridge roadway.

All three men stood at the side of the vehicle gazing at it. Remy stood between Kevin and Brockman.

"It's beautiful, no?" Remy asked both Kevin and Brockman.

"Like a fine Merlot ho," Brockman replied.

"How would you know?" Kevin asked with a dismissive tone.

"At least I can reach the floor pedals," Brockman shot back.

"Do they have a comic book that teaches how to drive?" Kevin sarcastically quizzed.

"It's on the higher shelves; that's why you can't see it," Brockman again retorted.

"Were you born an asshole or is it something you have to work at?"

"Were you born a midget, or do you prefer dwarf?"

"That's enough!" Remy shut the conversation down.

Brockman wanted to get in one more comment.

"Don't mock the Brock, little man. Or you're gonna find my shoe up your little ass."

"Bring it on, little girl," Kevin told him with a sinister look, ready to begin hand-to-hand combat. "I'll come and talk to ya when you don't have your bodyguard around." The bodyguard he referred to was Remy.

"Let's go inside," Remy told them and led the way.

As soon as Remy entered the building, he called out to the other men.

"Emile, Pike, Hazz, Philippe. Get over here."

Within 6 seconds, all four men appeared from the production side of the building. Remy waved them over to Brockman's computer table. Brockman took his seat. Remy was on one side of Brockman and Kevin was on the other.

"Philippe, you charge the air tanks?" Remy asked.

"All set," he replied.

"Pike, the template ready?"

"Ready to go," he answered.

Pike had made a template outline of the steel-reinforced container that would be filled with Semtex explosive and bolted to the side of the 2 towers, which Remy planned to demolish.

"Alton is coming over this afternoon, so we can get the frequencies off the CHP car," Remy told them. "Tonight, we'll all go out to the water. Pike, you stay topside with the boat. We'll take the template and sink the concrete anchors to bolt the containers on to the side of the towers."

"We gonna bolt the containers tonight?" Emile asked.

"No. I wanna do that tomorrow night. Last possible moment. Hazz, Philippe - you guys test everything one more time. All the harnesses and the connections to the explosives. Work with Brock to make sure everything goes smoothly." Both men shook their heads affirmatively. "Pike, what else do we need for the trucks?"

"I'm puttin' a winch at the end of each vehicle that abuts the outside of the bridge. We made a special grappling hook to snag the side of the bridge. Any problem with that, were gonna have to have Philippe repel down to catch it. I've got it weighted properly. We shouldn't have any problems."

"Sounds good," Remy acknowledged. Anybody got any questions?"

Brockman looked at Kevin.

"Is it really a small world after all?" Brockman asked, referencing the Disney attraction and smiled at the other men.

As Brockman turned back to Kevin, Kevin's right arm moved like an industrial piston and clocked Brockman squarely in the jaw. He flew out of the chair to the floor right at Remy's feet. Remy looked at Kevin and both were unsure if the other was going to make a tactical movement. Brockman sat up on the floor and shook off the punch.

"You know," Remy told Kevin in a deadly serious tone, "what we have had to do to get to this point. What we all had to sacrifice. And now you wanna throw it all away?"

"I'm not gonna put up with his shit anymore," Kevin retorted and his tone matched Remy's.

"You're gonna put up with his shit until this job is done. You understand me?"

As Remy spoke, Brockman stood up.

"I want him dead," Brockman declared. "We can finish it without him," Brockman spoke as he gave Kevin an angry stare.

"SHUT YOUR MOUTH!" Remy barked at Brockman.

"Hold it," Kevin interjected before anything further was said. "I can put up with him until the job is done."

"I told you once before," Brock again raised his voice, "don't mock the Brock. I take care of business."

Brockman was making reference to the tattoo on the back of his bald head that was in 2 inch high letters of I.T.C.O.B. It stood for 'I took care of business.' It was supposed to imply that he had killed someone.

"I'm shakin' in my boots. I'm gonna go take a nap, ladies. All this tough talk is wearing me out."

Kevin walked away and held up his middle finger to Brockman, while not even looking at him. Kevin feared no one, but

Remy did concern him. He knew Remy would kill him without thinking twice. Kevin knew from experience that Remy had no interest in self-preservation. His focus was the objective. If his life was part of the price, so be it. Anyone who blocked his path to the objective was expendable. To Remy, everyone was replaceable.

CHAPTER 58

Roger Legion and Luke Cordel returned from a case management conference dealing with a car accident that caused a pre-teenager facial trauma, a broken leg, and a broken arm. Roger observed while Luke handled all the questions from the Judge and the plaintiff attorney, as well as astute questions put forth by Luke. Roger kept a poker face until they were in the elevator rising to the law firm.

"That case has to settle," Roger told Luke with a tone of sorrow.

"Even with the comparative liability of the mother?" Luke wondered.

"That would be dangerous to pitch to a jury," Roger warned. "She wasn't doing anything outrageous and her kid was smashed up pretty bad. I'm sure on the stand she'd say that she wishes it was her who went to the hospital that day."

"Did you read the deposition of our driver?"

"On paper, he comes across as a shithead. I can imagine what he's like in person. Let's tag team this one for a settlement conference. I know this plaintiff attorney. He may want to go to mediation."

"Where should we put our energy then?" Luke asked.

"When you do the report to the insurance company, ask for settlement authority of $250,000. Before you send the report, call the claims handler and set up a lunch with the three of us. They have to do a lot of paperwork, so the sooner we get goin' on it, the better."

"Understood," Luke acknowledged as the elevator doors opened to the 24th floor lobby of Legion & Associates.

As both men stepped off the elevator, they saw the white-shirted back, and could hear the voice, of another Legion attorney interrogating Nina, the receptionist.

"Well, where is he? I need to talk to him. Now!"

With that, Nina pointed in the direction of the elevator, and the attorney turned to see Roger Legion emerge from it.

The voice belonged to a Legion lawyer named Ethan Paul. If Roger Legion could select one attorney to clone for an army of lawyers, he would select Ethan Paul. He was 32 years old, 6 feet, 2 inches tall, 240 pounds, with black, wavy hair and thick, black, Wayfarer glasses.

What Roger admired most about Ethan was his imposing, intimidating look. Before he even opened his mouth, he could elicit fear from an adversary that would never be acknowledged, but always gave him an advantage. Like a bouncer in a bar, he looked like he was ready to crack a skull if anyone said the wrong thing to him.

In reality, Ethan was more of a gentle giant, who was very compartmentalized. He would like to say that he knew a little about a lot of things, so he could converse with anyone on any topic. This was another valuable skill that Legion always sought out and continued to hone in his attorneys. Ethan knew his limitations, but no one else did. This added to his mystique and his danger factor.

"Ethan?" Roger asked as he approached him. "What's goin' on?"

"We've got a problem," he countered and let a moment pass for Roger and Luke to stop within arm's length of Ethan. "Remember that case where the guy was showboating in the roller rink. He tried to go under another guys legs and flipped him?"

"Yeah," Roger acknowledged.

"The plaintiff attorney set his deposition 3 times. He told me he was gonna show up 3 times. He never did. Plaintiff brought a motion for sanctions. The excuse was that his grandmother was sick and then she died. The judge denied the motion for sanctions, but required us to produce her obituary. I couldn't find it. I called his house and guess who answers?" Ethan's voice echoed surrender.

"The grandmother?" Roger said bitterly.

"You got it, but it gets better," Ethan told him sarcastically. "When I tell the grandmother that I'm his lawyer, she said that she's left a lot of messages and why didn't I call? I didn't know what she was talking about. She tells me that her grandson, our client, killed a guy in a bar last night."

Roger's mind moved into overdrive and a series of questions, demanding direct answers, followed.

"Has it been in the paper?"

"A small article. No names," Ethan replied.

"Who's the plaintiff attorney?"

"A guy up in Los Angeles."

"Where's the plaintiff located?"

"Boulder, Colorado."

"Who's the claims handler?"

"Bernadette DiMeo at O-RISK-A. She knows about it. She wants to talk to you."

O-RISK-A National Insurance was a large, general liability insurer located in Oriskany, New York. They had a local claims office in San Diego and all of their defense work went to Legion & Associates.

"Get the file and meet me at my office," Legion told Ethan then turned to Luke. "Let's go to work."

Roger and Luke scurried to Roger's office at a pace that would seem to indicate that the building was on fire.

CHAPTER 59

Union Street separated the Hall of Justice Courthouse at 330 W. Broadway from the San Diego Main Courthouse located at 220 W. Broadway. The buildings were connected by a glass walkway bridge located 4 stories up and across Union Street.

A black, late model, Cadillac Escalade drove southbound on Union Street. The driver was Hazz, the member of Remy's crew proficient in electrical engineering, in particular, the collapsible circuit. When the Escalade reached the corner of Union and Broadway, Remy stepped out from the passenger seat and his brother, Emile, who was sitting behind Remy, also exited the vehicle.

Both men wore suits and sunglasses. They also carried thin briefcases. Remy's suit was charcoal with a light blue shirt and a darker blue tie with white stripes. Emile's suit was a blue pinstripe with a white shirt and a blue, paisley pattern tie. Remy headed to the Hall of Justice, while Emile crossed the street toward the entrance of the Main Courthouse.

Remy and Emile both produced a State Bar of California card, along with a picture ID, and they were allowed admission through the attorney entrance to each of the buildings.

Remy proceeded to the center of the first floor, where he stepped onto an escalator that brought him to the second floor. He began a slow trek around the perimeter of the floor, noticing the various courtrooms, attorneys, and any San Diego County Sheriffs or bailiffs. He also noted the location of the men's room.

Remy then stepped onto a second escalator and proceeded to the third floor. He once again began his slow trek to observe activity and stopped at the Department 62 courtroom. Outside the courtroom, on a corkboard, was posted the court's calendar for the day. Remy looked through it, not with any interest, but to observe the activity in Department 63. This was the department of Judge Gene Garubo, the man who was the target of Alton's ire and Remy's reason for being in the courthouse. Outside of Department 63, there were two sheriff's deputies posted. One was a woman and the other was a man with a walking cast.

Remy knew it was a set-up. The Sheriff's Department was setting up a decoy. Judge Gene Garubo was not going to be in Department 63.

In the main courthouse, Emile had ascended two escalators and took a seat on a bench outside the closest courtroom. He removed a newspaper from his briefcase and began to read it. Emile's cell phone rang.

"Yeah," Emile answered.

"Tell Hazz, it's gonna be a little while," Remy advised.

"Your friend said 12:00," Emile warned.

"It'll be done by 12:00." Remy was not concerned.

"Okay. Just tell me when you're ready," Emile replied and disconnected the phone.

Remy decided to take another walk around the perimeter of each floor of the courthouse, but he did not have to go very far. As he walked around the 4th floor, two men in suits were sitting outside the doors to Department 64, one floor up from Gene Garubo's assigned courtroom. One man was totally bald and the other had a flat top haircut. Their suits were ill-fitting because, upon closer examination, they were wearing bulletproof vests. Remy also noticed that they wore wireless earpieces for a cellular phone. He could see the coiled cord that went behind them and into their suit coats. The earpieces were for their service radios.

Now, Remy knew that Judge Gene Garubo was in Department 64. He went into the men's room, entered the only stall, and closed the stall door. He set down his briefcase, removed his suit coat and the belt from his pants. He took the end of the belt and put it through the buckle. He pulled it until it was snug around his right hand and palm. Remy then put on the suit coat. The belt ran from his hand up his right arm. He exited the stall and the men's room.

Behind all of the courtrooms on a particular floor was a common hallway, only accessible to courthouse personnel. A person would travel through this hallway to proceed from the courtroom to a judge's chambers.

In addition, each courtroom had a small vestibule that separated the courtroom doors from the public hallway doors. This area served to minimize noise from people entering and leaving the courtroom.

Remy looked inside Department 64 and could see a flurry of activity. He then moved to Department 65 and the only person inside the courtroom was a bailiff, named Toby Wilkes, sitting at a desk on the right side of the room, talking on the phone and reading pending protocol modifications. The bailiff was in his late 50s, 5 feet, 9 inches tall, 210 pounds. He looked heavier due to his bulletproof vest. Remy entered the courtroom and walked toward him.

"*Excusez-moi, monsieur*. (Excuse me, sir.)" Remy said with a smile. The bailiff looked up at him and scanned him up and down, then smiled.

"Can I help you?" he asked.

"*Parlez-vous Français?* (Do you speak French?)" Remy wondered.

"*Un peu,* (A little,)" the bailiff responded, then added, "No, not really."

"I need," Remy's French accent was thicker than usual and he acted as if he was struggling for the words, "to go." Remy acted frustrated like he could not pull up the word. He then pointed to a piece of paper in his hand.

"Let me see it," the bailiff requested and Remy handed it to him. "This is in the Main Courthouse. The next building," Wilkes told him and pointed toward the eastern end of the building where the walkway bridge was located.

"*Où est-il?* (Where is it?)" Remy asked. "Where?" Remy again struggled for the word.

"Let me show ya," the bailiff told him as he stood up from his seat.

Wilkes walked toward the entrance doors and Remy followed him. As they walked, Remy loosened the belt around his hand and slipped it off. As the bailiff went through the first set of doors, with Remy close behind, Remy swiped the belt around his neck and snapped it back with a powerful tug. The belt closed tightly around the bailiff's neck and began to strangle Wilkes. Both men were now in the vestibule area. The bailiff struggled for breath and initially was trying to pull the belt off his neck. Remy wrapped the other end of the belt around his right hand, while still pulling it and put his back against the bailiff. Remy leaned forward and lifted the bailiff off his feet. All of the bailiff's weight was on his neck as he was being hung by the belt.

Wilkes' face had turned beet red and Remy noticed that he was trying to unholster his Glock G22 chambered in a .40 caliber. While still holding him on his back, Remy was able to keep Wilkes' hand away from the gun. He let him roll off his back, to the side, and slam to the floor. Remy grabbed the Glock and placed his left foot on Wilkes' throat. He put all of his weight on that foot and began to bounce on it like he was crushing a can.

When Remy was satisfied that there was no more fight left in Wilkes, he stepped off his throat. Remy pulled the slide on the Glock back far enough to make sure there was a live round in the chamber. Remy then removed a 2nd magazine clip from the bailiff's belt and locked the doors, so no one could enter from the public hallway. He then straightened his clothes and hair. He took a handkerchief from his pocket to dab a minimal amount of perspiration from his forehead.

Remy looked down at Wilkes and saw he was not moving. He noticed that the bailiff also wore a Taser gun. Remy removed it from its holster and fired it point blank into the groin of the bailiff. Wilkes did not move. Remy lightly tossed the Taser at him.

He took out his cell phone and dialed Emile. It was 11:55 a.m.

"Yeah," Emile answered on the second ring.

"Showtime," Remy told him.

CHAPTER 60

Ethan converged on Roger and Luke at the door to Roger's office, carrying a thin file, all three men moved at a brisk clip. Roger led the way in and began by snapping his fingers to request the file. Ethan handed the file to Roger and all three sat around Roger's desk. Ethan leaned forward in his seat in anticipation of questions and orders from Roger. Luke was there as a student, so he would not open his mouth unless requested.

"Do we have a demand?" Roger queried.

"Nothing official. He told me he was looking for $15,000," Ethan replied.

"Have we offered anything?" Roger again posed his inquiry.

"No. I told him I was thinking about $2,500." Ethan retorted.

"What are the meds?"

"Mainly, soft tissue. After the incident, he's only been seen by a chi-ro."

Ethan was advising that the plaintiff suffered a 'soft tissue' injury, which is generally the result of a sprain or strain. Since the incident, this plaintiff had only been seeing a chiropractor for treatment.

"What's the dollar amount for the total meds?" Roger demanded.

"Forty-seven hundred."

"Are there any hard meds?"

'Hard' meds are costs incurred that would generally not be subject to negotiation of costs because they are demanded by the injury.

"The ambulance ride and the emergency room," Ethan told him.

"How much?"

"Fourteen hundred."

Roger thought for a moment as he lightly pulled his right hand down along his cheeks to his chin.

"Is there a lien for the fourteen hundred?" Roger asked.

A third party involved in an accident, such as a hospital, medical provider, or ambulance company have a right to recover their costs from any settlement by placing a lien on the settlement. The amount is often reduced or compromised to expedite payment and reduce recovery costs.

"Yeah. Either Cindy Striblen or Janice Hooks at Watson-Rowland has it. They job share."

"What?" Legion exclaimed, repulsed by the notion. "Whatever. We'll take the lien. They'll take 50 cents on a dollar, right?"

"If we shut it down quick, they should do 40 cents on a dollar."

"Shut it down quick, then." Ethan immediately arose from his chair. "This attorney, did you check his trial provenance?"

"Yeah. Nothing in Southern California," Ethan stopped, wondering if Roger had any more questions.

"All right. You get going on the lien. I'm gonna call the carrier before I call the attorney. You need the file?" Roger asked.

"If you don't need it, I'll take it." Roger handed the file back to him.

Luke was impressed that Roger did not need the file and he was going to undertake so much activity without having it in his possession.

"I've never heard the term 'trial provenance.'" Luke pointed out.

"When you take a case to verdict, you own it. Not the firm. Not anybody else who touched it. You take the glory. You take the blame. It becomes part of your ownership history," Roger explained. "Now, I want you to go into the hallway and grab the first attorney you see. Tell'em to get in here."

Luke moved with urgency and found Randy Newsom, one of the seasoned trial lawyers at Legion & Associates. Randy was 5 feet, 10 inches tall, 190 pounds, slightly pudgy. He wore a gray, pinstripe suit and matching tie. He had an uncompromising knowledge of American history, in particular, the Civil War.

Luke followed Randy into Roger's office. Roger was scribbling something down on a post-it note stack. He took the top sheet off and held it out to Randy. Randy took it from Roger.

"There's an attorney's name on there. I want you to check with the State Bar and see if he's ever had any disciplinary action. Also, there's an address. I want a picture of the place. Bird's eye view." Roger hesitated for a moment. "I need it now."

Randy did an about face and hustled out the door. Luke reclaimed his seat. Roger found a number in his telephone's directory and pressed a single button on the phone. He then pressed the speakerphone button and returned the receiver to its cradle.

Roger and Luke stared at the phone, while waiting for it to be answered.

"O-RISK-A, DeMeo!" The voice sounded like it belonged to a truck driver instead of a claim handler.

"Bernie, it's Roger Legion. How are ya?"

"About two smokes away from a coronary. What's my favorite ambulance-chasing shyster up to?" Bernie's voice beamed with bravado.

"Just crankin' the billing machine," Roger told her with a smile.

"Hey, any lawyer tells me different is lyin',"

Bernadette DeMeo had worked for O-RISK-A National Insurance for the past 30 years. She was trained in the old school claims handling method that begins with the premise that the claim is not covered. She specialized in making claimants work for their money.

"Bernie, I've got you on speaker because we have a new attorney listening in," Roger advised.

"You got fresh meat over there! When were you gonna tell me, Roger, you dirty bastard?" Bernie always enjoyed a conversation that allowed her to talk like a drunken sailor. "Is he good lookin'?" she demanded.

"Bernie, you gotta decide that," Roger told her.

"Now, I don't give a shit what you called about, when you takin' me to lunch to meet this new guy?"

"You tell me when," Roger suggested, enjoying their banter.

"Tuesday. 12 noon. Come and pick me up." Bernie responded without thought.

"It's done," Roger commanded.

"What's this new guy's name?" Bernie asked.

Roger pointed at Luke, then at the phone.

"Luke Cordel, ma'am," Luke told her.

"Ma'am! I like that! Jesus H. Christ, Roger, what are ya startin' to hire gentlemen over there? Listen, Luke, when you come over here, wait in the car. It's all women over here. It's an estrogen cesspool. A real bitch ditch. And they're all in heat. Now, it's not for me, mind ya, but I got daughters. So, don't forget, I got first dibs."

"We won't forget," Roger told her.

"Hey, Luke, you know I'm just bustin' balls, right?" Bernie joked.

"Oh, yeah," Luke chirped in.

"Now, Roger, what are we gonna do about this turd showboatin' in the roller rink?" Bernie demanded. "Should we just roll over and pay this guy what he wants?"

"Bernie, you know me," Roger pontificated, "if I'm gonna go down, I'm gonna go down swinging."

"That's why you're the best man for the job. Now what's the plan?"

Bernie eagerly awaited Roger's plan of action to achieve settlement.

CHAPTER 61

As soon as Emile disconnected his call with Remy, he dialed Hazz.

"What?" Hazz answered.

"Time to go," Emile told him.

"I'm on my way."

Emile then stood from the bench, picked up his briefcase and proceeded to the down escalator, where he stepped on for a ride to the 2nd floor.

Remy re-entered the courtroom and moved quickly with his briefcase in one hand and the Glock in the other. The door to the hallway that ran behind the courtrooms was open. Remy went up to it and tried to see as far down the hallway either side without exposing himself. He removed a small hand mirror from his briefcase and he held it at an angle to obtain a greater line of sight down both sides of the hallway. In front of the doorway entrance to the next judicial chamber down, Department 64, was a uniformed San Diego County Deputy Sheriff.

Remy again opened the briefcase and removed a water bottle that had a sports cap on it. He placed the Glock in the waistband of his pants behind his back and pulled a pack of matches from his pocket. Remy opened the pack and folded the center match down and around the bottom of the pack, so that the head of the match was on the striker for the pack. He then pulled the top of the sports cap up, as someone would do if they were about to start drinking the water.

Remy waited inside Department 65, just to the side of the entrance from the courtroom to the common hallway.

Emile walked off the escalator and directly into the business office for the courthouse. There were a number of lines to conduct business and at the far right end, there was a segregated area where a person could review court files. A person would look up the court index number for a file, write it on an order form, along with the person's identification information, and give it to a clerk, along with either a State Bar card or driver's license. The clerk would retrieve the file, give it to the person requesting it, and they could sit at a countertop desk area to review. When a person was done with the file, they returned it to a bin on the main desk that said, 'FILE RETURN.'

Emile entered the segregated area and placed his briefcase on a countertop area away from other patrons. He picked up a form to request a file for review and sat down in front of his briefcase. He opened the briefcase and removed a volume of a file, perhaps 2 inches thick, and closed the briefcase. It looked like one of the thousands of files within the courthouse records department.

Emile stood from the counter and picked up the file and his briefcase. As he left the segregated area, he placed the file into the 'FILE RETURN' bin and immediately walked out of the business office.

Emile hastened his gait to the escalator that would take him to the first floor. On his ride down, he took a key fob from his pocket. The key fob was a non-descript type that would be used to lock or unlock doors on a car, or pop the trunk. As Emile stepped off the escalator, he pushed one of the buttons on the fob.

Seconds earlier, one of the business office clerks placed all the files from the return bin onto a cart where they would be taken to an area for re-shelving. The clerk was almost to the door of the file room, when Emile pushed the button on the fob.

A massive explosion and fireball erupted with a radius of 50 feet from its point of origin. Bodies, papers, and desks were strewn about and every place that had paper or something that was a flammable source, raged with fire.

A fire alarm sounded throughout the building and Remy heard it. He stepped out into the hallway and began his trek approximately 20 feet toward the guard standing post outside the door.

The deputy began speaking to someone inside the office and Remy could hear a part of the conversation.

"Stay where you are until I find out whether or not it's a false alarm."

The deputy turned and saw Remy walking toward him. He took no evasive action, because Remy did not appear to be a threat. When Remy was within 6 feet of the deputy, he lowered the water bottle, with the sport's top aimed at the deputy and squeezed it. This caused a stream to strike and hit the deputy. In the same moment, the deputy went for his service revolver and Remy struck the match head, lit it and tossed it at the deputy.

The liquid in the bottle was 190-proof grain alcohol called Everclear. As soon as the match touched the deputy, he fully ignited. He let out a life-threatening scream. It happened so quickly that the deputy had not even cleared his gun out of his holster. The deputy dropped to the floor and began to roll as he was fully immolated.

Remy then began to move like a man on fire. He pulled the Glock from his waistband and shot the deputy once in the head. He stopped moving and simply burned.

Moving at lightning speed, Remy entered the chambers where Judge Gene Garubo and a guest, he was meeting for lunch, were waiting for an escort to a local restaurant. They were both attempting to seek shelter in the bathroom when Remy entered. Within the same second, he shot both of them and they went down to the ground. In the next moment, Remy put a 2nd bullet in the head of each man. Remy left the chambers of Department 64 to return to the courtroom of Department 65, where he had entered.

The confusion caused by the fire and bombing caused all personnel to move into rescue mode. Once the deputies were alerted to shots being fired on the 4th floor, they converged with a tactical team, weapons drawn searching for their gunman. They were hampered by the evacuation of the building in the chaos.

From the men's room emerged a man, who appeared homeless, 5 feet 10 inches tall, 165 pounds, wearing a black garbage bag, soiled, dirty clothes, unshaved and unwashed. His foul odor wafted for 6 feet around him. What made him even more unique was that he was carrying the gun that Remy just used to kill the deputy, Judge Garubo, and his lunch partner.

As soon as he was seen, a voice yelled out, "GUN!"

The homeless man took off toward the eastern end of the floor where the walkway bridge was located. He was now being chased by 4 deputies from within the Hall of Justice and one of the deputies requested back-up from deputies in the Main Courthouse to cut him off.

As the homeless man ran, he reached the end of the floor and dropped the gun before proceeding across the walkway bridge. By then, 6 other deputies were coming at him from the Main

Courthouse. The man stopped in the center of the bridge and looked out onto Union Street and Broadway. Just as the 1st deputy was about to tackle him, he slapped his hand onto the glass. He went down and 5 more deputies piled on top of him.

Before the tattered man hit the floor, two explosions were heard and felt. These were much more powerful than the one that took place in the business office. The explosions occurred at each end of the walkway bridge. The Semtex explosive was placed around the perimeter of the bridge walkway at each end that connected the buildings. At the Main Courthouse end, there were additional steel girders, located several feet from the building and those were also blown.

The explosions caused the bridge to dislocate from the building and it plummeted 4 stories and crashed to the ground with 10 deputies, the homeless man, and several attorneys, who were simply trying to get out of the building because of the original fire alarm.

By the time the walkway bridge fell, Remy, Emile, and Hazz were on their way back to the Deus X Machine Shop.

CHAPTER 62

Randy Newsom returned to Roger's office just as he was ending his call with Bernadette DeMeo of O-RISK-A National Insurance. Bernie wanted to give Roger $15,000 of settlement authority to settle the roller rink case, but Roger told her that $10,000 was sufficient.

"What did you find out?" Roger posed his inquiry to Randy.

"The only thing with the State Bar was that he was suspended from practice 12 years ago for failure to pay dues. Here's the picture of his address," Randy disclosed and handed a sheet of paper to Roger. "It's a UPS store."

The attorney's address was a mailbox drop located within a United Parcel Service store.

"Thanks, Randy," Roger told him.

As Randy left Legion's office, Ethan re-entered returning to his original seat.

Roger then raised his reading glasses from the desktop and put them on. He reviewed a phone number that he wrote on a Post-it note, and then pressed the corresponding digits on the phone. He turned on the speakerphone and it was answered on the 3rd ring.

"Law Office," a male voice said that had a distinct Asian accent.

"Mr. Cheyapanta, please," Roger requested.

"May I ask who is calling?" His accent slowed the cadence of his speech.

"This is attorney Roger Legion calling regarding his client, Tom Nguyen."

"Oh, this is Paul Cheyapanta."

"Hello, Paul, my firm represents Tenzory Entertainment, they operate the roller rink, where the incident occurred. How are you today?"

"I am good, sir. How may I help you?" Paul asked with his thick Thai accent.

"Well, I was just reviewing this file. I believe that you've been dealing with an attorney in my office named Ethan Paul," Roger advised.

"Very nice man," Paul told him.

"Thank you. I wanted to talk with you about this file."

"Mr. Legion, I want to apologize for the motion for sanctions."

"There's no need to apologize. I would have done the same thing."

"I think a $15,000 settlement is quite fair."

"I was thinking Paul, why don't you let us take care of the lien."

"Really?" Paul was intrigued. "That would help me out."

"Now what do you want to settle this case?"

"$12,000?"

Legion knew that because he said it in the form of a question, there was room for movement.

"$5,000," Legion told him. "I can have the check to you the day after tomorrow."

The noise on Paul's end of the phone indicated there was some fidgeting and the sound of a calculator being used.

"I can do $10,000," Paul told him.

"I'll go $6,500, but that's it." Roger was succinct. "Otherwise, we can go to trial."

"May I ask: Who will try this case in your office?" Paul wondered.

"I try all the cases for this insurance company."

There was a long pause on the phone.

"So, Mr. Roger, just to re-cap. If we agree on a settlement amount, you will have the funds to me the day after tomorrow?"

"We can do that. But I want the dismissal filed today."

"I don't know if I can do that. I don't have a secretary today."

"We'll help you with it. Ethan will send you a dismissal for your signature." As Legion spoke, he pointed to Ethan to take notes.

"And he would send me a letter acknowledging the settlement amount and that you will be responsible for the lien?" Paul asked.

Ethan took notes as Paul spoke.

"Absolutely," Roger confirmed. A moment passed.

"I can do $7,500," Paul acknowledged.

Roger allowed a moment to pass.

"Paul, you seem like a nice guy. Let's split it: $7,000."

Another moment transpired.

"Mr. Roger, I can do that," Paul conceded.

"All right. Ethan will contact you shortly and we will order the check immediately. Ethan is going to need your tax ID number."

"I can fax that to you now," Paul advised.

"Very good. Ethan will call you in a few minutes."

"Thank you, Mr. Roger. I have enjoyed working with you."

"Same here. Take care." Roger disconnected the call. He pointed at Ethan.

"Help him get the documents filed. Definitely get the dismissal filed today," Roger demanded. "Tell your secretary, this is a rush. I'll call Bernie and let her know."

Ethan quickly moved out of the room. Roger never liked to tell anyone that something was a rush. He felt a 'rush' situation was generally caused by someone slacking off along the way. Luke stood and began to walk to the door.

"Luke," Roger called out requesting his attention. "That's how it's done."

To some, it may have appeared elementary, but to a novice attorney like Luke, it was a mastery class in crisis management. Especially, when you consider that 15 minutes earlier, Roger Legion knew no details regarding the file and had never met the plaintiff attorney.

CHAPTER 63

At least 10 minutes before any of the activity commenced at the courthouse involving the firebomb, murders, and the walkway bridge falling to the ground, Detective Jeff Elkins stood outside of his cubicle on the 3rd floor of the downtown San Diego Police Headquarters waiting for his partner, Skylar Stubbs, so they could go to lunch.

"Hey, Sky, when you gonna be ready?" Jeff wondered.

"I'm almost done. Let me finish the last paragraph on this part of the report," Skylar answered typing away.

"What's the mood for lunch?" Jeff asked.

"I caught you a delicious bass," Skylar said with a smile.

"*Napoleon Dynamite.* 2004. That's an easy one," Jeff exclaimed with urgency.

"Yeah, but the quote's got to fit the moment."

"So, where we goin' for lunch?" Jeff again asked.

"I don't care. Anything, but Mexican. We had that yesterday."

Then a voice spoke up from the cubicle next to Jeff. It was Detective Margaret Byrne, who they spoke with when Roger Legion visited their office.

"Jeff, did they ever find the van those guys were in from the murder of the police captain?" Margaret asked without standing or leaving her chair.

"Yeah," Jeff replied with a disgusted tone. "They found it on Torrey Pines Road. It was torched."

"What about the next guy?" Margaret asked.

"He's a judge. County boys say they got it. He's on their turf. Our track record hasn't exactly wowed anybody's socks off. Skylar and I both told 'em not to underestimate these guys. They are brazen."

As Jeff spoke, Skylar's cell phone rang. The Caller ID indicated 'County of San Diego.'

Skylar answered the phone without thought.

"Homicide. Stubbs."

There was a moment of silence, and then music began:

> *If you're the victim of a slip and fall,*
> *There's really only one, guy to call.*
> *Hearing his name will make them sigh,*
> *Tell 'em your lawyer is Dexter Frye.*

Skylar looked up as the blood was draining from his face and sprinted into action. He immediately wrote down the number, put it on speaker and stood up.

As he started to speak, the following verse played:

> *Insurance companies go round and round.*
> *Dexter will knock them to the ground.*
> *So, if you need a lawyer, don't be shy.*
> *We both know that Dexter's your guy.*

"CAP-TAIN!!!" he screamed and everyone on the floor stopped what they were doing and looked. Captain Shood raced out of his office. Skylar stood and started to speak and wanted to run to the elevator.

"They're in there, now, at the courthouse," he told the captain. "Call over there and tell them to lock the building down. Both buildings. Jeff, let's go!"

As Jeff and Skylar raced to the elevator, the jingle concluded:

Dexter Frye, Dexter Frye, Dexter Frye,
The Litigation Guy.

CHAPTER 64

Jeff and Skylar raced down Broadway in a marked San Diego patrol car with their lights blazing and siren blaring. As they drove, news came over their police radio of an explosion and fire at the Hall of Justice. They traveled 12 blocks ignoring all the lights and avoiding 2 near-miss traffic collisions. Part of Broadway in front of the courthouse was cordoned off, so Skylar parked the car as close as he could to the Hall of Justice and began to run toward it. Jeff got out and walked at a brisk clip.

Skylar approached the first uniformed deputy sheriff and flashed his badge.

"Hey, sorry to bother ya," Skylar told him. "I'm with the City P.D. Did you hear anything about anybody gettin' shot?"

"I just heard a radio transmission; they heard shots on the 4th floor. I don't know too many details. Hold it," the officer said and touched his finger to his ear to listen to the latest transmission. He looked at Skylar. "They say they got the guy cornered on the walkway bridge."

Just as Jeff caught up to Skylar, the officer pointed up to the walkway bridge. All three men looked up and saw a lone palm slap the glass. As soon as it happened, the bridge connections to the buildings exploded. All three men covered their eyes as glass flew and the bridge smashed to the ground. First responders appeared at the scene to help those injured in the fall.

Skylar wanted to run and assist the people who were on the walkway bridge, but Jeff grabbed his bicep to get his attention.

"That palm on the glass: that was a signal to somebody on the ground. Whoever it is, could still be here," Jeff told Skylar.

Jeff's analysis made sense. Skylar and Jeff began a slow scan of the area, looking for anyone suspicious, anyone who may fit the previous suspect descriptions, or anyone enjoying the fruit of their work.

Skylar crossed Broadway for a closer examination. When he looked down the pedestrian walkway on Union Street, he saw a tall, thin man wearing a hoodie with the hood up and the draw strings pulled tight around his face. He wore sunglasses and a fake beard. He was filming the falling of the walkway bridge and its aftermath on his cell phone camera. It was Alton Burchesky.

Skylar stared at him for a moment and Alton noticed him. Alton took off running followed in high pursuit by Skylar Stubbs.

Jeff ran back to the car and was forced to make a U-turn to follow both men. Because Union Street had a pedestrian walkway and did not allow traffic access, Jeff was forced to drive around the block. All the while, the patrol car's overhead beacon was glaring and its siren was whaling.

Alton ran south on Union Street away from the Hall of Justice then cut across the plaza of the Metropolitan Correctional Center. The Metropolitan Correctional Center is a 23-story federal detention facility for both men and women of all security levels.

Skylar continued to shorten Alton's lead on him as they made it to State Street, located one block to the west and turned the corner. They ran up the center of the street north toward the Hall of

Justice moving like there was Olympic gold in their future, with one man focused on escape and the other on capture.

Jeff followed as closely as he could in the patrol car but had to go around the block because Alton and Skylar cut through the plaza. Jeff radioed into San Diego Police Headquarters and advised them of all the activity involving the foot chase.

Alton turned the corner onto the Broadway sidewalk heading west. At Broadway and State Street, the streets were closed to accommodate emergency vehicles. As Skylar turned the corner, a San Diego County Sheriff's Deputy popped out from between 2 vehicles, with his Taser drawn.

"Stop, or I'll tase ya," the officer commanded.

"I'M A COP!" Skylar screamed, not slowing down, but raising his arm to push the officer out of the way with an arm block. Skylar's action caused the officer to take defensive action.

When Skylar was within 2 feet of the officer, the officer pulled the trigger on the Taser. The electroshock weapon fired 2 electrode darts attached to the Taser by a conductive wire into the top right quadrant of Skylar's chest. Skylar had started to pivot away before the darts were deployed. As the darts struck him, he felt the electrical current attempt to incapacitate him, and he called upon his adrenaline and determination to yank the dart wires and rip them from his body, while still in motion.

Skylar slowed for a moment, but then went back into full sprint mode. He was forced to stop before he could cross Broadway and he saw Alton enter the America's Finest City Building through the car entrance to the garage under the building. Once he crossed the street, he was flying.

Alton ran to the elevator lobby, opened the door, but before entering, he took a spray can of black paint from the pocket of his hoodie and sprayed the lens of the camera over the entrance door.

He then went to the computer pad and pressed the necessary buttons to request an elevator to the 24th floor, the floor of Legion & Associates. He held the spray can in his hand and zipped down his hoodie to expose the handle of his Beretta 92FS. He was told that his ride to the 24th floor would be in the 'C' elevator. He waited for the doors to open and continued to look at the entrance to the garage to see if Skylar may show up.

A bell went off indicating that the 'C' elevator had arrived and the doors opened. Before entering the elevator, Alton reached his hand in with the spray can and sprayed the lens of the camera inside the elevator.

When Skylar arrived at the elevator lobby in the parking garage, he was able to tell from the computer screen that the last elevator requested was headed to the 24th floor. Skylar raced up the stairs to the lobby of the building and immediately saw one of the building security officers.

"I need you to stop the 'C' elevator now!" he commanded, holding up his badge.

"Stop the 'C' elevator now!" the security officer ordered into his walkie-talkie.

"Where is it?" Skylar asked.

"What's the 20 on the elevator?" the guard asked into his walkie-talkie.

"It's between the 17th and 18th floor," a voice answered.

"I need to get on the 24th floor now," Skylar told him.

"Send a car to the lobby for non-stop to the 24th," the guard again spoke into his walkie-talkie.

It was then that Jeff walked into the lobby and he could see Skylar's white shirt with a red patch from where he was bleeding from pulling out the Taser darts. A bell was heard that announced the requested elevator had arrived.

"Sky, you all right?" Jeff's voice echoed concern.

"I'm okay." He then turned to the guard. "Is there any way outta that elevator?"

"No," the guard answered.

"When I call you, send it up," Skylar told him.

"Here," the guard said, "take my walkie."

Skylar and Jeff raced onto the elevator. On the ride up, both men took out their service weapons. Jeff checked to make sure he had a bullet in the chamber.

When they reached the 24th floor, they stepped off the elevator with their guns drawn, sweeping the lobby, looking for anything suspicious.

"Excuse me," Skylar called over to Nina, "has anyone stepped off this elevator in the last few minutes?"

"No," she said, slightly trembling, with a spooked look.

The two officers turned and faced the 'C' elevator.

"Send the 'C' elevator up," Skylar spoke into the walkie-talkie.

"It's on its way," a voice responded.

"I'll take low, you take high," Skylar told Jeff as he crouched down. Both men had their arms fully extended holding their service weapons aimed at the elevator door.

"Sky, watch the corners," Jeff told him.

Roger Legion appeared from the hallway to witness the events.

"Nina, come here," Legion said, calling her over. "Go down the hall."

She started to go, but was being nosey, wanting to see what happens. Legion saw what she was doing.

"Stand behind me," he told her and she stood behind him able to see the action with one eye from the side of his shoulder.

The elevator bell rang announcing its arrival. The doors opened. The elevator was empty.

"DARN IT!" Skylar yelled and wanted to punch the wall, but thought again before doing it.

Jeff put his foot out to hold the elevator door open and looked inside. Skylar saw Roger Legion standing at the end of the hallway in the corner of the lobby. Their eyes locked.

"You're next you know," Skylar told Legion with an angry gaze, and turned to Jeff. "Let's go."

"We can't," Jeff replied pointing to the elevator. "It's a crime scene."

Jeff used the emergency stop on the elevator to lock the doors open. Skylar looked inside wondering what made it a crime scene. He saw what Jeff referenced. In the middle of the elevator floor was a business card from Dexter Frye, the Litigation Guy.

CHAPTER 65

FBI Special Agent Oliver Love was in his Orange County office finishing up a conference call that was on speakerphone with FBI Headquarters in Quantico, Virginia. It dealt with a computer virus spread through unsolicited e-mail that claimed to originate with the Federal Bureau of Investigation. As soon as Oliver had concluded the conference call, Special Agent-In-Charge, Joseph Rossi, appeared in his doorway, holding several pieces of paper.

"Ollie, they got a hit off that photo you sent for a facial recognition scan," Joe advised as he handed the papers to Oliver.

"Who?" Oliver asked before reviewing the pages.

"Remy Kalm." Silence filled the air.

"I knew that I saw him someplace before. I was part of a task force dealing with a possible terrorist attack on the Willis Tower in Chicago," Oliver recalled. "That's the old Sears Tower. His name came up as a possible suspect. He's smart and he's slippery."

"Well, Interpol has a warrant out on him for a series of bombings in Helsinki. If he's in our neighborhood, I suspect he's up to no good," Joe warned.

"With the dead girl, the story about the radioactive material, the cell phone photo, the San Diego address from the phone, and

Remy's background, I think we got enough for a warrant," Oliver suggested.

"I agree," Joe concurred. "Call the San Diego office and see if they have any investigations going on him or that location. If not, let them know you're coming. While you're waiting on the warrant, get a tactical team on standby."

The tactical team was essentially a Special Weapons and Tactics or SWAT team of officers that would be able to make a quick entrance into the Deus X Machine Shop and their show of force would intimidate the people within the building and mitigate any potential violent interaction.

"What if the San Diego office wants to get involved?" Oliver wondered.

"It's their turf. Invite'em to the show."

"One thing about this guy, Remy," Oliver warned. "I remember reading on his sheet that his nickname was 'Remy the Hemi.' Basically, he will destroy anything that gets in his way. His people or anybody else. He always leaves a trail of bodies."

"Bag'em and tag'em. Keep your finger on the trigger and make sure the warrant is a no knock," Joe elucidated.

Oliver began making phone calls in preparation for service of a warrant.

Part 3

CHAPTER 66

Shortly before dawn, on this Thursday, Remy Kalm assembled his team around Brockman's computer desk in the machine shop. All the men looked tired. They had just returned from their final underwater excursion where the steel reinforced containers loaded with Semtex explosive were placed onto a 38-foot Boston Whaler 350 Defiance fishing boat. This boat was modified to allow off-loading from a compartment under the vessel.

This particular type of boat was selected because it had a Duobond construction that allowed it to maintain buoyancy during the off-loading process.

Pike lowered the containers using a winch on the boat and Remy, Hazz, Emile, and Philippe bolted them perfectly onto the anchor bolts they installed on the land side of the 18th and 20th towers the day before. Hazz made sure that the circuitry was operational once the containers were in place. The containers were covered with the camouflage shield they used while they performed the underwater drilling. Remy also had Hazz place a motion sensor on the outside of the containers, so they could be monitored by Brockman at the machine shop.

"Pike," Remy commenced, "is there gas in the trucks?"

"About a half tank in each one," Pike answered. "We can start to load the Semtex whenever you give the word."

"All right," Remy said. "Hazz, watch the harnesses when they're put in the truck." Remy then turned back to Pike. "What kind of clearance do the harnesses have?"

"It's one inch," Pike answered. "I hot rolled the steel to keep it relatively form fitting. We placed the explosive in the trucks once before. It won't be a problem."

Within the box of the trucks, where the Semtex would be placed, Pike installed a sheet of diamond pattern plate steel that he 'hot rolled' or bent to create a metal cover over the explosives. The purpose of this was to force more of the energy of the blast downward into the weakened bottom of the truck and, ultimately, into the road of the bridge.

"Let's make sure before we leave here that the circuitry is all able to come on line," Remy declared. "Brock, we won't move those trucks until you give the green light."

"You got it, man! You got it," Brockman shouted. His head gave off a slight twitch and he looked like he was about to play a video game for the championship of the world.

"Pike and Emile will drive the longer trucks, the eastbound trucks," Remy advised. "You guys are gonna drive down Interstate 5 and take the Palm Avenue exit, then you drive up the Silver Strand into Coronado. That's where you catch the bridge. Hazz and Philippe, you guys are in the smaller, westbound trucks. If we do this right, everybody should be in place at the same time. Brock will monitor all 4 trucks with a GPS. Kevin and I will be waiting in the Escalade for the eastbound trucks in Coronado. When we see the 1st truck pass, we get in front of the 2nd eastbound truck and proceed across the bridge. Once the trucks are in place, we secure them to each other and the bridge. Then, we just turn on the power for the circuits and we're done."

"Remy," Pike interjected, "I'm not a very good swimmer."

"Don't worry," Remy told him. "We'll make sure you make it."

"Are we coming back here?" Philippe wondered.

"No. We're going right to the airport in Carlsbad. A private plane will be waiting." Remy then turned to Brockman. "Brock, once it's detonated, walk out the door. Take one of the trucks to Carlsbad. This guy, named Farnsworth, is gonna come and clean this place out."

Brockman shook his head affirmatively, while gazing forward, without focus.

"We'll communicate on the bridge with walkie-talkies. We got all the frequencies off Alton's CHP car. By the time they find our frequency, we'll be 'eading out of town." Remy's French accent dropped the 'h.'

"One final thing:," Remy uttered with critical tone, "You each have a submachine gun. One clip – 30 rounds. Don't waste the bullets, but don't be afraid to use them."

Remy panned his eyes across all the members of his team.

"Gentlemen, let's burn down the forest."

All the men proceeded to their assigned tasks and Remy walked back to oversee and assist with the loading of the Semtex into the trucks. Kevin Camballa walked next to him.

"Remy, Brockman's losin' it," Kevin told him.

"That's just the way he is. Don't worry about it."

Remy continued to the production area and Kevin turned back to look at Brockman. He sat at his desk wildly engaged in playing the air drums without any music and he was not wearing earbuds. Kevin walked back over to him.

"Brock, are you all right?" Kevin asked.

Brockman stopped playing the air drums and perspiration was gathered on the top of his head. He was looking forward and turned suddenly, in a millisecond, to look at Kevin.

"Why would you ask me that question?" Brock serenely inquired.

"Just makin' sure you're ready."

"When I was a kid, my father was angry at me for cracking the windshield on his new Monte Carlo with a baseball I hit. He took my bat and hit my dog, Ruthie, over the head with it. Right in front of me. Then, he looks at me and says, 'Are you all right?'"

Brockman looked at Kevin, who was somewhat mesmerized by the story.

"So, whenever I hear that sentence, I think about the only girl that I ever loved. The only girl who ever loved me, the only girl who ever kissed me, and the only girl who would die for me."

Kevin stared at Brockman. Brockman turned away from him and pressed several keys on one of his keypads. An episode of *Speed Racer* began to play on one of the screens and Brockman gave it his total attention.

CHAPTER 67

Shortly after 1:30 p.m., Luke Cordel walked around the perimeter of the 24th floor, looking for attorneys in their offices to see if he would be able to get a ride to the Kia dealership in National City, located in the southern portion of San Diego County. Luke could not find one lawyer traveling in that direction and this was the day he promised Karla that he would take her to pick up her dog from the veterinarian.

The dealership had a shuttle service that allowed him to drop off the car, but they had no return shuttle service. They promised Luke that the car would be ready by 4:00 p.m., which would leave enough time to pick-up Karla's dog before 6:00 p.m., when the vet closed.

Luke would not disappoint Karla. He would call a cab if necessary.

As Luke rounded the corner in front of Roger Legion's office, he quickly looked in and saw Roger sitting at his desk, reviewing a pleading. He put the brakes on and decided that he had nothing to lose by asking him. He knocked on the door as he walked in. Roger looked up and lowered his glasses to the desk.

"What's goin' on?" Roger asked.

"By any chance, are you heading toward National City later today?" Luke wondered.

"As a matter of fact, I'm going to pick up our old friend, Lester Abrams, in Coronado," Legion advised.

"What time are you going?"

"I told them I'd pick him up at three o'clock."

"Can I get a ride to the Kia dealership in National City?" Luke asked.

"Kia? Why don't you have an American-made car?" Roger inquired.

"It's what I could afford at the time."

"When you were 'in country,' did you see alotta guys die?" Roger queried.

Roger's reference to 'in country' denoted the time Luke spent in a foreign country during his military service.

"Yeah," Luke answered.

"Think about it the next time you're buying a car."

Luke shook his head in acknowledgement.

"So, can I get a ride?" he requested.

"We'll go get Lester, then I'll drop ya off."

"Is it okay if Karla comes with us?"

"Who?" Legion questioned.

"She's a paralegal on the 23rd floor," Luke sheepishly advised.

"Oh, your friend who gave you the tour. Absolutely. Tell her to be ready and up here by 2:45."

"Thank you," Luke hesitated a moment, stuck on whether to call him 'sir' or 'Roger.' He stared at Legion, looking at him differently for some reason. In that instant, Luke realized just how dangerous Roger Legion was. Something had happened that would change Luke's opinion of Roger Legion forever.

Luke did an about-face and made a hasty retreat out of Legion's office.

CHAPTER 68

At 2:43 p.m., Karla Mulry stepped off the elevator onto the 24th floor. She wore an indigo, blue trumpet skirt, with a marigold, crème stripe crewneck tee shirt and a blue sweater jacket. On her shoulder, was a black, leather handbag, large enough to carry files that matched her suede and leather flat shoes.

Nina greeted Karla with a smile.

"Are you ready for the weekend?" Nina asked.

"I was ready on Monday," Karla replied with a smile as she walked over to Nina's raised granite countertop. She put her elbow on it and then rested her chin in the palm of that hand. "Is it a busy afternoon?"

"The usual. You takin' off early?"

"Going to pick up my baby from the vet."

"How is little Sophie?" Nina inquired.

"I just love her to death. Let me show you the latest pictures."

Karla reached into her bag and removed her cell phone. She found a series of pictures of her dog and handed the phone to Nina. Luke walked up behind Karla and announced his presence.

"Good afternoon, Miss Mulry," Luke exclaimed.

She turned to look at him. He wore his suitcoat and carried a black, canvas, tactical bag that was approximately 34 inches long. Karla had seen the bag once before when Luke took her, along with Pat Madore and his son, to the shooting range. Luke kept at least one rifle in it, along with ammo and shooting supplies.

"Good afternoon, Mr. Cordel," she uttered rather dismissively. "I'm ready," she told him and began walking to the elevator.

"We just have to wait for one more person," he told her.

"Who?" she quizzed.

Just then, Roger Legion appeared from the hallway. He looked at Luke and then Karla.

"Let's go," Legion declared.

Karla was slightly shocked, but knew that she had to keep her cool. She wondered if there may be some ulterior motive hatched between Luke and Legion. Luke spoke up.

"My car is in the shop and Roger, eh, Mr. Legion, said he would give us a ride to pick it up."

"Thank you, Mr. Legion," Karla told him.

"You're welcome," Roger answered with a smile.

They entered the elevator and rode to the parking garage without anyone uttering a word.

In Legion's Cadillac, Luke sat in the passenger seat and Karla sat behind Legion, who was driving. Luke's bag was stowed in the trunk and Karla kept her shoulder bag in her lap. As they crossed the Coronado Bay Bridge, both Karla and Luke admired the awe-inspiring view from both sides of the bridge. As they neared Coronado, Legion glanced at Karla in his rear-view mirror.

"What kind of dog do you have, Karla?" Legion asked.

"A West Highland Terrier," she replied.

"A Westie," Legion acknowledged with a hint of enthusiasm. "That's the kind of dog I have."

Karla was somewhat surprised that Legion had a dog. She did not envision him to be a dog person.

"What's your dog's name?" she wondered.

"Daisy. We also have a bichon frise named Susie," Legion told her. "My wife likes small dogs."

Karla was amazed that Legion had two dogs and that he was married. Probably not his first wife, she thought. But then, maybe he was really a nice guy who put on an act at work. She thought that Roger Legion was definitely a curiosity.

The Cadillac swept down from the bridge into Coronado. Right behind the old toll plaza, that all the cars on the bridge had to pass, was a large center median. The California Highway Patrol posted two cars on the median to warn drivers to obey all driving-related laws on the bridge. The officer in one of the patrol cars this day was Alton Burchesky.

CHAPTER 69

Legion parked his Cadillac on Orange Boulevard directly in front of the Coronado Paradisio. Karla and Luke stayed in the car while Legion went inside to retrieve Lester. Karla stared out at the ocean.

"Coronado's nice," Karla said with a serene calmness. "Have you ever been to the Hotel del Coronado?" she asked Luke.

"A long time ago," he answered, "when I was a kid."

"Was it nice?"

"It was nice," he responded and looked over his shoulder at her. "I know you'd like it."

"Do you know if they take dogs?"

"I don't know."

Karla smiled, shook her head affirmatively, and returned to gazing at the ocean.

Roger Legion and Lester Abrams emerged from the Coronado Paradisio. Lester appeared disheveled as if he was doing a perp walk to the car. Roger said something to him and he knew that he should sit in the back seat of the car. Lester entered the vehicle and noticed Karla.

"What are you doin' here, Karla?" Lester asked as if she was not good enough to ride in the same vehicle with him.

"Mr. Legion is giving me a ride, so I can go pick-up my dog."

"Is this your boyfriend?" Lester inquired pointing to Luke.

"No," Karla replied.

"You know he dislocated my jaw. Asshole!"

"Lester, shut up," Legion told him.

Legion started the car, put it in drive, and immediately performed a U-turn to return on the same route they took to get there. Lester wanted to continue the conversation with Karla.

"He hit me while I wasn't lookin'," Lester said.

"Lester," Legion again spoke up with anger percolating, "you either shut up, or I'm gonna stop the car and let him finish what he started."

Lester looked like he bit his tongue and let out an exasperated sigh. He then began to peer out the window like an angry child who was not getting his way.

Legion turned onto Orange Avenue from Orange Boulevard and Alton's police cruiser was less than a block behind him. When Legion passed in front of East Plaza Park, Alton turned on the overhead lights and turned on the siren in short bursts, just enough to get Legion's attention. Legion pulled over at the east end of the park, near the corner of 6th and Orange.

"What's this guy want?" Lester declared after staring over his shoulder.

Legion lowered his window as he saw Alton approach, wearing mirrored sunglasses.

As Alton reached his window, Roger asked, "Is there a problem, officer?"

"License, registration, and proof of insurance." Alton's reply was cold and detached.

Legion took his license from his wallet. Then, he reached over to the glove box and removed his registration and proof of insurance card. As he performed this task, Legion had a sudden realization, an epiphany. He handed the requested documents to Alton.

"I'll be right with you," Alton told him and he walked back to his car.

As Alton walked back to his police cruiser, Legion reached into the inside breast pocket of his suit coat and removed his phone, trying to give the appearance of minimal movement. Luke looked over his shoulder and saw Alton sitting in his patrol car.

"What's up with this guy?" Luke asked Roger.

"Luke, listen to me," Roger's voice pulsed urgency. "If I'm not mistaken, this guy is going to arrest me and take me outta the car right now."

"What?" Luke was shocked at Roger's claim.

"Listen to me!" he demanded in a succinct fashion without raising his voice. "My cell phone is on the floor, if you need it. If he takes me, I want you to call the San Diego Police Department 9-1-1. Tell them to get a message to Detective Skylar Stubbs. Tell Stubbs that the killer he is looking for is a California Highway Patrol officer named Alton Burchesky. Tell him Alton took me and we're heading across the bridge now. You got it?"

Alton reappeared at Roger's window.

"Would you step outta the car, please?" requested Alton with an eerie, monotone voice.

Legion stepped out of the Cadillac and began to walk back toward Alton's police cruiser. Alton then addressed the remaining occupants of the vehicle.

"Keep your hands where I can see them. Don't attempt to exit the vehicle. Any attempt to exit the vehicle will be seen as an act of aggression. Just sit tight."

Luke watched the activity between Alton and Roger. Alton placed Roger in handcuffs and escorted him to the backseat of his vehicle, without patting him down. Alton closed the door on Roger and walked back to the driver's window of Legion's Cadillac. He leaned against the door and looked in.

"I'm gonna need everyone's cell phone and the keys to the car."

Initially, no one in the car moved.

"NOW!" Alton shouted and, in the same moment, pulled his Smith & Wesson .40 caliber service weapon and aimed it at Luke. Luke handed his cell phone to Alton and Karla pulled her cell phone from her purse. Before handing the phone to Alton, she fidgeted with the phone to remove the cover.

"What are you doing?" Lester asked impatiently.

"I'm keeping the cover," Karla told him. "It has a picture of my dog."

"Where's yours?" Alton asked Lester.

"I don't have a cell phone." Lester stated with an angry stare.

Alton turned his attention to Luke.

"Car keys."

"It's a keyless start. Roger's got the fob."

"Don't get out of the car while I'm here," Alton articulated. "If you do, I'll view it as an act of aggression."

Alton holstered his weapon and walked back to his car. His cell phone rang and he answered as he entered the vehicle.

"Where are you?" Remy asked.

"I'm on Orange Avenue," Alton told him.

"Get to the bridge. The eastbound trucks will be here in less than 2 minutes."

As Remy finished his sentence, the 1st eastbound truck, with a D-A-Go Trucking logo, passed Alton's patrol car.

"I see the first one, I'm on my way."

Alton pulled out at a high rate of speed and Luke immediately sprang into action. He quickly moved to the driver's door, opened it, and pushed the release to open the trunk. He grabbed his tactical bag and placed it on the passenger seat. Luke started the car. The 9-1-1 operator was still on the line.

"What are you doing?" Lester asked, rather incredulously.

"I'm gonna go get him," Luke replied, referring to Legion.

Luke hit the gas pedal and the Cadillac roared. Karla was trying to comprehend this series of events. When Alton stood outside of Legion's window, she could see on his name plate that his last name was Burchesky. That was all that was written on it. She wondered how Roger knew that his first name was Alton.

CHAPTER 70

On the 3rd floor of the San Diego Police Headquarters, Skylar Stubbs stood outside Jeff Elkins' cubicle discussing the known information regarding the courthouse bombings and murders. It was national news, and media trucks surrounded the headquarters waiting for the next briefing. Members of the FBI were scheduled to meet with both detectives and Captain Shood at 4:00 p.m. this afternoon.

Skylar wore a short sleeve white shirt with a red tie. Jeff wore a light blue shirt with a yellow tie that had blue stripes.

"Did you ever deal with the FBI before?" Skylar asked.

"A coupla times over the years. They think they piss champagne and crap gold, but at the end a the day, they just have more toys to play with," Jeff ruminated.

"They're gonna spend the entire time telling us everything we did wrong," Skylar observed in frustration.

"Sky, I just realized," Jeff spoke up as if he had a brainstorm, "you forgot your badge."

"What are ya talking about?"

"Your Mormon badge. Don't you need that to complete your uniform, Elder Stubbs?" Jeff boasted a big grin. "If the FBI gets on our back, we'll tell'em that's not very Christian, then we'll give 'em a *Book of Mormon*."

"If it was only that easy," Skylar pondered. "Jeff, you have an open invitation to come with me any Sunday."

As Skylar finished his sentence, Captain Shood bolted out of his office and did an immediate scan searching for Skylar.

"Skylar," the Captain's voice was rushed, "9-1-1 dispatch just received a call from one of Legion's lawyers for you. They said that the killer you're looking for is a CHP officer named Alton Burchesky. He's got Legion and they're going over the Coronado Bay Bridge now."

"Let's go," Skylar barked at Jeff wanting to move at warp speed. He turned to the elevator and turned back to see Detective Margaret Byrne, standing in her cubicle, looking to see if she could provide any assistance.

"Maggie, call CHP," Skylar requested of her. "See what you can find out about this guy. Tell them to stop him if they see him. He's got Legion."

"Legion?" Margaret's tone was serious. "Are you sure you wanna stop him?"

"Please, Maggie," Skylar's voice telegraphed that there was no time to discuss it.

"It's done," Margaret told him as she regained her seat and looked up the CHP phone number.

Skylar and Jeff both moved at high speed to the elevator and parking garage in the hope that they could cut Alton off at the bridge.

Meanwhile, FBI Special Agent Oliver Love and 12 members of the San Diego FBI Field Office SWAT team entered a large, unmarked white van for a trip to the Deus X Machine Shop to serve a warrant.

Oliver wore a standard, military-issue bulletproof vest with identifying patches on the front and back. The rest of the men were dressed in green, paramilitary, tactical gear that included a Heckler & Koch MP5 submachine gun and a Springfield .45 caliber handgun. Their tools included a breacher, or battering ram, a Halligan pry tool, and a collapsible sledge hammer.

The warrant that Oliver obtained did not require them to announce their presence prior to entering the structure. Their plan was to breach the 4 man doors, or regular doors, located on each side of the building at the same time. Any resistance would be initially met with flashbang or smoke grenades.

Bob Brockman sat at his desk monitoring the location of the westbound trucks as they proceeded across the bridge. The eastbound trucks were nearing the entrance to the bridge.

CHAPTER 71

On the inside of the bridge railings, from the east to the west, the numbers 1 to 30 were painted in sequential order at various distances across the entire span of the bridge. The numbers indicated the location of the concrete tower or pylon situated directly under the number. The point where the trucks were to be parked perpendicular to the traffic would be between the 17th and 18th tower and the 20th and 21st tower. The 18th and 20th towers were targeted by Remy for demolition.

Pike drove the lead truck, 32 feet long, in the eastbound direction which consisted of 3 lanes at this time of the afternoon and he stopped the truck in the far right lane as he passed the number 18 written on the inside of the bridge railing. Emile was driving the 2nd truck in the eastbound direction and also stopped his truck in the far right lane after he saw the number 21 on the railing.

In the westbound lanes which were 2 lanes wide, Philippe drove the lead truck, 20 feet long, and Hazz drove the 2nd truck. They also stopped shortly after they sighted the numbers on the bridge railing. The 2nd truck on each side was on a slight incline as they were both proceeding toward the 19th tower, which was the highest tower.

In both directions, horns started blaring as cars went around the stopped trucks. Kevin and Remy rode in the Escalade and slowed down to assess the events. Both wore sunglasses. Remy called Alton. Alton had just turned off Orange Avenue onto 4th Street for entrance to the bridge. Luke, Karla, and Lester were in close pursuit.

"Yeah," Alton answered his phone.

"Run the traffic break now!" Remy demanded.

"Done," Alton responded.

Alton turned on his overhead emergency lights and would intermittently blast his siren just enough to gain the attention of motorists preparing to enter the bridge. He then began to swerve his police cruiser across the 3 lanes of traffic and motorists knew not to pass him. He continued to slow down the traffic as he proceeded onto the bridge. Emile could see when the traffic behind him was starting to clear. Luke stayed as close to Alton's patrol car as possible.

When all the cars had passed Emile in the 2nd eastbound truck, he began to make a tight left hand turn. The truck moved slowly, as it needed to power up for the incline from a stopped position. As the truck began to move, Alton accelerated to pass the truck while it was in mid-turn. Legion's Cadillac matched Alton's speed and Luke barreled around the front end of the truck.

Emile drove as far to the left as possible, backed up, and straightened out. The first 32 foot truck was in place.

Remy had Kevin stop the Escalade at the 19th tower, the highest point, so he could watch all the truck activity from one vantage point. As soon as Remy saw Emile's truck start to move, he called to Hazz over a walkie-talkie.

"Hazz, do it."

Hazz checked his mirrors and put the 20 foot truck in 1st gear, and began to ease up on the clutch. When it started to move, he pushed the accelerator to the floorboard. Horns began to blast, cars could be heard skidding, and white smoke could be seen from various tires and brakes of motorists trying to avoid a collision. Hazz made a tight left hand turn across the 2 lanes, backed up and straightened out.

The 2nd westbound truck was in place, but not before an ensign from the Coronado Naval Air Station, driving a late model Yamaha Raider SCL between the lanes of the bridge, was caught completely off guard by Hazz's truck maneuver. In an attempt to avoid a collision with the truck, the motorcyclist swerved and went down. The velocity of the bike caused it to continue under the truck and the driver rolled across the pavement under the truck as if he was chasing it. The rear wheel of the motorcycle was still turning when it finally came to a stop. The driver of the motorcycle tried to get up, but fell back to the bridge roadway.

Now the 1st truck in each direction was able to pull into place once the traffic had passed. Like a synchronized swimming team, Pike and Philippe both positioned their trucks in line with the other two trucks. Traffic was now cut off totally on the bridge.

Once a truck was stopped, the driver took an 8 ½ by 11 piece of paper and taped it to the inside of the driver's window, so it could be read from the outside by police or nosey motorists. It read: DO NOT MOVE! DETONATOR IS MOTION-SENSITIVE!

Remy removed the hearing transmission device from his pocket. This was the device he used when he was on the maintenance walkway of the bridge to install the splice hijacker. It was in plastic and germ-free as Remy demanded. He also put on the video glasses that allowed Bob Brockman to have the same line of sight as Remy. In addition, all the men wore a corded earpiece to hear the walkie-talkie transmissions.

"Brock," Remy declared, "can you see and hear me?"

"Brock and roll, baby," Remy heard clearly.

"Take away their eyes," Remy told him.

With 4 keystrokes, Brockman connected to the power source of the splice hijacker. With one additional keystroke, Brockman redirected the optical feed from the bridge cameras and he now controlled all of them.

"It's done," Brockman told Remy.

From one of the cameras, he could see Hazz's truck moving into its final position. An evil smile came over Brockman's face as he perused the 6 screens. Brockman wore a headset and he pushed a button that allowed his voice to be blared throughout the building.

"Ladies and gentlemen. For the comfort of all our patrons, please silence your cell phones. Refreshments are available in the lobby. Enjoy the show!"

CHAPTER 72

In the traffic control center of the California Highway Patrol Border Division, Sergeant Michael Demma reviewed traffic volume reports and training modifications set to be instituted within the next 30 days. Sergeant Demma's desk was in the corner of the room. The center of the room consisted of 12 work stations, manned by 12 officers, who monitored live camera traffic activity throughout southern San Diego County. Each officer had 2 monitors to review and they would be able to alert patrol officers to accidents and any other traffic-related incidents.

"Sarge," one of the officers called out and Demma looked up to acknowledge his name. "There's something going on on the bridge."

Demma walked over to look at the screens. Just then his phone rang. He walked back to answer it.

"Control Center. Demma."

"Mike," Demma recognized the voice as Lieutenant Leonard Brown, "what's going on with the bridge? 9-1-1 is blowing up. They say trucks are blocking all the lanes and some of the people claim they're wired to blow."

"Let me call you back, Lieutenant."

"Mike, I'm gonna call the Terrorism Threat Assessment Center. I want them activated for this. Let me know what you find out." Demma returned the phone to its cradle.

"Pull up all the cameras on the bridge."

"They're all dark," one of the officers said.

"Did you call over there? Is it a mechanical problem?" Demma asked with urgency.

"We called. They can't find a problem."

"Did you re-set them?"

"We did. Nothin'. The maintenance people just received an order to evacuate."

"See if there's an airship in the area. Let's find out what the hell is goin' on." Demma's voice flared in frustration.

Once the trucks were in position, the drivers moved with mechanical precision. The first thing they did was to remove an industrial chain from the cab of the smaller truck. Pike had modified the front bumper of all the trucks to allow the chain to be wrapped around it and hooked. Then they would proceed to attach a grappling hook to a winch that Pike mounted on the rear of each truck. The winch would lower the grappling hook to catch the side of the bridge and secure the truck to it.

Kevin and Remy proceeded to the eastern end of the blocked off portion of the bridge in the Escalade. Alton slowly followed them, tailed by Luke in Legion's Cadillac. Remy stepped out of the vehicle to survey Hazz and Pike as they worked to secure the longer truck to the bridge.

"We got it," Hazz said to Pike in a raised voice. Even with no cars on the bridge, the wind made communication difficult.

"We retract it until it pulls on the truck a little bit," Pike replied and he pulled the winch cable back in until it tugged on the truck. Pike gave a thumbs up and the men moved to the smaller truck.

"Emile, how's it coming?" Remy asked into a walkie-talkie.

"We gotta connect one more truck to the bridge," Emile answered.

"Remy," Brockman's voice could be heard through the hearing transmission device. "You've got company. A police helicopter and a news helicopter."

The sound of helicopter rotors filled the air.

"Kevin," Remy called out. Kevin Camballa looked in his direction.

"Don't let him do it," Brockman pleaded with exigency. "He'll screw it up. You have to lock it on a heat signature. Just slide the panel out. I can do it from here."

Remy raced back to the passenger side of the Escalade. Under the glove box, he pulled forward an instrument panel on a track that was complete with a single, steering-arm, control stick and small, radar-like screen. A small green light on the panel turned on.

"I got it," Brockman told him.

"Tell me when the police helicopter is within range," Remy said as he looked up and waited for the arrival of the CHP Eurocopter AS 350.

"It's within range," Brockman told him.

"Light it up," Remy exclaimed.

On Brockman's screen in the machine shop, he could see the outline of the helicopter on a radar screen. The outline moved, then stopped, and the word 'LOCKED' appeared at the bottom of the screen. Brockman was maneuvering the image with a control stick and when it locked, his thumb pushed down on the top button of the stick.

Immediately, the top of the Escalade burst open and up popped an unmanned, computer-guided, .50 caliber machine gun. It locked on the police helicopter's position within a second and began firing .50 caliber tracer rounds at it. Tracer ammunition has a small pyrotechnic charge in the base of the round to allow the naked eye to follow the bullet.

Brockman strafed the helicopter and focused on the rear rotor as the bullets pulsed from the weapon system. The tracers provided a deadly reminder of the ammunition's power. The bullets completely sheared off the rear rotor.

"He shoots, he scooooooores!!!" Brockman proudly screamed with a fist pump. "The crowd is going wild."

Inside the helicopter, a 'May Day' distress signal was put out and the helicopter continually swung around in a circle, spiraling downward faster and faster. The helicopter crew prepared for a hard water landing. Within 5 seconds, the helicopter crashed into the bay and the water stopped the main blade from turning.

"What about the news helicopter?" Brockman asked.

"Leave it," Remy told him.

Inside the traffic control center of the California Highway Patrol Border Division, Lieutenant Leonard Brown was advised that the airship was down and the condition of the crew was still being assessed.

"See if we can pipe the TV coverage in here," Brown said. He picked up his phone and dialed 3 numbers. "Our airship is down. Get me somebody at the Coronado Naval Air Station, Miramar Naval Air Station, and Camp Pendleton, in that order. Tell them we have a terrorist threat. See if they can scramble a couple of jets over the bridge. Then, get me the Department of Homeland Security."

Alton, Legion, Luke, Karla and Lester all watched in horror at the capabilities of these individuals.

At the Deus X Machine Shop, Bob Brockman prepared for round 2.

CHAPTER 73

Detectives Skylar Stubbs and Jeff Elkins raced down Interstate 5 in a marked Ford Crown Victoria Police Interceptor hoping to stop Alton Burchesky as he came across the bridge. Both detectives knew from the radio traffic that something major was going on involving it.

Once the California Highway Patrol realized a criminal incident was taking place on the bridge, they immediately closed it and placed two patrol units at each entrance and exit of the bridge. Additional units provided traffic support to guide cars that were stuck on the bridge after Remy and crew closed it off. In the eastbound direction, there was a relatively small number of cars and they were quickly escorted off.

In the westbound direction, there was over a mile of cars on the 2 lanes that needed to be turned around and driven back to Interstate 5.

Skylar saw the police cars barricading the westbound entrance and the line of cars returning to the freeway. This process was slowing down all movement on the freeway. Skylar turned on his overhead lights and siren. Cars allowed him to move to the center breakdown lane, where he drove down the freeway, adjacent to the median. This was not a lane of the freeway.

Once the traffic congestion started to ease, Skylar cut across the lanes, still blaring his siren, and saw the two CHP cars blocking the exit to the bridge.

"What are you gonna do?" Jeff asked with concern.

"Get on the bridge," Skylar answered with laser focus. He knew that if they could arrest Alton Burchesky, they would salvage their investigation.

Skylar turned the wheel for a hard right hand turn and the car went up and over the median and the berm that was covered with groundcover plants. Skylar and Jeff were now heading westbound in the empty eastbound lanes of the bridge. The two CHP units called in the event. Because it involved a police vehicle, they awaited instructions before engaging in pursuit.

Bob Brockman saw Skylar and Jeff's vehicle get on the bridge.

"Remy," Brockman called for his attention.

"Yeah," Remy answered.

"A cop car's coming at you in the eastbound lanes at high speed."

"We got it," Remy said and called out to Kevin. "Kevin, get the SAW from the back seat and get on top a this truck." Remy referred to the larger truck on the eastern side of the blocked off area. The SAW or Squad Automatic Weapon that he wanted Kevin to grab was an M249 light machine gun. This gun was .556 caliber and could cycle bullets at a rate of 775 rounds per minute. "A cop car is coming. Greet it."

Kevin moved quickly as he retrieved the weapon. He went to the truck, opened the driver's side door and was able to climb onto the cab of the truck, then to the top of the box of the truck. He opened the folding bipod attached near the front of the gun and set it down. He then got down on his stomach and looked through an Eotec sighting system to find his target.

Skylar and Jeff were traveling at a speed in excess of 100 miles an hour. As they reached one quarter mile from their destination, the parked truck came into sharper focus and they could see the bipod legs of the gun. Their assassin was looking through the sighting system to place them in his crosshairs.

"Sky, that's a sniper! Stop the car!" Jeff exclaimed as his voice bellowed.

Skylar hit the brakes with both feet. The front of the car pushed down as the tires started to skid and the brakes started to smoke. As soon as Kevin saw that the car was trying to stop, he opened fire on it.

Jeff and Skylar tried to cower down inside the vehicle as the bullets mercilessly rained down on it. All the windows in the car were blown out and dozens of large holes were blown into the side of the police cruiser. The hood of the car suddenly popped open and bent back over the area where the windshield would have been. The front tires blew out and the rear of the car fishtailed, then the car rolled one full revolution, landing back on its rims. As it flipped, Kevin took his finger off the trigger. The car came to a stop several hundred feet and parallel to the truck where Kevin was firing.

CHAPTER 74

While Kevin dealt with Skylar and Jeff, Remy focused on completion of the mission. Once the trucks were secured to the bridge, the final item was to turn on the power to the electronic harnesses that would place the explosives in any particular truck on the same circuit with the other trucks and the explosives mounted on the towers below the water.

"Brock, what's goin' on downstairs?" Remy asked.

"On the first floor, the rent is paid. We're live and hot," Brockman proclaimed with serious bravado.

As soon as the trucks were on line, Remy and the men would jump off the bridge. Remy looked off in the distance and could only see the top of the larger truck. The bridge inclined to its apex at the 19th tower from Remy's location. Remy saw Alton standing next to his CHP police cruiser staring at him.

"Kevin," Remy spoke into his walkie-talkie, "watch this side. Keep an eye on Alton."

Kevin stood from his lying down position and picked up the SAW machine gun. He held it at waist level. From his vantage point he could watch all the activity at the eastern end of their blockade and he could see the trucks on the western end of the blockade located approximately one-half mile away.

"Pike," Remy called to him while watching Alton, "are we all set?"

"These two trucks should be online," Pike advised. Hazz jumped out of the shorter truck and gave a thumbs up.

"Brock," Remy spoke up due to the wind volume, "Are we set with these trucks?"

"The first westbound truck is not online, Philippe's truck," Brockman responded.

Remy immediately returned to his walkie-talkie.

"Emile, what's the problem with Philippe's truck?" Remy's rushed voice demanded an answer.

"It's got juice," Emile said, "but it won't power the circuits."

"Send Hazz down there," Brockman told Remy in his ear.

"Hazz," Remy called to him, "go down there and see if you can get Philippe's truck online."

"You want me to take the Escalade?" Hazz asked.

"No," Remy replied. He looked around. "Take that motorcycle." Remy pointed to the motorcycle that slid under the second westbound truck while it was maneuvering into position.

Hazz straightened the motorcycle and the right side was extremely dented and scratched. With the push of one button, it started.

While Remy gave orders and received information from Brockman, Luke removed a Colt AR-15 type assault rifle from his tactical bag. He slammed a fully loaded magazine clip into the weapon and made sure a live round was ready to be fired. He turned around and looked at Karla.

"You stay here. Don't get outta the car."

Karla looked at him and nervously acknowledged his command. Luke then looked at Lester.

"Don't touch her." Luke's word had a seriousness mixed with a primal anger that Karla appreciated.

Luke opened the car door and Karla spoke up.

"Luke, be careful." It was the first time that she had ever called him Luke.

"I will, Miss Mulry." Luke exited the vehicle.

Luke immediately raised his weapon and aimed it squarely at the back of Alton's head.

"Alton," Luke yelled out. Alton did not turn, but knew a gun was trained on him. "Don't go for your gun or I'll view it as an act of aggression. Let Legion out of the car and take off his handcuffs."

"You don't want to be involved in this," Alton yelled out, still not turning. Remy watched the events unfold.

"Remy," Brockman's voice bellowed forcing Remy to re-direct his attention.

"Yeah," Remy responded, now covering his mouth, so his voice would not be drowned out by the wind.

"The cavalry is comin' over the hill," Brockman told him. "They're sending two F/A-18 Hornet jets. The ordinance on it are Sidewinder missiles. It's got an internal cannon that can fire 6000 rounds of 20 millimeter ammo per minute."

"What direction?" Remy demanded.

"The north. They're gonna buzz you once, then they're gonna come in hot. Do you want me to engage 'em?" Brockman's voice was fast and focused.

"Can you take it down with a 50 cal?" Remy wondered if the .50 caliber machine gun on the Escalade was powerful enough to shoot down an F/A-18 jet.

"I don't know." Brockman's voice echoed surrender. "Maybe one, but not both."

"Don't engage it," Remy ordered. "They won't open fire on us. Americans don't like to see blood while they're eating their fast food."

"Alton," Luke yelled to him, "back up now or I'll engage in an act of aggression."

While Alton backed up, Lester reached into the front seat of Legion's Cadillac and grabbed Luke's tactical bag to review the contents. The first thing that caught his eye was a Colt 1911 .45 caliber semi-automatic pistol. Lester found a loaded clip for the gun and inserted it.

"What are you doing? You shouldn't touch that stuff," Karla told him with disdain.

"Just in case I need it," Lester told her as he continued to watch the events involving Luke and Alton. "There's one more in there. You should take it."

Karla looked in the bag and found a Colt Peacemaker. This gun was a .45 caliber, 6-shot single action revolver that looked like a cowboy gun. Karla was familiar with this gun because she fired it when she went with Luke, Pat Madore, and his son to the shooting range. Karla opened the loading gate at the rear of the cylinder of the gun and loaded 6 bullets into it. She closed the loading gate and watched Luke.

"Hazz, what's goin' on?" Remy screamed.

"One of the circuit boards is cracked," Hazz told him. "It must have broke on the way over here. I can fix it."

"Hurry up." Remy's demand was exigent. "Emile, bring Philippe over here."

Roger Legion had stepped out of the CHP police car and Alton took off his handcuffs. He wrung his hands around his wrists in the area where the handcuffs had been.

Alton suddenly pulled out his pistol and aimed it at Remy.

"It's over, Remy. You're under arrest." Alton spoke with a stern countenance.

"Our business is over," Remy told him. "Kill Legion and they're all dead. Then Dexter Frye can rest in peace."

Alton turned to Legion while still keeping the gun aimed at Remy. He then looked back to Remy and pulled the hammer back on his gun. In the distance, a jet's roar could be heard.

CHAPTER 75

Back at the machine shop, Brockman continued to check the circuits on the last truck hoping it would come on line. Abruptly, a computerized voice filled the air.

"PERIMETER COMPROMISED," repeated over and over.

Brockman looked up, with no time for shock, threw off his headset, and moved at warp velocity. He immediately pulled up the video from the outside cameras and could see the FBI SWAT Team preparing to make entry.

"NO! NO! NOOOOO!" Brockman screamed with voracious anger.

Brockman saw the SWAT team members had raised weapons and breaching tools in hand. His face displayed vitriolic frustration. Brockman started typing furiously, while intently viewing one screen. The display on the screen said, 'SELF-DESTRUCT SEQUENCE INITIATED.' Under those words appeared a box that had the words, 'SOFTWARE' and 'HARDWARE.' Brockman put a check mark in front of each word. The computer then requested an authorization code. Brockman typed in 'JOHNNY_QUEST.'

Brockman got out of his chair and raced over to a large, industrial circuit breaker panel that was located on the wall closest to his computer table. He opened the door to the circuit breakers and pulled out a large circuit breaker that had a handle, known as a fusible pullout. It was located directly in the center at the top of the circuit breaker panel. His momentum was in high gear as he squatted down to a large toolbox situated at the base of the panel. He opened it and retrieved a piece of copper wire that was approximately 3 feet long.

With geometric precision, Brockman wrapped the wire on the prongs of the fusible pullout where it interfaced with the circuit box. He rushed to replace the fusible pullout to its previous position within the panel, but did not press it in. A copper wire ran out on both sides from the back of the fusible pullout. He wrapped those wires around two steel handles located on each side of the circuit breaker display. The steel handles were perpendicular to the ground, 3 feet long, and located 3 feet off the ground. The top of the handle was 6 feet off the ground.

Brockman again squatted down and pulled out two pairs of handcuff restraints from the toolbox. He connected one of each pair of handcuffs on each of the handles.

All the while, the computerized voice blared 'PERIMETER COMPROMISED' with precise repetition.

Brockman walked back to his computer table and put his headset on.

"Remy," Brockman's voice was cold and detached, "now, I have company. *Bon chance, mon frère* (Good luck, my brother)."

Brockman stood up and looked at the door and the outside cameras. The SWAT team members were in place, but holding their position. They were awaiting approval for entry from Special Agent

Oliver Love.   On the screen where he typed the self-destruct password, a loading bar was filling.

Brockman again typed feverishly and brought up the radar screen for the .50 caliber machine gun turret on the Escalade. He moved the control stick to allow a 360 degree view around the Escalade. He found his target.

CHAPTER 76

From the back seat of Legion's Cadillac, Karla saw Kevin on top of the truck holding the SAW machine gun aimed at Alton. At the rear of the smaller eastbound truck, Pike aimed his MP5K submachine gun at Alton, but also moved it to aim on Luke. Lester opened his door.

"What are you doing?" she asked.

"I'm gonna take my chances outside," Lester told her. He stepped out of the vehicle and crouched down behind it.

With the door open, the jet's engines bellowed their thunderous power. Karla slid across the seat and contemplated stepping out of the vehicle. Her eyes nervously moved from Luke to Alton to Kevin, then Pike.

"It's over, Remy," Alton declared. "Let me see your hands."

The Escalade, Alton's CHP cruiser, and Legion's Cadillac were lined up in the center lane of the eastbound lanes. They were on a slight decline as the bridge was descending from its highest point at the 19th tower.

Remy began to raise his hands and he held his walkie-talkie in his left hand. He passed his left hand in front of his mouth and he spoke into the walkie-talkie.

"Kill him."

Kevin's SAW machine gun came to life as he slaughtered Alton. The bullets ripped apart his skull and the center of his chest. Kevin stopped firing and stood at the edge of the truck with light, white smoke coming out from the barrel end of his weapon.

Then, Kevin and Pike aimed their machine guns at Luke. Luke swept his rifle from side-to-side ready to open fire on either one.

"Mr. Legion," Remy screamed out and walked closer to him. "It's unfortunate that we had to meet this way. Alton never told me why he wanted you dead."

The wind blew up Legion's suit coat and tie.

"He didn't want me dead. I wanted him dead," Legion spoke and stood in defiance.

Legion's sentence hit Remy like a runaway bus. With just a few words, Legion promulgated his power and his danger. Remy was uncomfortable. He quickly raised the walkie-talkie to his mouth.

"Kill them all."

Luke saw a burst from the muzzle of Kevin's gun. The firefight was on. Luke was only able to get an occasional shot off at Kevin because of the velocity of fire from the machine gun. Even though Pike had a submachine gun, he fired in one shot bursts, to conserve his ammo. Pike was also conscious of taking cover from Luke's fire. Legion ducked between Alton's police cruiser and his Cadillac.

Karla got out of the car through Lester's door with the Colt Peacemaker and raced to a position behind the car. Lester was crouched down next to her. The sound of the shooting was being drowned out by the booming noise of jet engines.

From the westbound direction, Karla saw a motorcycle on the roadway coming over the 19th tower. Emile was driving and Philippe sat behind him. As they approached, Philippe leveled his MP5K submachine gun to open fire on Luke. Luke was about to be trapped in a triangular crossfire.

Two F/A-18 Hornets were bearing down on the bridge with an intimidating presence.

As the jets passed, a fast shadow covered the action on the bridge. The jet engines drowned out all the gunfire. As the motorcycle came up parallel to the Cadillac in the westbound lanes, Karla stood up, took one step and held the Peacemaker out with her right hand, aimed at the motorcycle, slightly above waist level, ready to fire. With her left hand, she pulled the trigger once and then began fanning or slapping the hammer of the gun, as fast as possible, 6 times in a row. Fanning is a shooting technique that allows the cylinder of the gun to turn and hit the firing pin to allow for semi-automatic fire in a single-action weapon.

The motorcycle and the men went down, mortally wounded.

As Karla was firing, the turret of the Escalade moved with computer precision from its aim over San Diego Bay to straight ahead. The barrel of the gun was aimed at Kevin Camballa. Within a second, it was in position and fired mercilessly. Fifty caliber tracer bullets pumped out of it. The first bullet carried Kevin off the truck and he continued to be hit while his body was in motion. He was struck 4 times and his body landed 20 feet away from the truck. His chest was torn apart and his face was unrecognizable, due to a head shot.

CHAPTER 77

As the bullets ripped Kevin Camballa apart, at the Deus X Machine Shop, Brockman took his thumb off the button at the top of the control stick and the Escalade's gun was silenced. He looked at the screen that displayed Kevin's dead body.

"I told you, I take care of business, bitch," Brockman uttered with finality.

It was then that Brockman heard the FBI SWAT team begin the process to breach the doors. The loading bar on the self-destruct display was almost full. He typed another flurry of keystrokes and the banging on the doors became louder.

Brockman ran from his computer table to the circuit breaker panel where the handcuffs hung and the fusible pullout that was attached to the handles with copper wires was located. He looked at the set-up. He was now shaking uncontrollably, trying to maintain a grasp on what was left of his sanity.

"I gotta admit, this is gangster," he concluded with inevitability.

He put one set of handcuffs on each wrist and grabbed the handles at the highest point. He pulled his legs up and, with his right foot, slammed the fusible pullout into place. It closed the circuit and

200 amps, 600 volts cruised through the copper wires, the steel handles, the handcuffs, and Brockman. The voltage in an electric chair for execution ranges from 500 volts to 2000 volts.

Brockman's body tensed up like he was hit by a Taser shotgun. The lights in the entire building flickered and the 4 doors on the building were breached at the same time, allowing the SWAT team entrance.

The fusible pullout circuit tripped and the electricity stopped flowing through Brockman's body. He hung by his wrists from the handcuffs with the bottom half of his body on the floor. Blood trickled lightly from every orifice in his head including his eyes. A spotlight, directly overhead, shined down on him. It illuminated his bald head and the letters, I.T.C.O.B.

FBI SWAT team members began their sweep of the building before Special Agent Oliver Love would be allowed to enter. On one of Brockman's video screens, a series of messages popped up as events transpired.

When the SWAT team came through the doors, the words, PERIMETER BREACH, appeared on the screen. When Brockman was being electrocuted, the first message stated, POWER LOSS DETECTED, while the lights were flickering. When they stopped flickering, the next message was BACK-UP POWER INITIATED – RE-BOOT AVOIDED.

Suddenly, large metal gates dropped down from above the 4 man doors and the overhead doors. These were large, heavy, welded doors that were not mechanical and dropped under their own weight. When they fell, the next message on Brockman's computer screen was EXITS SEALED.

The next message was DELUGE ACTIVATED. A sprinkler system went off throughout the building and it started to rain intensely. It did not rain water. A liquid ran through a glass piping system within the building. The liquid that ran through the system and rained down on everything, including the FBI SWAT team, was sulfuric acid.

Oliver Love heard the screams of the men inside, but could do nothing until firemen and rescue personnel arrived.

Before Brockman's video screens were totally destroyed, the next message read DETONATION SEQUENCE ACTIVATED. This would begin the process to detonate whatever Semtex was online on the bridge.

The next message stated SELF-DESTRUCT SEQUENCE COMPLETE and then there was the final message: BROCKMAN HAS LEFT THE BUILDING!

CHAPTER 78

Remy knew that Kevin was hit because even though the jets drowned out the sounds of gunfire, he saw the barrel aim from the Escalade's turret and the tracers fly. One of Luke's bullets then hit Pike. Pike retreated farther behind the 2nd westbound truck, but collapsed onto the bridge railing behind the truck.

Remy and Luke locked eyes. Luke knew he was almost out of ammunition. Legion watched the action as the gunfire ceased. Luke turned and looked behind the car. He saw Karla and gave her a smile and a wink. In the second that Luke glanced away, Remy pulled his Glock C18 machine pistol. As Luke returned his gaze to Remy, Remy fired one shot at him. It was a headshot. The bullet struck Luke near the left eye socket. It spun him around. As he spun, he dropped the rifle and went down to the roadway face first.

Legion saw it all happen and he mouthed the words, "Oh, no."

Karla watched in horror and the cacophony of sounds from gunfire to jets to the wind whirling, went silent. She trembled uncontrollably and her mind would only let her see the image of Luke's face smiling and winking. Then, she heard her mother's voice.

"You don't deserve him. He was too good for you. That's why he was taken away. Face it, you're gonna die alone."

Karla let out a primordial scream and dropped to her knees. She sobbed hysterically as she slowly brought her forehead down to the roadway.

Remy looked inside the cab of the larger truck on the eastern end of the blockade. On the power box for the detonator, he saw a green light blinking. This meant that Brockman had started the detonation sequence. The Semtex was about to explode.

Suddenly, from behind, an arm came around Remy's throat and yanked him back. Legion had hooked Remy from behind with his right arm and took his left arm to grab Remy's face in an attempt to snap his neck.

"It makes no difference," Remy struggled to speak, referring to Legion's attempt to kill him while fighting to pull his arm away. "It's gonna blow."

Remy slammed Legion's back into the truck twice, but Legion would not let go. Legion's face tensed up trying to find the strength to end Remy's life. Remy still held the machine pistol and he thought he may be able to shoot Legion in the head or the foot to force him to release his grip.

Their struggling brought them near the bridge railing. Remy raised the gun and fired it once toward Legion's head, but missed. He desperately tried to reposition his hand for a 2nd attempt when a gunshot filled the air.

Detective Skylar Stubbs shot Remy in the center of the chest. Skylar stood there ready with his gun aimed at Remy. His clothes were dirty and blood trickled down onto his white shirt from a cut on his forehead. Legion let go of his grip and Remy fell to the roadway. Legion looked at Skylar.

"Come'on. We gotta go. These trucks are gonna blow," Legion told him.

Legion picked up Remy's gun and threw it off the bridge. Skylar raced back to the front of the truck, where his partner, Jeff Elkins, was leaning against the front end of it. He was in pain from his hip being slammed and was having difficulty walking. Jeff put his arm around Skylar and they moved as fast as possible to Legion's Cadillac.

As Legion ran up to the Cadillac, he took off his suit coat and folded it. He knelt down next to Luke. The circle of blood around his head spoke volumes regarding his condition. He saw Lester standing there with a horrified expression on his face and Karla nearly in a state of shock.

"Lester, get over here," Legion ordered. "Karla, open the back door."

Both followed his commands. Legion removed a handkerchief from his pocket and placed it on Luke's wound. Legion and Lester slid Luke into the back seat and Legion had Karla kneel down on the floor of the back seat. She looked at Luke and started sobbing.

Legion stuck his head in the car from the back door near Luke's head.

"Karla, bend his knees," Legion told her. She complied. "Lester, shut that door."

Legion knew Karla was overwhelmed and he reached over to her face with both hands and lifted it, so she would look at him.

"You've gotta stay with me, sweetheart. We can save him."

"Okay," she cried as she tried to control her tears.

Legion stood up and ripped his shirt open like Superman would do in a classic comic. He removed his tie and put it on top of the car. He then ripped each arm of the shirt off.

"Karla, wrapped this around his head," Legion rapidly moved, now wearing a white t-shirt, and gave her the arms of the shirt. "Hold it in place with my tie." He tossed the tie to her and closed the door.

Lester was in the passenger seat and Legion arrived at the driver's door just as Skylar and Jeff reached the Cadillac.

"You guys jump in the trunk," Legion told them and popped the trunk open.

As fast as they could move, Jeff, then Skylar, fell into the trunk. Skylar pushed a button on the trunk lid and it closed automatically. Legion started the car, put it in reverse, and slammed the gas pedal. The car moved backward at high speed.

A hand reached up and grabbed the bridge railing. Like a zombie that refuses to die, Remy stood up. His coat was blood soaked and he saw the Cadillac backing up toward the 19th tower. He held his chest and moved as quickly as he could to the passenger door of the Escalade. He got in and moved the joystick on the control panel in search of the heat signature for Legion's Cadillac. No one in the Cadillac knew that Remy was still alive.

The Cadillac reached the apex of the bridge, the 19th tower, and Legion parked the car perpendicular to the lanes and parallel to the trucks. He lowered all the windows. Legion grabbed Luke's tactical bag and saw a pair of shooter's earmuffs for hearing protection. Legion took them from the bag and also found headphones that were *Beats by Dr. Dre*.

"Karla," Legion said turning to her, "you put one a these on and put the other on Luke. Hold it on his ears." She followed his orders. Legion then made a general statement, "Everybody, get down! Cover your ears!"

In the Escalade, Remy found the Cadillac on the radar screen. The word, 'LOCKED,' then appeared on the screen. As

Remy pressed the button on the top of the joystick to commence fire, the Semtex exploded.

CHAPTER 79

The concussive energy of the blast caused the trucks to launch. At the eastern end of the blockade, the longer truck blew 25 feet straight up in the air. The frame of the truck was blown apart and the remaining portion looked like a meteor crashing back into the bridge roadway. The shorter truck also had its frame blown apart, but blasted up on more of an arc sending what remained of the fiery box and cab of the truck into the bay.

At the western end, the truck that Hazz was attempting to bring online did not explode. The front end of the truck was on fire from the shorter truck blowing up in a similar manner to the longer truck at the eastern end.

Hazz was not prepared for the explosion. He was killed when a portion of the reinforced steel from the adjacent truck flew through the windshield of the cab where he was working. Hazz was decapitated.

Approximately 40 feet of the bridge railing behind the exploded trucks was gone.

As the trucks exploded, they generated a sonic boom and caused a concentric ring of energy to actuate away from the area of the trucks. Its power lifted the front end of the Escalade and toppled the vehicle up and over onto the top of Alton's police cruiser. It was upside down and it slid off the police car onto the open lane, next to the bridge railing. As the pulse of energy passed through each vehicle, all the windows shattered with a sudden pop.

The boom was accompanied by a shaking that felt like a massive earthquake was about to unleash its reckoning.

In Legion's Cadillac, the passengers were ready as the windshield and rear window popped into thousands of smaller pieces followed by a wave of heat. Karla held the *Beats by Dr. Dre* headset on Luke and she could see the area around his wound start to redden. Her tears had not stopped.

In the darkness of the trunk, Skylar and Jeff were quiet, except for the low voice of Skylar praying.

At the bottom of the bay, the reinforced container attached to the 20th tower exploded apart and blasted away from it. On the 18th tower, the container blew off like a bullet firing from a shell, slamming the 17th tower while releasing a ginormous explosion and fireball that matched the explosion between the 20th and 21st towers.

From nearly 50 feet below the water, the ardent fireball raised up to slightly above the bridge surface, approximately 200 feet above the water. From inside the Cadillac, Legion and Lester could see two walls of fire arise on either side of the car, as if the doors to Hell had been opened. After a moment, the flames began to recede.

Fire raged on the bay over the area of the explosions. The remnants of the Semtex that did not explode continued to burn.

When the explosion occurred, the underwater area below the bridge became the epicenter for a mini tsunami. Boats within 500 feet of the bridge were capsized and those docked near shore were lifted onto it. Any vessel within eyesight of the bridge felt the wrath of the explosion.

Inside the upside down Escalade, Remy was crumpled on the ceiling amidst broken glass. The turret of the gun raised the rear of the vehicle. He looked up, surveyed the bridge, and realized that his plan had failed. Remy could see that the Escalade was on fire in the engine area and in the rear of the vehicle. As he started to move, his chest was in excruciating pain. The Escalade tipped toward the railing side of the lane, but the railing had been blown off.

"*Viva La France!*" he uttered in a weakened voice.

The gas tank on the Escalade exploded and the vehicle catapulted off the bridge providing Remy with one last fiery ride into the blazing waters below.

CHAPTER 80

Legion stepped out of the Cadillac and popped the trunk open. The waning sunlight of the afternoon shined down on Skylar and Jeff as Skylar jumped out and assisted Jeff with a labored exit from the car. A magnificent sunset enveloped the city landscape and a mild breeze exuded a zephyrean tranquility.

From his position near the top of the 19th tower, Legion was able to gaze upon all the destruction that took place on the bridge. He called over to Lester, who also stepped out of the vehicle.

"Where's my cell phone?"

"Luke had it," Lester told him.

Roger briskly returned to the car and opened the door near Luke's head.

"How is he?" he asked Karla.

"I don't know," she answered while trying to stop her tears.

"Karla, see if you can find my cell phone," Roger requested.

She found the phone inside Luke's suit coat pocket and handed it to Roger. Also in his pocket was her address and phone number on a piece of paper.

Roger dialed 9-1-1 and waited for a response.

"This is Roger Legion," he told the 9-1-1 operator. "I'm on the bridge with the survivors. It's over. We need an air ambulance immediately."

Jeff had his arm around Skylar and they leaned back against the trunk of the car. Jeff looked at Skylar with a devilish smirk. Skylar returned the glance.

"Well, ain't we a pair, raggedy man?" Jeff told him.

Skylar smiled. "*Mad Max: Beyond Thunderdome*. 1985."

"You're good," Jeff replied. "You know what I was wonderin'?"

"What?" Skylar asked.

"What time is church on Sunday?" A smile filled Skylar's face.

Air ambulances had been on standby waiting for the 'all clear' signal before proceeding to the bridge. An air ambulance was on the bridge road near Legion's car within 4 minutes. Luke was loaded onto the helicopter and Legion stood there with his arm around Karla. Legion stopped the main nurse.

"She's gonna ride with him," Legion told her with a raised voice to overcome the sound of helicopter rotors, referring to Karla. He turned to Karla to escort her to the helicopter.

"I'll come over to the hospital as soon as I can," Roger said.

Karla looked at him with her eyes reddened by her abundance of tears and nodded. Roger then gave her a kiss on the cheek and looked her in the eyes.

"You saved him."

She immediately came at him for a tight hug like a loving daughter and he reciprocated. Karla knew who Luke's savior was and she was hugging him. Karla would never return to Legion and Associates because she did not want to remember Roger Legion as the tyrannical king of a legal empire, but rather as a hero who saved all the survivors that day on the bridge.

Part 4

CHAPTER 81

7 Days Later

On the 24th floor of the America's Finest City Building at Legion & Associates this afternoon, Lester Abrams sat back in his chair with his feet on the desk, talking on the phone, and reminiscing about the events on the bridge. He was basking in the limelight as he would regale the story to anyone who would listen about the gunplay, the explosions, and the .45 caliber Colt that he held in his hand. The same Colt that did not even have a live round in the chamber that day. He could not get enough of the news media or the congratulatory words that were being heaved upon him.

His wife, Diane, had commenced divorce proceedings and Lester moved in with Clare Luconi, the court reporter that he had been having an affair with for the past year. They planned to marry as soon as his divorce was final.

Roger was intentionally keeping Lester away from his old accounts and any direct contact with an insurance company. At present, he was performing the same work as a paralegal.

Roger Legion had no comment about the bridge after he was debriefed by the police, the FBI, and the Department of Homeland

Security. The city wanted to give the survivors of the bridge event a parade, but Roger would not allow it. He felt too many people died needlessly that day, including five members of the FBI SWAT team and Alton Burchesky.

Video surveillance linked Remy and his brother, Emile, to the courthouse explosion and the murder of Judge Gene Garubo. Patrolmen Accendo and Rivers linked Kevin Camballa and Philippe to the murder of Captain Kyle Bober.

As soon as Lester hung up his phone, Nina, the receptionist, called.

"Yes," Lester answered.

"The parking garage just called. Your car alarm is going off."

"Again?" Lester retorted in disbelief. "This is the 2nd time in the past week. Lousy beaners down there, lookin' to see what they can boost. All right, I'm on my way."

He stood from the chair and walked out to the lobby. Lester waited for an elevator and caught Nina's eye.

"If any media calls, put them on hold, I'll be right back. Make sure they don't hang up."

A bell indicated that an elevator had arrived. When the doors opened, Glenn Edgarian, Roger Legion's private eye extraordinaire, stepped off the elevator. He wore a blue suit, white shirt, and a blue striped tie.

"Hey, Lester," Glenn beamed with recognition and a smile, "How are ya?"

They exchanged a quick handshake.

"I'm good, Glenn," Lester answered as he entered the elevator and held the doors open. "Ya gonna be here for a while?" Lester asked.

"Yeah. I gotta talk to Roger. I saw you the other night on Fox News."

"Come and see me when you're done. I'll tell you all about it."

"All right," Glenn replied and the elevator doors closed.

Glenn and Nina exchanged smiles as he walked up to her counter.

"Hey, Mister Glenn."

"Hey, Miss Nina. Where's the boss?"

Nina pushed 2 buttons on her telephone.

"Glenn Edgarian is here to see you." She waited a moment for a response and looked up at Glenn. "You can go back."

Glenn had been to Roger's office many times before, so he did not need an escort. As soon as he left the lobby, Nina reached into her purse to retrieve her cell phone. She dialed a number that she had on speed dial.

"He's on his way down," she said and ended the call.

Roger was sitting at his desk reviewing mail when Glenn knocked at his door.

"Come on in," Roger said as he stood and walked over to Glenn for a handshake.

"Roger, how are ya? Keepin' a low profile?"

"It's a sideshow," Roger told him referring to the bridge media coverage as he returned to his chair. "I don't make a good media whore. Have a seat."

Glenn sat across from Roger.

"How's Luke?" Glenn asked in a serious tone.

"He's in a drug-induced coma."

"That's terrible," Glenn reflected and eased into the next topic. "Remember that little assignment you gave me regarding somebody trying to hijack your files? I found out who it was." As

Glenn finished his sentence, a mischievous grin filled his face and he crossed one leg over the other.

"Who?" Legion wondered.

"Who did you think it was?"

"Walter Stoller," Legion responded with certainty.

Walter Stoller was a partner from the law firm of Bantree, Tasker & Matast. He had met with Lester Abrams at the Bistro West Restaurant in Carlsbad to advise him of his law firm's plan to steal away clients from other law firms and offered Lester a partnership position.

"Bingo," Glenn remarked as if Roger had just answered a game show question. "You heard what happened to him, right?"

Glenn began to answer his own question and Roger began to remember.

CHAPTER 82

As Lester stepped off the elevator on to the 'P2' level of the parking garage, he could hear his car alarm in the distance. Lester entered the garage from the elevator lobby of the parking level and made the trek to his black Porsche 911. It was located straight down an aisle approximately 30 cars from the doors to the elevator. He was able to turn off the alarm with his key fob. None of the windows were broken and all the doors were locked. He looked to see if there was any exterior damage as the alarm was also motion-sensitive. There was no sign of any damage.

Without the alarm blaring, the garage had an eerie calm. Lester noticed several high-end vehicles and stopped to admire a new Bentley. It did not yet have license plates and the interior appeared to have been carved by a craftsman.

As he resumed his return, he saw a $20 bill on the ground. He stopped and crouched down to swipe it. As he reached for it, he heard a pop and in the same moment felt that he had been hit in the head with a lead pipe. He went to one knee and then to the ground as the strike to his head was a muffled .22 caliber bullet shot point blank in the back of his head. It was soon followed by 3 more shots.

Approximately 10 cars away, a 1992 Lincoln Continental started and backed out of its parking space. Then, a 2010 Chevy Malibu, parked further down the row also started and began to back out.

The Lincoln Continental stopped alongside the shooter and the trunk popped open. The Chevy Malibu pulled up closely behind the Lincoln. The shooter got into the trunk of the Lincoln and pulled the trunk down to close it. Both cars proceeded to the exit where they paid their parking fee and left the building.

A man in his late 60s, gray hair, thick glasses, wearing a cap and windbreaker coat drove the Lincoln. When his car reached the street outside of the building, he took out his cell phone and dialed a number. The call was answered on the 2nd ring.

"Tell Jimmy, it's done," the driver said into the phone and ended the call.

Javier Jimenez' son was a drug dealer who wanted to be a movie gangster. He was also Lester Abrams' drug dealer. When Javier's son found out that Lester had talked to the police, he feared Lester would incriminate him. He told his father and his father sought the assistance of Jimmy Flowers, another high-powered crime boss.

Lester Abrams name along with the law firm name and address were on the piece of paper that Javier gave to Jimmy when he went to visit him while his grass was being cut.

Jimmy Flowers did not charge Javier for this hit because he still harbored some resentment against the Legion law firm. Eighteen months earlier, 8 of his men died in a shootout in the Legion and Associates conference room in an attempt to retrieve drug money that was stolen from Jimmy.

As the synapses in Lester's brain were futilely firing, while in the process of shutting down, Lester wondered if this was

Legion's final act of retribution against him. His final thought was something Roger Legion once told him. Legion said, "If you want to win a battle, you gotta get bloody." As Roger Legion had always been in the past, he was right.

CHAPTER 83

Legion recalled standing in the driveway of an old, City Heights home and knocking on the side door. Roger also carried a briefcase. The door opened and there stood Alton Burchesky.

"Hey, Mr. Legion, come on in," Alton offered and Legion entered walking into the kitchen of the home. "Would you like some water, or a beer?"

"No, thanks," Legion told him. "I'm fine."

"We might as well sit here," Alton advised pointing to the 50-year-old Formica kitchen table.

Legion took a seat at the head of the table and Alton sat on the right side of the table adjacent to Roger.

"You sure you wanna do this?" Legion asked in a deliberate tone.

"Yeah. I'm sure," Alton responded.

Legion placed his briefcase on the table and opened it. He then turned around and snagged a napkin from the kitchen counter. From the briefcase, he used the napkin to grasp and remove 3 newspapers, all with the same date, and all containing the article regarding the 25th anniversary of Dexter Frye's jump from the Coronado Bay Bridge and placed them on the table. With the napkin, he then removed a snack size Ziploc bag that contained approximately 10 Dexter Frye business cards. He placed the bag on the table, closed the briefcase and returned it to the floor.

"Be sure you use gloves when you touch this stuff," Legion cautioned. "The ink on the newspaper will smudge. It could leave a print. For the cards, use the top card first. That's got a clean print."

"All the names are in the newspaper article?" Alton inquired.

"Yeah."

"They're all cops?"

"Except for Dexter Frye, me, and the judge, Garubo. He's the guy that needs special handling."

"What's needed for him?"

"Every Tuesday, he goes to lunch with this lawyer. The lawyer comes to his court chambers a few minutes before noon. If you're gonna do it in the courthouse, that's when it's got to be done. That's probably the cleanest place. It's gotta look like the judge is the target and this guy is just collateral damage," Legion stopped speaking and looked Alton in the eye. "That's what I want."

"All right," Alton nodded his head in agreement. "I'll start casing these guys immediately. What's the other guy's name?"

"Walter Stoller."

"You gonna tell me what happened to Dexter Frye after he jumped from that bridge?"

"You take care of this for me and I'll tell ya."

Alton extended his hand and Legion shook it to seal the deal.

Roger Legion met Alton Burchesky 4 months earlier, when he personally delivered a check to him for $12,000 in regard to the settlement of an estate. It was from the estate of Lucila Necioro. Mrs. Necioro's husband and 9-month-old child were killed as a result of errant police conduct and she had retained the services of Dexter Frye to represent her for her claim against the City of San

Diego. Dexter's dogged prosecution of that case caused the police to attempt to frame Dexter for the murder of his wife and ultimately resulted in his jump from the bridge back in 1980.

At the time of her husband's death, Mrs. Necioro was pregnant. After the death of her 9-month-old infant, her mental state was fragile and she decided to put her baby up for adoption. Dexter Frye and his wife agreed to adopt Mrs. Necioro's baby. After Dexter jumped from the bridge and his wife's murder, Roger Legion handled the adoption of the baby. The baby's adopted name was Alton Burchesky.

At their first meeting, Roger told Alton about his history. What bothered Alton the most was not the murder of his biological father and brother, but rather the lost opportunity to be the son of a successful lawyer. For that, he wanted revenge. Initially, Roger dismissed Alton's ramblings as idle puffery. Then, Roger Legion found the opportunity to capitalize on Alton's bloodlust.

CHAPTER 84

"I guess Stoller was just in the wrong place at the wrong time," Glenn pondered as he told the story of Walter Stoller that was available for public consumption. He then ruminated, "He could never have taken you on, one-on-one."

"I like to think so," Roger added. "How did you know it was him?"

"If you're dealin' with a lawyer, you always start with the telephone. It's like catnip to a bullshiter. No offense. Called my guy at the phone company. They put some traps on the lines at Acitu – here and up north. Stoller met a Vice-President of Claims from Acitu on a cross-country plane ride. That's how it began. Apparently, Stoller promised them the world. What about you? How did you suspect him?"

"Lisa Leffort at Acitu," Legion revealed. "Stoller kept wanting to take her to lunch, but she kept refusing. Then he started telling her various bits of information, which she kindly relayed to me."

"It's a good thing we live in a civilized world," Glenn proclaimed with his trademark smile as he stood.

Roger stood up from his chair and started to walk around the desk, "What do I owe ya?"

"Nothing," Glenn responded and he shook his head. "It's goodwill."

"I don't like that," Legion acknowledged and removed a money clip from his wallet. "All you have to sell is your skill and that has value."

Legion peeled off three $100 bills and tossed them on the desk in front of Glenn.

"Take your wife to dinner."

"If you insist." Glenn's smile was infectious and it brought a smile to Legion's face. Their hands met with a stern handshake.

"I'll be calling you again," Roger told him.

"You better," Glenn said and then added as he walked out the door, "Take care."

As Roger walked around his desk, he surveyed the ocean and, in particular, he looked to the south to see the Coronado Bay Bridge. Since the incident, it had been closed while being inspected and tested for any structural deficiencies. Roger thought about where he was a week earlier and began to remember.

While Roger sat in the back seat of Alton's CHP police cruiser, shackled with handcuffs, he wondered what Alton was doing. Nothing like this was ever discussed with Roger.

Alton returned to the car and entered with cell phone in hand.

"I see the first one, I'm on my way." Alton was speaking to Remy and referring to the 1st eastbound truck. The plan was for Alton to run a traffic break for the 2nd eastbound truck.

Alton ended his call and Legion's perturbed voice filled the car.

"Alton, what are you doing?"

"I'm helping out these guys and I'm gonna deliver you to them."

"What are you talking about?" Legion demanded.

"Hear me out. These guys I'm following right now, they're gonna blow up the bridge. They killed the last 2 guys for me, including your friend. I'm gonna deliver you to them, then I'm gonna arrest them for everything. All the murders, the explosion at the courthouse, and the bridge. Finally, I'll get what I deserve."

"Unless you kill these guys, they're gonna trace it back to you," Roger pleaded with him.

At this point, Alton was running the traffic break, with Luke on his tail, and about to pass the 2nd eastbound truck who was maneuvering into position.

"I'll take care a that, too," Alton advised. "Now, before I make any more decisions here, I wanna know what happened to Dexter Frye after he jumped off the bridge. Start talkin' or you're gonna join him in the bay."

Roger let out an exasperated sigh and looked to the rear-view mirror, where Alton would glance at him while driving.

"Dexter made it to the shore in Coronado and he called me. I was living in Coronado at the time. I picked him up, but he was hit and bleeding bad. I took him to a clinic down in Tijuana. I thought he was gonna make it, but he developed an infection and died. So, that's what happened to Dexter Frye after he jumped off the bridge."

Alton was introspective as he heard the rather non-climactic ending of Dexter Frye.

"Let me ask you something, Mr. Legion. If Dexter Frye had been alive all these years, would he have been a rich man today?"

"I have no doubt in my mind that he would." Legion's answer was definitive.

"That's all I needed to know. Shut your mouth and let me handle this."

Those were the last words that Roger recalled Alton saying in the car. Within minutes after the car parked on the bridge, Alton would be cut down by Kevin Camballa's machine gun, thus eliminating Roger's concern that his plan might blow up by Alton's misguided strategy.

As the final moments of Lester Abrams life force drained from his body, Roger Legion continued to peer out the window of his office and gazed at the ocean. He contemplated the events that took place on the bridge and wondered if he was a hero or a victim to his own form of madness. The reality was that he had a law firm to run. The sound of the phone's ring returned him to that reality. He walked over to the phone and pressed the intercom button.

"Yes."

"Lisa Leffort is on line four."

Lisa Leffort was the claims manager at Acitu Mutual Insurance Company. Roger pushed the blinking button.

"Lisa, how are you?"

"Good, Roger, how are you doing?"

"I'm doing well. It's been a while."

"I know. I've got alotta files here for ya. Do you wanna send someone to get 'em?"

"They're on their way."

It was in that moment that Roger realized that his efforts had value and any threat to his dominance was totally vanquished.

Walter Stoller's fatal flaw was that he underestimated Roger Legion, just as Remy had underestimated the strength of the bridge. Walter underestimated what a certain attorney would do to keep business, so that his firm would continue to generate billings, one-tenth of an hour at a time.

EPILOGUE

O'Hare International Airport
Chicago, Illinois

25 Years Later

At Gate 6 of Concourse H, Rae Leff sat calmly, sipping coffee, and watching hoards of people board and disembark from various scheduled flights destined for a location other than the airport. Rae was 83 years old, white, curly hair, thick glasses, and was always conscious of sitting up straight. She learned proper etiquette at Sears, Roebuck & Company in the North Park section of San Diego, when she took elocution lessons as a young girl.

Heavy rain was causing continual flight delays and Rae was hopeful that her flight, destined for Boston, would begin boarding at any moment. She scanned the crowds without focus and when her eyes perused the seating area, a woman's face caught her attention. She had seen the face somewhere, but the name was eluding her. She felt such a strong connection, coupled with the fact that she was bored of sitting, that she found no harm in getting up and walking toward her.

Rae pushed a button on her carry-on suitcase and a metal arm extended to assist in wheeling it around the terminal. She stared at the woman as she approached her, occasionally looking down, so her efforts would not be so blatant. When Rae was within 6 feet of the woman, a name popped into Rae's head.

"Excuse me," Rae spoke up to garner the woman's attention. The woman glanced up at her with a smile. "Is your name, Karla?"

Karla Mulry's classy charm and alluring appeal had not faded one iota. She was resplendent from her brown hair that covered occasional gray roots to her simple red patterned dress and crème colored sweater. The delicate way her arms rested on the arms of the chair and the way she slightly touched her face would lead you to believe cameras were going to start clicking and snapping at any moment.

"Yes, it is," Karla appeared to be happy to see the woman, even though Karla had no idea who she was.

Rae sat down next to her with a big smile as she believed her discovery bore fruit.

"Didn't you use to work at the Legion law firm in San Diego?" Rae excitedly asked.

"I did," Karla acknowledged.

"I don't know if you remember me, but my name is Rae, Rae Leff. I was a secretary there."

Then the bulb went on in Karla's mind.

"I remember. How are you, Rae?"

"I'm fine. Going to visit my sister in Boston, if the weather lets us out of Chicago. But what about you? How are you doing?"

"I'm heading back to San Diego. My son just graduated from Loyola here in Chicago."

"I never saw you again after all that stuff on the bridge. What happened?"

"I couldn't go back to the firm," Karla smiled. "At the time, it was just too much."

"Do you ever think about it?"

"What? The firm or the bridge?" Karla wondered.

"Either one."

"Sometimes."

"I still have a copy of the _Time_ magazine with your picture. Are you working?"

When Karla fell to her knees in tears, after Luke was hit, a cameraman on a news helicopter captured that image on film. The next week it appeared on the cover of _Time_ magazine.

"No. I've been a housewife for nearly 25 years."

"How many kids?"

"Five. And I'm a grandmother 4 times over with a 5th one on the way."

"I bet when you walk with those grandkids, they think you're the mom."

"Rae, you are too nice."

"Look," Rae said as she took a piece of paper from her purse and scribbled onto it. While she wrote, a voice came over the intercom and announced the boarding of her flight. "This is my e-mail. I'm very technologically-challenged. Drop me a line. I'd love to catch up. Maybe, you could sign my copy of _Time_ magazine."

"Absolutely," Karla assured her. Karla and Rae stood and gave each other a strong hug. "Thanks so much for stopping by, Rae."

Rae turned, rolled her bag, and disappeared into the moving crowd. As Karla watched her disappear, she heard a voice from behind her.

"Did they call our flight?"

Karla shifted her direction and there stood Luke Cordel. He wore an eye patch over his left eye that served as a daily reminder of the events on the bridge. He was still tall and lean, but his hair was more salt than pepper.

"May I sit next to you, Miss Mulry?"

Luke never lost his enjoyment at simply looking at her.

"Yes you may, Mr. Cordel." They both sat down at the same time. "Do you remember a secretary at Legion and Associates named Rae Leff?"

Luke thought for a moment and shook his head affirmatively.

"Yeah. I do remember her. White, curly hair. Really, nice lady."

"She just stopped by to say 'hello.' She's on her way to Boston."

"I'm sorry I missed her." Luke said.

"She gave me her e-mail. I'll look her up when we get home," Karla paused for a moment. "She asked me if I ever think about the bridge."

"Do ya? I know we haven't talked about it in a long time."

"You know what I remember?" Karla was ponderous. "Roger Legion called me 'sweetheart' and he gave me a kiss."

"You know what I remember?" Luke asked to pique her curiosity. "It was the first time you called me 'Luke.'"

"It's funny how certain things stay with you. Remember all that stuff you told me about, involving that guy who jumped from the bridge like 30 years before," she paused to collect her thoughts, "Spenser Frye."

"Dexter Frye," Luke corrected her with a smile. "That's a name I haven't heard or thought about in a long time."

Luke became lost in that thought and began to remember.

It was 25 years earlier. The morning of their fateful ride across the Coronado Bay Bridge. Luke waited for an elevator in the lobby of the law firm, when he was seen by Roger Legion.

"You goin' downstairs?" Legion asked while also gaining his attention.

"I was gonna go grab some lunch."

"Can you drop this off to Roux?" Legion handed him a large, yellow envelope. "It's kind of important. He's got a doctor's appointment, so see if you can catch him before he takes off."

"Will do," Luke answered as he accepted the envelope and entered an elevator, which conveniently arrived.

The envelope was thick and must have had at least a quarter inch of papers within it. As soon as the elevator doors opened, Luke made a hasty dash to the America's Finest City News.

Luke entered the convenience store and saw Mathias, the young employee, stocking one of the shelves.

"Mathias, where's Roux?"

"He just left," Mathias told him. "His ride's here. You can probably catch him. It takes him a while to get to the car."

Luke made a beeline out the front doors of the building and gave a quick scan to the cars parked along Broadway loading and unloading passengers. He saw Roux opening the door of a late model Honda Civic with white cane in hand.

"ROUX!" Luke yelled and Roux was discombobulated by the sound of his name.

Roux continued to enter the vehicle, and Luke arrived at the vehicle just as Roux was shutting his door.

"Roux, Roger wanted me to give this to ya." Luke handed the envelope to Roux.

"Is that Luke?"

"Yeah," he answered.

"Thank ya, kindly," Roux beamed his trademark smile. "Don't forget me, Mr. Luke."

As Roux spoke, Luke locked eyes with the driver, nodded his head, and gave him a simple, "Hi. How are ya?"

The man was bald, with a white beard, and thick, prescription glasses. Luke took a step back from the car onto the sidewalk, while continuing to gaze at Roux and the driver.

"Take care," Luke told them as the car drove away.

Luke stood there and watched the car drive west on Broadway for approximately two blocks before it turned north onto Pacific Highway. He watched it until it was totally out of his sight. He was familiar with the man who drove the car. He had seen his picture many times before. Even with the features that characterize advancing age, his face was recognizable. It was Dexter Frye, the Litigation Guy.

THE LITIGATION GUY

If you get in trouble, my oh my,
And all you really wanna, do is cry.
Well, there's one thing that you oughta try,
Tell 'em your lawyer is Dexter Frye.

Dexter will get you a settlement,
So you don't have to worry, about the rent.
You can afford him, wait and see,
'Cause Dexter works on contingency.

Dexter Frye, Dexter Frye, Dexter Frye,
The Litigation Guy.

If you're the victim of a slip and fall,
There's really only one, guy to call.
Hearing his name will make them sigh,
Tell 'em your lawyer is Dexter Frye.

Insurance companies go round and round.
Dexter will knock them to the ground.
So, if you need a lawyer, don't be shy.
We both know that Dexter's your guy.

Dexter Frye, Dexter Frye, Dexter Frye,
The Litigation Guy.

About the Author

Vince Aiello grew up in upstate New York before moving to Southern California where he attended California Western School of Law. He is admitted to practice law in both New York and California. *The Litigation Guy* is his second novel. His first novel was the acclaimed, bestseller, *Legal Detriment*. Visit his website at www.vinceaiello.com.

ACKNOWLEDGEMENTS

I would like to thank the following individuals for providing support and, in some instances, the use of their name for a fictional character in *The Litigation Guy*:

Paniz Abbaspour	Troy H. Geisser, Esq.
Diane Abrams	Janice Hooks
Ethan P. Aiello	Alan Horton-Bentley
Sarah Rose Aiello	Uschi Horton
Valerie R. Aiello, RPh	Beth Jurecki
Kyle Bober	Mark Jurecki
Keith Bremer, Esq.	Robert Kalm
Robert Brockman, Esq.	Rae Leff
Leonard Brown	Lisa Leffort Reynolds
Jill Burdick	Oliver Love
Margaret Byrne, Esq.	Clare Luconi
Kevin Camballa	Pauline Murray
Paul Clifford	Vic Nagpal, Esq.
Bernadette DiMeo	Bill Piersol
Glenn Edgarian	Joseph Rossi, Esq.
Michael Eiffert, M.D.	Russ Shood
Nina Eiffert	Cindy Striblen
Jeff Elkins	Skylar Stubbs
Karla Mulry	DeAnna Versteeg
Angelo G. Garubo, Esq.	Patty White

www.ingramcontent.com/pod-product-compliance
Lightning Source LLC
Chambersburg PA
CBHW070801180626
46818CB00001B/43